FEAR OF THE DARK　　　　　　　*Erik Jayce Landberg*

FEAR OF THE DARK   *Erik Jayce Landberg*

FEAR OF THE DARK

By

ERIK JAYCE LANDBERG

FEAR OF THE DARK   *Erik Jayce Landberg*

Victoria Publishing Ltd.

ISBN 978-1-105-64256-2

FEAR OF THE DARK   *Erik Jayce Landberg*

Thanks to Xandra Alkemade.

FEAR OF THE DARK   *Erik Jayce Landberg*

TABLE OF CONTENTS

FEAR OF THE DARK   *Erik Jayce Landberg*

FEAR OF THE DARK

By

ERIK JAYCE LANDBERG

FEAR OF THE DARK   *Erik Jayce Landberg*

IMMORTAL

FEAR OF THE DARK   *Erik Jayce Landberg*

IMMORTAL

In a time devoured by the sole and absurd obsession of eternal youth, Mike seizes the microphone not quite in enthusiasm. His shirt is of a dazzling blue, his tie undone just beneath the collar streak. His forehead is ghastly with sweat, yet not so much out of nervousness as of enthusiasm.

Outside autumn leaves are falling to a certain fate as the wind unleashes gusts of air against the frail window blinds of the lecture room. It whistles through as if to remind of the sour demise of a summer that once was but no longer is. It does so only to hush seconds later, entailing that nothing lasts forever. Or does it?

The year is 2047. A year consumed by progress. That of Botox, hair transplant solutions, anti-wrinkle creams, and many other breakthroughs, the essence of which has driven society to the inevitable dependency where growing old, or at least being perceived as such is no longer an option.

It is a year in which promises of eternal youth and the supremacy of words are more highly sought after than the boredom or reality.

"What if I told you," Mike began. He paused briefly, seeking to meet gazes. "…that there is a way you will never grow old? Would you believe me?"

There were half a dozen or so in the crowd whose faces could be recognized from the previous lecture, the week earlier.

"Would you be willing to do whatever it takes to achieve eternal life?

Mike always started his lessons with those very two sentences, as if he wanted to catch the attention of his apprentices all at once.

And they kept coming back, week after week, month after month. His listeners, same faces every time. Several were new of course, and while some were used to the stark, almost rusty voice of his, others were discovering his fervor for the very first time.

They had heard of him of course. How couldn't they when so many notorious scientific newspapers and magazines had covered him at least once over the past three years.

Had it not been for thundering roars thumping across from afar, silence would have dawned on the room and roared across its dark wooden walls. Everyone in it held their breath in attentiveness, as though fully absorbed by the magic of his words.

Yet some remained unconvinced, attending his speeches with narrow-mindedness and prejudice. After all, the press had referred to him as *"the ultimate mad scientist"*, a stamp strong enough to arouse the curiosity of even the most sceptical amongst them, it seemed.

Rain started to beat down on the grey streets about the block as Mike dashed down the concrete steps of the building opening on Grosvenor Street. One of the attendees hastened behind him in a staggering motion as though to avoid the slippery stains.

Casting a swift glance beyond his shoulder, he tried to head her off as he often did with seemingly stalking critics or journalists.

"Mr. Heathrow?" she bellowed as he leaped around the corner heading for the other side of California street.

She stopped short of the zebra crossing, to her chagrin the light faded to red. From afar she could still make out his black soaked umbrella disappearing beyond the park. She might still stand a chance she thought, yet panting for air and craving for the light to turn back to green.

As seconds leaped and cars hummed through, her hand dug into the leather of her worn, black purse seemingly in an endeavor to conceal a device.

Lights turned green.

She cast a quick glance to her right, at the skyscrapers overlooking Chinatown as though to remind herself how to head back to Grosvenor Suite where she temporarily rented a flat. Rain began to pour all the more as she dashed after her prey.

She was now in the park, the French Cathedral on her left. Before her eyes the street began to get steeper all the way down to Fisherman's Wharf. Her ankle was aching and she thought what an ordeal it would be to walk back up again would Mr. Heathrow decide to stroll down the avenue.

In the meantime he was nowhere to be seen. She had paused, panting for air and reaching down again into her leather purse. Her gaze drowned in it as though in chase of a hiding prey.

She dug out the device but dropped it inadvertently as it fell down on the crosswalk with a thud. Raindrops began to stain its silver metallic shelf. She bent forward to pick it up when out of the blue a reddish ray lit up on the upper left. It looked like a screen display yet seemed to be something else.

She held it in her palm, her eyes examining it in awe. A passer-by cast a quick glance in her direction as he strolled past her. For a very brief moment she'd swear there was suspicion in his gaze. She didn't linger and tossed the device back into her purse when all of a sudden footsteps emerged. In a twinkle of an eye she had turned around to face the man behind her.

She opened her mouth.

"I… I'm not a–"

"I know you're not a journalist" the man answered still concealing his face beneath his umbrella.

"I followed you to–"

"I know why you followed me," he interrupted, his face still in the shadows.

"How do you mean?" Her voice quivered a bit.

"The device."

"You forgot it in the auditorium… I just wanted to return it to you," she smiled in nervousness.

"I left it there on purpose to attract you here," he answered now revealing his traits.

"You left it on my table on your way out, Mr. Heathrow and…" She paused. "To lead me here…?"

"Precisely."

"I… I don't understand," she stammered in her sweet British accent.

He didn't answer.

"What is this all about Mr. Heathrow?" she sighed as her gaze tensely ran down and stroked her feet.

"Call me Mike."

"What is this all about, Mike? What exactly is it that you want?"

"You want to know what that device is and I want to know–"

"What makes you think I want to know anything Mr. Heathrow?" she rose her voice as though gaining confidence.

"Look let's stop pretending for a minute, " he smirked in wryness. "You've been attending each and every one of my lectures, sitting in the exact same place every time, hearing me rehash the same old speech over and over again, each time for new students, each time for different faces save for yours. Your face was always there, identical, perpetual," he paused, "obsolete."

"So...?" she smiled and waved her head. There is a couple of dozen who keep coming back to your speeches."

"They're journalists."

"I ain't–"

"I know you're not. See I couldn't help but notice your beautiful gaze and all the questions sparkling in it, dissecting with greed my gear from head to toe, longing for answers, dying for answers."

"What do you want to know?" she sighed as she shrugged.

Rain kept beating down on Mike's umbrella.

"I know you're not a journalist, nor an avid student. I'll tell you all you want to know if you tell me who you are and who you work for."

"Very well..."

"Over a coffee."

***

From the outside the Diner appeared forsaken. A few oaks swayed in the wind as though to attest the place was not entirely desolate. Although the rain had set at last, a muggy mist still prevailed outside as though to confine people in. Reminiscent of the tempest was the hush of the wind stroking the blinds and the wet sound of tyres of a few cars driving by on the other side of the green firs by the parking lot.

Inside a smoky atmosphere stanched and blurred the windows overlooking Union Square.

"Milk, sir?"

Mike answered the waitress with a slight nod for all to judge, yet absorbed by the discussion.

"I'm going to be totally honest with you," he pursued as he stirred the coffee. "I think I know exactly who your employer is, I just want it confirmed and hear it from your own mouth before we take this discussion any further."

She pulled a wry smile as her eyes were drawn to her cup.

"I would very much doubt so, Mr. Heathrow."

"Try me. What do you know about SIT?"

She raised her eyebrows.

"Not much except it's very classified from what I understand and that…"

"Yes?"

"Well there are a lot of rumors surrounding it."

"So I would believe," he uttered as he took a sip.

Silence dawned briefly on the moment until she dared to ask.

"What is it?"

"Does the term E.O.P.A. ring a bell?"

"No," she replied as though she was asking a question.

"Let's cut the crap here will you? I know exactly what your deeds are. They sent you on a mission to find out haven't they?

"Who?"

"The European Opposition Project against America, you know damn well what I'm talking about!"

Her eyebrows betrayed her once more. So did her gaze as she looked down again with panting breath.

"What would their interest possibly be in your program?"

"You tell me. What does the word Opposition entail?"

"Mr. Heathrow." She rose abruptly from her chair and grabbed her purse. "I think I'd better take my leave now, if you would excuse–"

"What if I told you I'm intending to divulge everything to you right here right now in this coffee shop."

"I don't think so…"

She turned around and began strolling towards the exit.

"Miss Crowney, you're forgetting something," he uttered out loud with such self confidence that she paused almost before he had finished saying her name. "My device's still in your purse."

Slowly, she turned around so as to face him.

"How do you know my na–?"

"Are you in or out?"

He took yet another sip, his eyes still avoiding hers.

"What's the catch?"

"You get to work for me. You tell them everything I tell you to. Whatever they pay you I'll double it."

"A twofold spy, huh?"

***

The next day bore the scars of the tempest. It rose above a rusty Golden Gate, the color of which was barely reminiscent of red. "Why did they ever stop to paint this bridge?" he mumbled to himself as he drove under the climbing towers soaring past above his head.

2023 was the year it all started. The ever-growing unemployment rate, the deficient economy leaving Europe and most countries outside the United States on the brink. 2023 also saw the fall of the European economy, the abandon of the Euro currency and the excommunication of several latin countries from the E.U. Wasn't it all inevitable after the big crash of 2017. At least it helped the United States re-assert its position as a world leading economy after the Bush Government. Yet the country was still unstable and its overgrowing population and crime rate didn't make it much easier. Did it?

As if that wasn't enough, dazzling conspiracy rumors about viruses implemented by the U.S. government with the aim of cutting down the population began to spread like the plague.

One thing led to another. Suspicion aroused obsession and before the end of the 30's the masses became infatuated with the notion of eternal youth and the postponing of death. All that contributed of course to Mike Heathrow's ingenious idea. An idea so ingenious that he had acquired a greater amount of enemies than friends over the past three years.

Among the foes, a specific group of readers of course; the ever-growing lefty E.O.P.A. who had, in this turbulent political and cultural climate, gained increasing respect here in the U.S. It is an anti-American movement counteracting newly born American values which they judge far too plastic and superficial and which they refer to as a national threat to European traditions.

And who could work as a darker menace than Mr. Mike Heathrow himself?

Long had their eyes dissected his manuscripts. Long had their ears lurked in dark corners and attended his lectures. Long had their minds apprehended the fact that his ideas were grandiose if not revolutionary.

Long had they realized that his scientific assets were jeopardizing their frail ideologies.

He parked the car on the steep road leading up to California Street. Nob Hill wasn't what it used to be anymore, he thought as he turned off the engine and threw a sideways glance in the rear-view mirror. If everything goes according to plan he pictured, this street, let alone the neighborhood would become a very different place. A smirk formed at the corner of his mouth as he locked the door behind him. This time he would use the back door he thought so as to avoid tabloid journalists and the scandal press. After all he had only invited what he perceived to be the real press. The big wheel as he often referred to it.

Mason Hotel glowed white in the morning sun. The conference room shrieked with inquisitiveness under the entering steps of a thousand or so curious lads invited to hear very special words (they were told).

She grabbed a different seat and this time her gaze was no longer drawn to the mysterious device of his. For she knew didn't she? She knew it all and he was going to use her as a diversion. As a means to not arouse suspicion or doubts as regards to the STI project, which he knew they would never let happen, if it came to their knowledge.

"What if I told you?" he began.

Before his eyes, hordes of bloodthirsty paparazzi glared as he spoke the next controversial words.

"That I have created a brand new world in which you all can live forever…"

Eyebrows frowned.

Faces lit up.

Smirks vanished.

"…and where death is obsolete?"

***

The door slammed as her high heels echoed on the marble floor of Lorry's Diner. The penetrating sun through the blinds cast her silhouette in a blend of shades and smoke.

At the rear Mike lifted his cup and brought it shy of his lips. He blew twice with an outstanding calm.

"Why did you divulge everything?" the silhouette questioned loudly.

There was anger in her voice and her lips shivered as she uttered the next words.

"I just can't believe you did it! How are you supposed to get the project approved by the White House? It is the most foolish–"

"Take a seat, Vanessa!" he countered flatly as he took a sip.

"Mr Heathrow!" she raised her voice.

"Please."

He waved at her, aiming at the seat in front of him, yet without the respect of meeting her gaze.

There was self-assurance and an ounce of arrogance in the way he waved.

Astonishing was the fact that she complied without much resistance.

Her tone smoothed when she continued;

"There where a hundred paparazzi or so there, some from major magazines and press institutions."

"The big wheel," he smirked.

"What would make you do something like that? You're digging your own grave."

"Because there is another spy from the E.O.P.A.! You don't seriously believe that they would rely entirely on your accounts?"

His gaze met with hers but only shortly.

"What?"

"I was forced to divulge part of it in order to dissolve any suspicion or distrust that they may hold towards me."

"I don't understand," she sighed as her eyes fell down to the table and she shook her head.

Instead of lying totally about the SIT project which they wouldn't buy, I chose to undermine it by means of you." He leaned forward towards her. "You see, you are gonna tell them there is no threat." His tone worsened. "You are gonna tell them my project is merely the work of a madman, a utopia that doesn't stand a chance and whose credibility is ridiculous. That this whole thing isn't feasible and that there is no more to it than an ordinary virtual experience, void of any consequences for humanity. To make a long story short, you will tell them my program doesn't work and that I'm only thirsting for fame scoops and financial gratification."

"Why me?"

"Because you're not like them."

She stroked her purse as though thinking it all over.

"Vanessa." He said her name as though he had known her for years. "All I want is to buy enough time for it to reach the White House. They are everywhere, among senators, lawyers, mothers, daughters. Like cockroaches. Would they only lay eyes on as little as the project's synopsis, the whole project would be over. Like this!"

He snapped his fingers.

She frowned at the sound as though scared or intimidated by it.

"Do you understand me? This is my only chance to get it through."

Had there been the slightest arrogance in his voice just a moment before, it was now as far as last winter's snow.

She shook her head only to stammer.

"I... I don't know," she whispered flatly.

"You're not gonna let the American conspiracy carry out this bloodless genocide are you?" he exclaimed with a deep sigh.

She kept her head down and brought her hands to her face. She sank it in her palms.

"God knows there is not enough place on this planet. Soon people will die everyday. The economy is dead. There will not be enough food to feed everyone. The threat is imminent. It's all over the place. An impending doom! They're creating this mass psychosis and obsession about eternal youth to create a diversion in people's minds so that no one sees what's going on under the mantel."

She raised her eyes and her gaze confronted his for the first time in several minutes.

"Don't you understand, Vanessa?" he pursued. "I'm offering the world an exit, a solution to everything where there will never be too little space. Where an overpopulated world is obsolete and where resources are infinite."

"You're also creating a problem," she countered with firmness in her voice.

He paused, leaned back on his seat, then leaned forward again.

"What do you mean?"

"You are creating a major problem for the establishment. They'll never let you go through with this. You'll jeopardize your life and the lives of others! Including mine."

"Oh so that's what puzzles you? You're frightened and more concerned 'bout your safety than the fight for a good cause?"

No sooner had he said the words than she pointed her finger at him.

"Don't even try, Mr. Heathrow!"

"I know it's not the case, Miss Vanessa Crowney. And therefore you have no excuse but to get involved in this," he smiled.

She returned the smile, nervously.

***

"What do you mean by '*program*', Mr Heathrow?"

"It's a virtual world where no mistakes can be made."

"A virtual world?" the former voice counter-asked.

"You can lower your hand, sir." He waved flatly making that hand-raised silhouette appear as though he was no more important to him than a little tabloid paper thriving to get *in* the game. Little did the others know he represented a major paper.

"Yes a virtual world."

"Critics have claimed the program doesn't work," another voice in the crowd uttered.

"How so?" Mike seized the water and took a sip without raising so much as an eyebrow, calm as an eye in a storm.

"Even *Post-modern Science Magazine* said it won't work because it lacks one essential motor, namely a device capable of refraining the program from rebooting and thus refrain all stored information from being lost would a general power failure occur."

"A power failure?" Mike coughed a bit as he jested in amusement. He put the little plastic bottle back by the microphone stand.

"I'm not talking about a standard power failure Mr. Heathrow, I'm talking about a general power seizure in which the continuity of the virtual time continuum would be altered and cease to exist."

"Here you go…" he shrugged. "Have you ever heard of the term Girophony, Mr…?" He paused as though genuinely interested in his name.

"No," the voice uttered flatly.

"It is a device imagined by an inventor about a little more than half a century ago."

"And?" another voice shouted from the far rear of the conference room.

"And…" Mike tucked a gum into his mouth. "…I suggest you do some research and put some thought into it. It's a device whose essential feature is to relocate, or redirect if you will, sound signals, as the source of the sound generically moves onward. In this case a similar engineering directly borrowed from the Girophony, redirects energy sources as the virtual time continuum proceeds forward. Thus any power failure would already be in the past when the failure occurs and becomes therefore obsolete. *O.B.S.O.L.E.T.E,* Mr. whoever you are."

He spelled the word with such sarcasm that silence dawned on the crowd. Whether it was in convincement or bewilderment before the arrogance of the man would be hard to ascertain but his egotism surely convinced some of them yet only caused a wry smirk to form in the corner of Vanessa's mouth.

***

The plane took off more abruptly than it landed. Vanessa had stared at the clouds passing by, finding it hard to believe that under this radiant sunshine, soaring above these clouds, mist and snow awaited below.

It was no little delusion when they finally vanished and gave way to a view of skyscrapers screaming above a realm of haze.

"Why did you bring up the Girophony?" she asked as they both stepped into the yellow cab.

"Because it's clear that it doesn't work." He lit a cigarette.

"So he was right?"

Mike threw a quick glance at the driver in front of him.

"Mind if I smoke?"

The driver answered by shrugging and waved his hand in the rear-view mirror as if to say *You already lit it didn't you?*

"Of course he was right," he exhaled as he took a deep drag on the filter. *More* had always been his favorite brand and he'd make sure those long brown cigarillo-look alike death sticks linger on in what he now referred to as *the new world* and occasionally as *the brand new world* to avoid Orwell's term *brave*.

"So what was the point in lying?" she asked in astonishment.

"You almost disappoint me, Vanessa."

"How so?" she retorted.

The cab driver's gaze stroked the rear-view mirror.

"You probably noticed the overconfidence of my tone during my speech," he lowered his voice almost to a whisper.

She answered with a nod.

"If I can convince them that I'm so self-absorbed as to believe a half decade old device can serve model to a whole computerized virtual reality, the only logical outcome would be for them not to take me seriously and therefore leave me be. They'll make one or two research attempts to verify the potential and efficiency of the device until they give up on me with a grin."

He grinned himself.

The driver glanced in the rear-view mirror with a staggering gaze.

Vanessa noticed and lowered her voice.

"So you're out to dissuade them from even bothering trying to refrain you," she whispered as though she was sharing a schoolgirl secret.

"We're on the right path. First I throw this meeting in the Big Apple and next stage's Washington. We sneak closer in to the target smooth and easy. It'll all go unnoticed to them."

"What makes you think you'll even get close to the White House?"

"I'll be throwing a few other meetings during the next few weeks in order to confuse them. We'll let the media do their work. In the meantime, as we get closer to Washington I'll start to reveal more and more about the true nature of the program which will catch the attention of essential, targeted politicians, while it'll dissuade the interest of the media and that of the E.O.P.A. and its administration. I'll start right here in New York."

"Targeted politicians?" she frowned.

He lowered his eyes but the driver didn't.

"Mr. Heathrow?" she paused. "Mike?"

Michael leaned toward her.

"Ever heard of Jason Patterson?"

No sooner had he mentioned the name than she raised her eyebrows almost instantly, seemingly in shock.

"Oh so that's what you had in mind! You were just out to use me all along weren't you?" she retorted waving at the driver and summoning him to stop the cab.

Mike grabbed her arm firmly in an attempt to still her down. His lips stroked her ear. His teeth showed as he murmured.

"Regain composure. I'm pleading you."

"Don't even think about it, Mister! I ain't gonna let you use my entourage to achieve your ends!"

She waved again, aiming at the rear-view mirror.

"Senator Patterson is one of your close relatives. He's my only chance to get the project to the Majestic 12 board and eventually to the president!"

His didn't raise his voice but his teeth showed again.

"What do I care! Stop the cab!" she uttered out loud, digging in her purse as though she was looking for keys.

"You know damn well what will happen if we let them go through with their plans! They have a program..." he stammered for the name as it escaped him, "Elite 11, in which they will let everyone die, save for the elite. They will choose eleven people from each race. They will be sheltered and kept in safety for future generations... There won't be any space left... there..."

He lost his words.

She picked up her cell phone and dropped it in inadvertence.

"Please don't leave this cab! I'll explain he's with–" he whispered but she was already shouting back.

"I ain't going nowhere! You're the one who's leaving the cab, Mister!"

"Vanessa... he's–"

"Get OUT!" she spat, emphasizing *out* with such conviction that Mike's renowned conference speeches would have passed for less than a teenager's school resume in front of the class in comparison.

"He's with them," he said out loud as the door slammed before his eyes and the engine roared with screeching tyres down Madison Boulevard.

A horn echoed from afar, leaving him stranded at the corner of Powell's and Fifth.

He turned around.

"Taxi!" he yelled.

***

The next lecture bore the scars of the day in that it was nothing like the former press conferences he had been throwing in California. Vanessa's seat was now empty and as he spoke, Mike seemed elsewhere, his forehead ghastly with sweat and a former self-assurance sadly substituted for a lack of wordiness.

In truth he could think of nothing else but her, and as the questions dashed from the audience like wry, stinging needles his mind was set on his cell phone, perpetually dissecting the screen after a text or a life sign.

"What exactly is the essence of this virtual world Mr. Heathrow?" one needle stung.

He tucked the phone back into the sheltering silk of his suit.

"It is a virtual world, very identical to ours save for one tiny little detail."

He stroked the shell of his costume as though to assure himself the phone was still there. *Just in case* he thought. *Just in case.*

"The magazines talk about a brand new world deprived of imperfection. Imperfection? What's that entail?"

"It means no diseases, no earthquakes, no disasters, no…" he paused, to all appearances agitated and unfocused. "To sum up, it means no negative things whatsoever. Next question please."

He pointed a finger toward a risen hand at the rear of the conference room.

"Is there any better word than *utopia* to qualify your program?"

Laughter burst out, instilling eeriness akin to that of a political debate leading nowhere.

"How would that be?"

"I mean come on!" He looked about as though to get the support of everybody else in the audience. "A perfect world without any negativity? How would that work?"

He shrugged with a smirk.

"I have created a program that is so close to perfection that it provides with the possibility to transfer all information stored in a human brain to the new virtual world in question."

"You mean memories?"

"Memories, data, your entire life as if it had never ceased."

"What do you mean by *ceased*?" a voice uttered from the rear.

"Why would anybody want to have their memories transferred?" another one questioned.

Mike seized his cell again, placing it back on the stand in a flat yet determined gesture, as though to adjourn the *meeting*.

"The good thing," he seemed to regain confidence, "is that neither the transfer nor the program requires the body to function in order for it to work. Hence," he paused.

Had they roared with laughter just a minute ago, they were now sitting in absolute stillness, mouths agape, staring glares, as if they already knew of the words he was about to utter next.

"Hence," he pursued. "The consciousness of the transferred mind will live on forever after the body ceases to exist."

He said the words with such calm and banality that it would have had a paraplegic fall from his chair – had there been paraplegics in the new world to come, that is.

Tumult and moans filled the room as his phrase dawned on them like a thunderclap.

He had clearly said too much. Perhaps even gone too far in his phrasing this time. Yet he stood now at the point of no return. A point where divulging the rest would seem to have no further impact as to the consequences he had unleashed upon himself. Blame it upon his inability to see clear that very day or the simple fact that the secret was too much of a burden to bare.

"Do you realize what you're saying?" a voice uttered from afar.

Somehow he had divulged too much to stop right there.

"In doing so they acquire a new virtual body, a perfect, young one, not the least subjected to diseases or mortality. "Is that what you meant by living forever, Dr. Heathrow?"

Mike let the question pass unnoticed. Instead, he went ahead, dissecting every corner of the program and its infinite advantages for human kind.

Now that Vanessa was no longer here, he thought as he glanced at his cell phone, there would be no use for her. Nor would it be necessary to conceal certain aspects as he had planned prior to her leaving. Might as well lay all the cards on the table.

"Even so, the newly acquired body will retain past memories and its former consciousness. Thus, in the eyes of the subject, it will merely appear like a faint transfer from the previous real world and the physical body. Some will not even notice a transformation took place. Such is the truthfulness of the new world. It is by its appearance so close to ours that it will basically go unnoticed.

"You keep pointing out the pros. But what are the cons of such a project, Dr. Heathrow?"

"Well, you tell me folks! In a world devoid of famine, natural disasters, poorness, wars, and I skip many. What can the cons possibly be?"

"There must be a catch!" a voice retorted from the first row.

"What about food supplies, and space?" another one asked.

"I return you the question, sir. What about food supplies and the growing lack of space here on Earth? How will you solve that ordeal in the physical world where such resources are physically limited?"

Silence dawned.

"Well?" he smiled, his confidence resurfacing.

Aside from the sound of one or two coughing among them, there was no answer.

"The advantages that I have provided only constitute the tip of the iceberg. Allow me to enlighten you as regards to the matter. The program is generated and maintained by a giant computer here in the physical world. But that's the one and only physical aspect to it. In other words, everybody–"

"Everybody gets a nice, big house and as much money and food as he wants to eat?" a voice interrupted.

Mike grinned.

"Something like that. Although I would have chosen more eloquent words to describe it."

"How can that be?"

"Yes how can all negative events and disadvantages be erased like that? It's a utopia!"

"I told you. Everything is computer generated in the physical world. Basically, to make a long story short, there are two computers working hand in hand. One of them is provided with an infinite hard drive storing all imaginable negativity. Hence, events such as earthquakes, deaths, disasters etc. have been programmed one by one in that very computer. It acts as a counterbalance to all positive equations stored in the second computer. And by no means have we omitted one single negative equation. They're all there, you name it!"

Before their astounded expressions, Mike realized he had created a perfect world for which there would now be nothing but a frantic mass hysteria.

Unsolicited, a voice spoke from nowhere;

"How is Miss Crowney involved in your plans?"

At the words, Mike peered out at the audience.

"Who said that?" he bellowed as he scrutinized every face he was able to see.

But there were many.

"What about the financial side of it? Have you found invest–"

"Who asked that?" Mike retorted but as voices mounted under unquenchable curiosity, question started to build up upon question, and before he could even try to discern his subject, he was soon overwhelmed with an uncontrollable chaos of snapshot flashes and jostling.

Without lingering, he profited from the tumult to make himself scarce, springing straight for the back-door.

In a twinkle of an eye he was out, bolting on Twenty-Third toward his Chevrolet. It was parked down the junction. He ran through the park, heading for Madison, and just as he was about to insert the key, his cell began to ring.

He cast a quick glance at the screen which read *unknown number*, then entered the car so as to answer.

No sooner had he put the phone against his ear than a tarnished voice spoke.

"I believe you are looking for me?"

In the background, Mike could hear traffic and sirens, only to draw a quick link with the street noise about him. At the other end of the line, he heard an ambulance. Then seconds later he heard and saw it drive past him on East Twenty-Third.

"Where are you?" were the only words that came to his mind.

"In the park," the voice replied flatly as the ambulance veered toward Flatiron.

With stapled breath, Mike threw the door open and jumped out of his car. He peered out at the trees, the benches, the people but to no avail.

"You won't find me," the voice continued. "I'm well hidden. But I can see you."

"Who are you? What do you want?"

The voice spoke with such flatness that it made the hair on Mike's arm stand on end.

"Let's put it this way," the voice puffed, as though it was smoking a cigarette, "You have something I care for, and... I would like to think that I have something you care for too."

Mike scrutinized every inch of the park, approaching slowly as he listened. From afar he saw someone take a drag on a cigarette but, as he looked more attentively, it turned out to be a woman.

"I don't know what you're talking about."

He peered all the more.

"Oh come on, Mikey! You didn't think you'd impress us with that silly, little speech of yours? Girophony? Who the fuck are you kidding?"

"I still don't k–"

"We know the program works. We know your intentions and we're not gonna let you go through with it."

In the background, Mike could still hear the same street noise that surrounded him.

"You can't stop me!"

"Once we get the code, we'll just change it so that you can't initiate it."

"The program's activation code is sealed. You'll never get it."

"Is that so?"

Mike could almost hear the voice at the other end grin.

His heavy Southern accent was too much to bare for him and, as he swore he saw someone with a cell, obscured by a tree, the obscure voice uttered in threat;

"Does the name Crowney ring a bell? Or perhaps it spells *Clown*ey?"

Mike pretended as though he hadn't uncovered him and took his time to answer so as to win time and sneak in closer.

"Are you blackmailing me?" he uttered after a brief pause.

"Smart guy for a scientist, Heathrow."

"If you hurt her I'll make sure to–"

"To what? You'll make sure not to include me in your delusional, virtual, brand new world?"

"How do we proceed?"

"You mail the code to *13@codex.com* along with the exact I.P. of the server powering the computer generator. Once we verify it and erase the entire hard drive, we'll release her and she'll be safe and sound. It's as simple as that."

"How can I trust you will?"

"I give you five hours. Beyond that she dies."

The voice hung up on him with a disturbing tick, and just as he did, Mike saw his subject let go of his phone and throw it in a wastebasket behind the trees.

On a whim, he began dashing toward him as fast as he could, praying he wouldn't turn around, praying he could catch his prey unawares. But to his dismay, the man in the black coat did, and as their eyes met, only a few yards apart, the same man pulled out a firearm shooting twice at him. Mike dove forward and crashed aside in a commotion of screams and shouts from passer-bys. and as he lifted his eyes from the concrete surrounding him, the man had vanished, leaving no clue behind but the cell in the trash.

Mike jumped to his feet and sprang for the basket with stapled breath. He reached with both hands and began digging as though he had been a bum starving his guts out. He ploughed and ploughed, but to his deception, the cell was nowhere to be found.

He turned around and saw a man tuck something in his shirt.

"Hey you over there!" he shouted but the man didn't so much as give him a sideways glance.

Instead the pace of his steps increased as he walked away from him, back toward East Twenty-Third. Mike did his best to follow, but his left leg hurt too much after his fall on the concrete. Hence, plucking up his courage, he staggered back to the Chevrolet thinking how lucky he was that the gunman missed him by a fraction. He sank into the front seat painstakingly and reached for the glove compartment. His hands were shaking but eventually he managed to dig out the mysterious device of his. He held it firmly in his palm and scrolled down along the silver-blue screen. Before his eyes, mysterious numbers passed, unheard of. It looked as if they were some kind of language or cryptogram that needed to be deciphered.

Mike pondered. Could he really give them the code? He had worked so hard for this to happen, he frowned. As much as the thought weighed on him, *what's one life sacrificed in order to save billions?* and even though science had taught him never to mix feelings with the tasks, that thought repulsed him irrefutably. *It was out of the question – come what may – but it was out of the question.*

– Period –

He raised his eyes to examine the street, as though in search of a clue, when all of a sudden, it dawned on him like a thousand bricks from above. Vanessa had dropped her cell. Had she not? Just before she left him stranded, there in the middle of nowhere, yet in the middle of New York. He recalled how she threw him out of the yellow cab and how he had wanted to tell her. But there was no time. For what he really wanted to tell her about, was the man, the driver in the rear-view mirror.

No holds barred, he inserted the key and turned the engine on. It roared heatedly as he embarked on Madison. Reversed gear in, he backed for East Twenty-Third under the screech of tyres and blowing horns, and no sooner had he braked than the tyres screamed again as he hit the gas toward the street his assailant had disappeared down.

With one hand on the steering wheel, he started dialling a number on his cell, then put it to his ear. He missed a Pontiac by only an inch or so, in an attempt to pass a truck expelling thick plumes of sooty diesel exhaust. Horns blew behind him as he roared past the junction and the red lights.

"Ronald? Ronald? Do you hear me? – Yes – I don't have time to explain – Yes – I need you to track her cell for me. Can you do that? – Two, One, Two – Five, Seven, Seven…"

He enumerated the numbers in a tense, yet confident voice.

"As I said – Yes – I don't have time to explain. They gave me less than five hours. Yeah – I'll be eternally grateful, man!"

As his Chevrolet dashed down the last junction of the avenue, the wait he was forced to undergo felt like an endless ordeal.

"Garment District? Yeah – I got that – Heading toward West Twenty-Third? That's only a few blocks away!"

"Mike, I have located your position too! The vehicle in which the cell is trapped is veering to the right now. You won't cross him but–"

"Tell me the street!"

"Alright, alright, I got it, Roland spoke in his heavy New Yorker accent. "The vehicle seems to have stopped exactly at 563 West 38th Street!"

"Thanks, *pal*!" he retorted as though he had been American himself, but the British intonation ruined the attempt.

In the fourteen years or so that Mike had know Ronald, he had never walked out on him. Not once. Not ever, since they met and worked on the M.C.Y.I.T. project development in Houston back in 2025.

Once at 10th avenue, Mike braked hastily and veered to the right where he began to slowly reverse down 38th. He drove past a few rundown buildings until he finally parked the car, just short of a large parking lot on the right. In the distance, rising above the skyline, two silver-blue skyscrapers reminiscent of the Twins before they collapsed forty-six years ago, soared with majestic pride, but they were too small to even compare, he thought as he slowly but surely snuck out of the car.

"This place hasn't been taken care of since the year 2000," he mumbled as his gaze wandered in search of a clue. The dire reflection of the towers blinded him, and just as his eyes were drawn to a yellow cab parked at the far end of the lot, in the corner, a mysterious pick-up truck swerved in and stopped right behind it.

Mike kneeled down, sheltered by an old rusty Mercedes, the tyres of which were rotten to the core. He observed as two men wearing black shades stepped out and sprang around the corner of the rundown building to the right. They wore dark silk suits and their shoes reflected beams of sunlight as they walked past the shabby two-floor hangar next to the lot. Above the entrance, a faded inscription read *537*. Mike understood at once who the men were, for the number above the door was a secret code used by the E.O.P.A. at the dawn of their arising, before infiltrating into every European establishment.

No sooner had they vanished into the building than Mike started bolting for the cab. He stopped shy of its door, panting for air. The heat surrounding him had become unbearable he thought, as he peered inside the back window. He tried to open the door but the handle wouldn't give. Moreover, the reflection of the sun made it difficult for him to discern anything inside.

He grimaced. Sweat was running down his temples and his mouth felt dry. He gazed to the left. The white pick-up truck caught his attention once again, as if to lure him in. He crawled toward it. The keys were still inside, hanging under the wheel as though to lure him even more.

"They will be back anytime," he managed to sigh as he plucked up the courage and pulled down the handle. The door gave in with a slight creek. In the glove compartment, there were two Nine Millimetres and some gadgets that looked like F.B.I. devices. Without lingering, he seized one of the guns and headed back for the cab.

The back window cracked almost at once, as he battered it with the weapon, and there, lying on the floor, screaming to be noticed; Vanessa's cellular phone.

"They won't be long," he thought as he placed the phone in the pick-up's glove compartment and closed the door so as to steer clear of any suspicion.

Under cover of an abandoned bus, he waited for the men to return, yet to no avail it seemed. Minutes passed and almost turned into what felt as a whole hour. The heat began to take its toll and eventually, Mike saw no other alternatives but to go for it. He found a silver ladder at the back of the building and began climbing with vigilance past the first floor which was plunged in shadows. Mike was able to look closely; nothing but a builder's yard inside. The second floor had now become the target, and as he drew near the windowpane he heard voices inside.

At first, he thought he perceived two male voices, one of which was the man he had spoken to on the phone back at Madison, by the park. But as discussions progressed he heard a third one. It sounded faint and pale, and aside from the fact that it wasn't a male's voice, Mike didn't recognized it straight away. It was not until one of the men asked her to shut her mouth that it dawned on him. It was that of Vanessa. Poor, weak Vanessa whom, judging from the timbre in her throat, had been mistreated badly.

Mike hoped for the best, yet deep inside he knew it would take more than a miracle to get her out of there alive. As a scientist, he had never been much of a believer in God, yet at that very instant, and perhaps for the first time in his entire life, he could swear he heard a quiet prayer pass through his mind. Almost unwittingly.

He frowned and peered inside cautiously, his eyes barely above the pane. There were two silhouettes. One to all appearances holding a gun, the other one, a cell phone. In the center of the room, tied up to a chair, head bowed down; another shadow. That of Vanessa.

They were a few yards away and their backs were turned against him. That gave him a chance to lift the window without being heard and sneak in unnoticed. He ran for cover behind a dusty shelf, almost relieved from the heat. He strove to breathe as little as he could and lent ears.

"Three and a half hours to go," one of them emphasized as he glanced at his watch.

Probably a Rolex, Mike thought as its reflection beamed before his eyes.

"He will never give you the code," Vanessa uttered in a faint, exhausted voice.

The other man walked up to her chair and slapped her forcefully.

"That's it! No more water for you, Ma'am!" he retorted before drawing a cigarette from inside his suit.

He lit it by way of a silver lighter which reflected Vanessa's disillusioned gaze.

"Of course he will, Mr. Glenn–," the other man replied almost shyly.

"How many times did I tell you never to call me by my name, you illiterate idiot?"

"Sorry–"

"You might as well go back to being a taxi driver, Hank! I ain't paying you to behave in such an unprofessional way!"

Mike did his best to remain quiet and pass unnoticed, but as the discussion took a more severe turn, he scarcely lost his temper.

"You're not really going to kill her, Mr. Glennhard? Now are you?

He pulled a deep drag on his cigarette and answered with a grin. "It all depends on Heathrow. It's all in his hands."

Vanessa grunted and coughed as he blew the smoke in her face, antagonizing Mike's wrath even more.

"But now that you mentioned my name in front of her, I have no choice, now do I?"

His grin didn't vanish.

He leaned above her again and just as he prepared to slap her one more time, Mike reflexively hit the edge of the shelf with his elbow, causing a carton box to dive to the floor.

"There's someone in here! Quick, pull out your gun!"

As their gaze wandered within four walls, wiping the whole hangar to and fro, Glennhard pressed the canon of his revolver against Vanessas's left temple.

"I suggest you reveal yourself before I put a bullet in her beautiful skull, Heathrow!"

"Then I might as well not give you the code!" Mike retorted, as he remained hidden in the shadows.

His voice echoed against the walls, which made it impossible for the two men to locate him.

"This is no joke, Heathrow! I'm counting to nine. You're not out by nine and I shoot her! Understand?"

"If you shoot her, you're shooting every chance to lay your hands on the code!" Mike shouted back from behind the dusty shelf.

"One, two–"

"You just don't get it do you? The code is inside of her. It was implemented in her system on a digital crystal screen!"

"Four, five–"

"The code is engraved on the crystal, you need a microscope to retrieve it," Mike bellowed again, but his words didn't seem to affect Glennhard in the least.

"Six–"

"Perhaps he's right, Mr. Glenn–"

"Seven… No he's not! He's only bluffing you fool! Eight!"

"What if he's not bluffing? You know how much's at stake."

Glennhard stopped counting. His eyes were glaring fiercely. He was biting his lips. The taxi driver stared back at him in apprehension.

"Are you ready to come out now, Heathrow? I'll give you the benefit of the doubt!"

Mike didn't make as much as a sound.

Glennhard waited, short of breath.

"Heathrow?"

The two men gave each other one last look.

"Very well, Mikey. I'll shoot her then!"

He lifted the gun towards her, released the magazine only to insert it back in with a loud click, and just as he was about the to pull the trigger, Mike stepped out of the shadows, both of his hands tucked into his pockets, as though utterly unaffected.

"Don't shoot, Glennhard. I'll give you the code."

The gun was still pointing at her right temple. Glenngard's eyes glared as he gazed back at him.

"But I want you to release her first."

"I thought the code was inside her," he answered in sarcasm.

"Bull, as you figured it out yourself. The code is with me. Right here, right now."

Glennhard stared back without a word, his gun still glimmering at arm's length. He gave the driver a slight nod as a command to untie her.

"Put your hands in the air!" he ordered as Vanessa was pulled up to her feet, sobbing. "Now the code, Mr. Heathrow?"

He dug out a crystal sheet no thicker than a credit card and held it up so that they could see it clearly.

"It's right there. Paved in stone!"

"Hand it over!" Glennhard yelled as he tightened the grip around Vanessa's neck, the gun against her temple.

"First things first. I want her over here!"

"I'm not in a kidding mood, Heathrow!"

His eyes fell on his left pocket.

"Pull your left hand out of the pocket!"

He didn't so much as move.

"Heathrow!"

"Shove her over here and I'll give you the crystal. All you need to do is insert it into the hard drive and it will erase the whole program," he shouted back.

"Go and get the crystal!" he ordered the driver.

Under pressure, Mike handed it over without resistance. He watched as the man walked back with the code, toward Vanessa and her kidnaper.

"Now let her go, Glennhard!"

He smirked.

"You didn't think I would let you two live after this little ordeal? Now did you?"

He dragged the gun down, along Vanessa's neck, yet just as his index finger was about to brush the trigger, Mike shot once through his left pocket, hitting the driver's leg almost instantly. He fell onto the cold concrete floor with a scream.

On a whim, Glennhard took off with his *detainee* through the rear door by which he had entered the room. Mike began to run toward them in an attempt to follow, but just as he reached the door, the driver shot two bullets, one of which scraped Mike's knee. He stumbled forward and fell down the stairs.

When he had gotten back to his feet with unspeakable pain and trousers soaked with blood, Glennhard was already on the lot, running toward the pick-up truck while thrusting his hostage forward. She was screaming. But the screams were all Mike could hear as the truck dashed through the barbwire fence and the engine roared on with fury.

Had he been able to run, he would have sprung for his car, but the injury was too much to bare for Mike, who scarcely managed to enter his vehicle and turn the engine on.

As he turned the wheel on 10th Avenue and the motor hummed down the junction, Roland answered his call with fervor in his voice.

"Mike? Did you f–?"

"I need the new location!" he interrupted, short of breath, his wound hurting all the more.

"Mike, are you okay?"

"Quick! She's in danger!"

Without lingering, Roland managed to give him an exact location.

Tyres screeched as he drew near the deserted building site and stopped just short of the ditch.

He pulled himself out of the car with soaring pain, gazing in desperation as he strove to locate the white pick-up truck in which he had cleverly hidden Vanessa's cell.

He staggered along the ditch. Roland was still on the phone.

"I can't see the van!" he shouted as he peered across the site, panting for air.

"It should be only a few yards in front of you. I don't get it, you should see it by now!"

Mike walked unsteadily. The heat weighed on his shoulders like a plague. Sweat ran down his forehead and filled his eyes.

"I don't s–"

At the other end of the line, Roland's pupils reflected his screen.

"You're right over it Mike! You're right there!"

His gaze fell to the concrete. There, at his feet, Vanessa's cell phone lay scattered under the sun.

He kneeled down to pick up the pieces.

"Mike? Are you still with me?"

"They threw her cell out of the van," he said with distress in his voice.

Just as he spoke the words and his gaze wandered up toward the dire horizon of skyscrapers gleaming in the heat, his eyes uncovered something in the ditch. He heard a sound. A moan.

He looked closer.

"Vanessa?"

"Oh my God," Roland sighed from the other end of the line, as though he was there to witness the scene.

"Help me," she cried, "I'm really hurt."

Her voice was weak and frail, her face covered with blood and injuries.

"Vanessa!" he shouted as he glided down the bank, hurting his injured knee a bit more.

"I can't feel my legs. Hey threw me out of the car Mike. They threw me out of the car at full speed."

Her face turned into a cramped grimace.

"Don't worry," he sighed as he laid a hand on her wounded cheek. "We'll take care of you!"

"She gave him one last glance. One he would never forget, then shed a tear before her eyes closed out the heat and its blinding beams of light.

***

The patio looked onto the sea. Beneath it, palm trees were swaying in the wind. A warm breeze brushed against the silk curtains with grace as their shadows danced against the white wooden wall. Mike walked past the flowers on his left and took a seat in the sun. The air smelt of salt and aged wood. It shed a sense of calm and serenity.

He pulled out a cigarette from the left pocket of his shirt. He had never been much of a smoker, but turning into a health freak now would come across as outdated.

The waves drifted ashore in pleasant harmony. Mike watched as they caressed banks of white sand, wiping away footsteps after strollers and passer-bys. The sound they shed rocked like a cradle. He took a sip of his drink. It felt fresh and new, just like everything else. Perfect.

Against the warm wooden floor, bare feet brushed graciously towards him. They were that of a female.

She drew near him from behind and laid her hands on his shoulders. His eyes remained closed, longing to feel the warmth of the sun, longing to breathe in the way that it felt.

She grabbed a seat next to him and sighed in relief.

"It's a wonderful day," she said as her fingers ran through his hair.

"Everyday is a wonderful day," he replied and touched her hand with affection.

She looked at him, pondering. The wind stroked her raven hair.

"There's something I would like to ask you," she said, hesitantly. "You never told me–"

"Vanessa, don't!" he interrupted.

His eyes remained closed, sealed like a secret not ready to be uncovered.

A brief silence followed, aside from the sound of the sweet morning breeze brushing against the leaves and the foliage in the trees.

"I need to know," she insisted smoothly.

Mike opened his eyes. His gaze met with hers only to uncover glimmering pupils not quite dying from curiosity.

He sighed deeply as he thought of the right words to say.

"Did I…?" she intended to ask, yet paused in the middle.

Mike's gaze fell downwards.

Silence dawned again.

"We tried to reanimate you. We did the best we could."

She stared back at him with a thousand questions in her eyes.

He rose from his chair and walked toward the fence where he peered out at the sea and its never-ending horizon.

"Mike…?"

He stood with his back turned to her.

"Doctors said the injuries were too severe. They had to put you in an artificial coma." He paused. "That's the state you are in now." He paused again. "In the real world, that is."

She gazed at him almost relieved, as though contented that she didn't *really* die.

"There's one thing I don't understand," she asked.

"Yes?"

His eyes were still stuck on the beautiful horizon soaring before them.

"How come Glennhard didn't succeed in erasing the hard drive? He had the crystal code didn't he?"

Mike dug out the mysterious device from his pocket. The one he had been carrying all along, since the very beginning until the end of the *physical world* as they now referred to it. He held it in the palm of his hand.

"You see this? This is a portal between this world and the former one. Without it, the code is worthless. Everything goes through this device."

She smiled.

"What happened to Glennhard?"

"He ended up like the rest of them."

"What do you mean?"

"Only people with no criminal record were transferred here. In other words, the entire humanity, save for the unworthy. We couldn't afford them in a perfect world.

They were left to die in the physical one. I believe they all died out by now. It's been years, has it not?"

"What if they reproduced and carried on the human race there?

"Not a chance. The only thing left *there*…" he said *there* with aversion in his voice, as though he was talking about a horrible place, eons from here, that no longer had the right to exist "…are animals and plants. And the generator of course. The others were all castrated and imprisoned until they faced final extinction."

She gave him a glance filled with apprehension.

He noticed and replied; "We couldn't have them in a perfect world. They had to go."

"I understand," she sighed.

The breeze cooled her down a bit as she leaned back in the shade cast by the parasol.

"What I don't understand is how you managed to get this thing through on time, before I… before I died."

Mike answered on a whim, not quite unwisely.

"You're not dead!" he retorted. You're in an artificial state of coma. And so am I by the way. We're the only ones whose physical bodies are still connected to the generator back there."

He grimaced again.

"But how did you manage to get the project through?"

"Before you d–" He stopped. "Before they sedated you, I was given one last moment with you."

Tears almost filled his eyes.

"Yes?"

"And there, I promised you that no matter what happens…" He hesitated. "No matter what! I gave you the promise that I will give you a new life, here in this brave new world. And that we will live forever, you and I, just like the other 10 billion people whose *minds* were also transferred."

"How did you get past the E.O.P.A? I mean how–"

"Jason Patterson," he uttered flatly before she even had the chance to finish her sentence.

She frowned, yet not in anger.

"You gave me his number. I told him we could save you. I told him we could–"

"Hush, don't speak."

She was close to him now. Standing behind by the fence, breathing against his neck, her forearm wrapped around his shoulder as if to say *I love you*. But the words never quite came out.

Instead, months passed by, each morning more beautiful than the last, the sea growing bluer everyday, it seemed, just like the sky which soared above it.

Months passed by and eventually they turned into years and then decades, the flavor of which exceeded all expectations. For there was no pain, no sorrow, no darkness nor shadows.

Until one day.

Until one odd and sad day when it all started, just like that, dawning on them out of the blue like a throng of clouds coming down from the skies.

Mike was the first who woke up to the sound of raindrops beating against the panes and that of the wind whistling through the blinds. He came to from a weary sleep, thinking it must be a nightmare. But the thought caught up with him, there were no nightmares in the perfect brave new world that he had created. He had seen to it that it couldn't happen.

Hastily, he leaped out of bed and sprang for the window. He stopped short of the glass and peered out at the horizon, squinting. The waves were relentless, collapsing upon one another with a fury only reminiscent of *the old world.*

"What the hell is that?" Mike mumbled as a thunderclap struck the sea in a livid yet beautiful lightning.

The wind seemed to blow harder now, shoving the water to an inescapable fate as it crashed against the shore in a crescendo of white, boiling foam.

This cannot be, he thought but didn't say.

"Mike, why are you not in bed? What's going on?" Vanessa asked wearily as she strove to open her eyes.

Michael didn't so much as turn around to give her a glance. Instead, he dashed for the phone, but before he even had the time to dial any virtual number, it rang with insatiable vigor.

"Mike! Mike?"

"Ronald what's—"

"Put on the news, mate! This is really worse than you think! It's all over the globe!"

Without lingering he turned on the TV which, ever since the very first day in the perpetually sunny virtual world, had not needed to abide to any weather forecasts. Up until now, breaking news reports had always been about good news or good things, save for that morning it seemed, as the silver screen depicted no other picture but that of dread and horror.

"They're talking about a storm. A major storm!" he said with stapled breath as he wiped his eyes.

"One never seen before," Ronald answered, not quite in dread.

"I don't understand! I can't grasp—"

"There's more to it, Mike. Much more to it," he said so flatly that it literally scared the hell out of him.

"What...?"

His voice quivered.

"They're after you, mate. They want explanations."

"What's going on?" Vanessa retorted as she witnessed her husband's pale visage and quavering lips.

Ronald carried on spitting painful words.

"What do you mean earthquakes, Ronald?"

"They're talking about a tsunami. It might hit the shore in eight hours or so. But we don't know yet..."

Speechless, Mike hung up, casting a sideways glance at his wife, one of those looks you only give when everything is–

"Everything's out of hand," he said flatly, mouth agape, almost unaffected now.

There was a scream, followed by the sound of breaking glass and that of shattered metal.

"It came from outside," Vanessa said as she tightened the belt of her dressing gown and crossed her arms above it as though they could shelter her.

Mike ran back to the window and gazed downwards. What his eyes encountered could not be explained in words. To his astonishment, what looked like a riot had developed down his street, giving way to a scene of sheer and total dismay, as if taken straight out of a horror movie.

Before his eyes, *they* were, plundering stealing, assaulting, stabbing and firing at will in a concussion of blood and pillage.

Children shrieked, women broke down in tears, tears that almost instantly filled his blood-red eyes.

He opened the door and walked out on the patio.

"Don't!" she yelled, but he was already out.

Gusts of wind slapped his face. He peered at the horizon, which used to be made of water, but as the sea retreated slowly before his eyes, he knew it would only be a matter of hours before land took its place, to eventually give way to that immense, highly dreaded tidal wave.

He fell to his knees, bowing his head in shame. Vanessa hurried out to embrace him. Lightning struck just a few yards from their patio as thunder roared in a blend of wrath and fury unleashed.

She dragged him inside and closed the glass door.

"Something went wrong in the old world. Something with the computer generator."

He dug out the mysterious device and held it in his trembling hands.

"I've gotta go back," he said, his voice quavering.

Vanessa kneeled down by his side.

"Let me come with you!"

"I wish it were possible, but you're…" He paused and sobbed.

"I'm what? Speak!"

"Your body in the physical world is way too injured to wake you up. And even if I could wake you up, it would only cause you tremendous physical pain."

She stared back at him, tears in her glimmering eyes.

"I'm the only one who can go back and fix this. I know I can fix this!"

"But–"

"There's no but! This is the only chance that we stand!" he bellowed as he began to dial numbers on the device, the silver screen of which seemed more grey and somber than ever.

***

Mike's eyelids opened to the sound of whistling birds and the hum of an otherworldly wind. Wearily, he sat up in bed – *or what served as a bed* – and unwired the cables from his body. It was not painful, yet unpleasant. He was wearing a white gown, the texture of which seemed as cold as the four walls surrounding him.

Above his head, a tiny window let faint beams of sunlight penetrate the computer generator room, embracing two giant hard drives, one of which seemed as dead as the rest of the planet – *save for the animal life that is –*.

He got up to his feet. His head was aching and his temples throbbing. Wearily, he strove as his eyes got accustomed to the frail light cast across the room. His muscles ached and his back felt frail.

He struggled towards the computer screen and turned the power switch on.

Without lingering, it lit up not quite like one of those thunderclaps in the brave new world. To his astonishment, the screen was blurred and shattered with interference.

Even though, he recognized the disfigured face of Rolnald. Beside him, Vanessa was staring at the screen in unspeakable unease.

"Do y- read me, M-?" Ronald shouted from behind the screen, his voice barely getting through the incessant noise.

"Ronald! I read you! I'm fine. I'm checking out the generator, one of the hard drives is completely dead!"

"This -s unb-rable Mi-e! Th- first -nami struck t-e shores of C-lif-rn-a. Half the -te is wi-d o-t!"

"Come again?"

"H-f -e sta-e is w-pe- out!"

"Hold on mate! I'm checking on the drive!"

"Hurry M-ke, this is unb-rabl-, unbear-le! We cannot st-d it anym-re!"

Mike kneeled down and did his best to uncover the hard drive failure, and before he laid eyes on the burned up, not to say carbonised, memory circuits, Ronald screamed all the more from behind the screen.

"Th- -s -ll!"

"What?"

"-is –s h-!"

"I don't read you Ronald! Come again!"

"Th-s i- hell!"

Mike glared back at the screen, holding the burned circuits in the palm of his trembling hands. His forehead ghastly with sweat, he didn't so much as speak when he heard the thunder strike behind their window and shattered glass filled their room almost instantaneously.

Although he could no longer see her face because of the noise on the screen, he heard Vanessa shriek. It was the most horrible shriek he had ever heard and as he heard Ronald's next words, he dropped the circuits which went crashing against the cold, bare floor.

"Ev-ryth-ng is worsen-ng for ev-ery min-te p--sed!"

And as Mike's gaze wondered to the screen of the second computer hard drive, revealing twice the amount of terabytes that it had initially, everything dawned on Mike with unspeakable horror.

The hard drive that had been used as a counterbalance to store and seal out all negative equations and events had crashed, causing all the stored information to get backed-up and transferred towards the other hard-drive, governing over all positive equations and thus the brave new world.

"We're b-rning out, M--e! The sun is c-m-ng on too strong! Th-re ar- fires now! M-ke Mi-e?"

The picture on the screen was gone now. Yet Mike glared at it with an empty gaze. The noise grew all but thinner and Ronald's voice began to fade away.

With tears in his eyes, he leaned over the microphone and said; " I cannot fix it!"

"Th-s -s hell! Pl-ase help -s! It's too h-t! Oh -y God. it's w-y too hot!"

"I cannot fix it!" Mike screamed at the top of his lungs! I cannot fix it!"

Once again, he heard Vanessa shriek out in pain amongst all the noise and interference. Yet he could no longer recognize her voice.

The only thing recognizable now were Ronald's words.

"W-'re burn--g out now! We'r- bur-ing out but we're n-t dy-ng!"

"What?

"W-'re not dyin-!"

"I can't fix it! I can't fix it!"

"M-ke y-u have g-t to help us! Th-s -s h-ll!"

"What?

His voice quavered.

"This his hell!"

Panic-stricken. he hit the keys randomly in an endeavor to crack the code, hoping for some kind of miracle and craving that God would see this and shed some light.

But tears blurred his vision and Vanessa's shrieks blurred his mind, the next words spoken by Ronald hit him like a thousand bricks.

"P-t an end to th-s endle-s s-ffering! Put an end t- this et-rnal h-ll! Turn o-f th- comp-ter!"

"Come again?" he pretended as if he didn't hear.

"Shut of- th- progr-m!"

"What?"

"Shut off the brave new world!"

LOST

FEAR OF THE DARK   *Erik Jayce Landberg*

LOST

The walls were as white as snow, their surface as smooth and virgin as their very whiteness. They screamed with luster and brilliance and so did the floor, impervious, nearly static. Silence devoured the moment like a hungry beast blinded by greed. It roamed about avidly as a ghost present yet unseen.

There were neither doors nor windows. No cavity by which they could possibly have entered. There was no smell, no scent reminiscent of any odour but that of their own and nothingness.

The ceiling reflected the floor, the floor the ceiling, the latter perfectly sealed to the four walls encompassing them. They were trapped, prisoners in a room devoid of any access or exit, left at the mercy of their memory, one seemingly failing them, for there was no remembrance, no recollection of the past. Just a feeling of impending doom and the present, that white unyielding present, and they had just come to, awakening before that eerily white sheen glancing back at them from those walls, those seemingly ever-closing walls.

Ken leaned toward one, stroking it with the palm of his hand in a desperate attempt to comprehend.

"It's perfectly smooth," he grunted, his voice quavering a bit as he spoke the words. "It's perfectly smooth and there isn't one single anomaly to it."

"No hack, no ditch?" Hughes retorted.

"No hack, no ditch, no nothing!"

"That's nonsense! There has to be at least one defect, one irregularity! I don't understand how we even got inside!"

"Well there isn't, try for yourself!" Ken rejoined.

"I've tried for hours now, do you hear me? For hours and there is just nothing I can say, nothing I can do to comprehend, to understand how we got in here, in this eerie, empty room white and void. Where is the entrance? There is no entrance!"

Tears began to fill his eyes. They were tears of exhaustion, blurring his vision all the more with abhorrence and unawareness, as though he had never seen. It confined his head in a vicious circle from which there seemed to be no escape.

"Calm down, Hughes. There is no use in getting upset okay?"

"Speak for yourself, Ken! Just look at the state you're in. You're on the verge of a nervous breakdown. You shouldn't give any advice," James uttered in annoyance, sweat drops running down his ghastly face and inundating his fear-red pupils.

"Gentlemen," the fourth of them urged them serenely. "Gentlemen, we will not solve anything by yelling at one another and letting our nerves overpower us. Let's just remain wise and try to understand what's happening to us."

"Yes he's right!" Ken's ever-betraying lips shivered.

"We need to recall."

James nodded in agreement, panting slightly as he strove to regain his composure.

"Eventually, the memories ought to come back to us and soon we will see clearer and elucidate this little enigma," Hughes smiled but his heart didn't.

"You said that two hours ago. It's been over three hours now since we came to and we still remember squat!"

"Besides," Ken pursued, "not remembering is one enigma, but what about there being no exit or entrance to this room?"

"I don't know!" Hughes yelled. "We'll find out! Give it a little time!"

"Find out what?" James bellowed. "Find out how the impossible has become possible? If there is no entrance to this room, then common sense would be that we cannot have entered this room. Yet we are in this room! So what are we going to find out?"

First, the question was aimed at Hughes, then getting no reaction, he laid eyes on the three others, gazing at them inquisitively, yet only to uncover devastated faces, visages coloured with fear and apprehension.

Ken laid eyes on the fourth one, the most calm of them, gazing at him inquiringly from head to toe as though he had been some sort of a prophet.

"What about you? Do you remember anything?" he spat out in an accusing tone.

"Me? No, I think I just came to. I have no recollection of the past whatsoever, believe me."

"Really? How come you're acting so measured then? It's not really normal if you ask me." Ken's heart began thumping at a faster pace now.

"Yes, how come you're not nervous like the rest of us?" Hughes added.

"I don't know gentlemen, I don't know. I have a feeling we will soon understand. Something has happened and we will soon find out what."

"Perhaps we've been kidnapped and placed here in some sort of sealed cell, left to–"

"Left to die!" Hughes shouted.

"Shut up! Don't be ridiculous. We must have had an accident and we have amnesia. Yeah, that's what we have, amnesia. And we're probably in some sort of hospital room under medical surveillance in quarantine–"

"You shut up James! Now how intelligent is your theory? Pathetic if you ask me!" Hughes yelled back.

"Is that so? Well Mr. Einstein, I understand you must have a better explanation. Well come on, don't stand there with your mouth agape, spit it out and enlighten us as to this ambiguity that we all seem to be victims of. Come on! I'm all ears and dying to hear it."

"Enough!" Ken retorted, his voice now quavering more than before.

Hughes' eyes wandered to the ceiling, dissecting and scrutinizing every visible inch of it, yet to no avail. "There aren't even any joints, I mean there is no physical way by which we could have entered this room, there just isn't," he knelt down, burdened by the weary weight of his own fatigue.

"Nor is there any law of physics that would have enabled us to end up here from the outside," Ken uttered, he too starting to sound as if he had given up.

"What if…" the fourth one began.

"What?"

"Nothing…"

"No speak!"

"What if there isn't any outside?"

Two of them gave him a sideways glance, raised eyebrows, as though to question whether he had lost his sanity.

"What if this is all there is? This very room, right here right now."

"He's right, what if *this* is all there is? What if *this* is reality and we just happen to be alive, alive and unaware of where we come from, where it all began and were we're heading," Ken pursued.

"But who would have created us then, where in time are we?"

"What if no one created us? What if we just happen to be, happen to exist right here right now in this very reality, one seemingly devoid of any explanations. What if we just can't accept that there is in fact nothing to explain, that there aren't any explanations."

"Nonsense! Someone must have placed us here!" James grunted, turning his back on the others so as to face the right wall, or was it the left one?

"I think Ken is right," Hughes pursued, "There is no beginning or end, no outside world. There is only this room. That explains why there isn't any opening, and why we don't recall anything. Before we came to, in this room, there was nothing to recall because there was nothing. Nothing before now, no existence. We didn't exist then."

"That would explain why we don't remember anything."

"But we remember how to talk. We remember words, sentences, expressions."

"So?"

"So someone must have taught us. We can't just know everything like that." James snapped his fingers.

"Perhaps you're wrong. Perhaps we were born with that knowledge."

"Now how could that be?"

"How could it be we're locked in a room deprived of any exit or entrance?"

"I have a better question for you, Ken! How come we know of the terms exit and entrance in the first place if there isn't any outside world? Surely, we must have been exposed to these aspects in the past, in the outside world," James reckoned.

"That makes sense."

"No it doesn't," Hughes counteracted.

"Why not?"

"Simply because we just invented those terms. We co-exist with the room and we invent words and expressions along with it. It's called evolution."

"Where did you learn the word *evolution*, Hughes?" James exclaimed in sarcasm.

"I just invented it."

"That makes sense."

"But we all remember our names. And if we do, who gave us our names?"

"What about him?" Hughes pointed at the fourth one. "What's his name?"

"Yeah, why doesn't he have a name?"

"Because he hasn't invented it. We invented ours."

"Are you all losing your minds? God help me, I'm locked in a room with fools!" James knelt down raising his voice toward the ceiling, the latter imperviously gazing down back at him as though he didn't exist.

"God!" he bellowed even louder, convinced that the vocal vibrations would unveil a ditch in the wall, uncover a fissure or a crack. He yelled at the top of his lungs, craving an answer, let alone a sign, but the only sign out there was the ever-widening eyes of the others, even of the fourth one, staring at him as he prayed, as though it was he who had lost his mind, as though there was no God.

Ken gave him a sideways look, his lips slightly bent as though in disgust, one blended with pity.

"Leave him be," he said flatly as James had exhausted his vocal cords. "Let him kneel down as the fool that he is."

"There has to be an outside world!" Hughes suddenly changed his mind.

"What if there isn't?" Ken replied all the more unaffected.

"Are you telling us that creation is constituted by nothing else but a few lousy square meters surrounded by four white walls beyond which there is nothing but oblivion?"

"Yes."

"How can you believe that?"

"If there was an outside world, Hughes, how come we don't remember it? Certainly, we must have been part of it once and thus remember."

"Perhaps we've been brought here against our will! Perhaps we've been drugged so as to not remember."

"By whom, Hughes? We're standing in a room filled with nothingness, and there is no way in nor out. This whole room is a fallacy, unless–"

"Unless what?"

"Unless it constitutes existence itself, everything there is, everything that has been created and that exists at this very moment in time. That would explain why there is no entrance. You see, we never had to enter, we just are, co-existing with the room."

"He's right, Hughes," Ken nodded with a calmness so observable that it almost scared James to death.

"Beyond these walls, there is nothing but nothingness."

"Nothingness and us."

"I can't cope with that thought," Hughes retorted, his gaze beginning to resemble more and more that of James.

"Well think about it. Behind these walls, there is nothing but nothingness, you said it yourself. Nothingness all over save for here. In an infinite world, everything is eventual, everything must happen sooner or later, everything must occur at one place or another. Even life must occur, and we just happen to be where it has."

"Lucky us," Hughes attempted to jest but his red-blooded eyes betrayed him.

"Lucky or unlucky?"

"You're all crazy!" James groaned, letting a little of his saliva drip onto the virgin-white floor reflecting his demented face.

"He's drooling!" one of them exclaimed. "He must have rabies!"

"Yeah, that's probably why we're here. We all must have rabies!"

"Shut up you fools!" Ken yelled. "He's drooling out of fear. Can't you see his widening eyes? His trembling lips? His chattering teeth? He's going nuts!"

"Look at his pupils, they're becoming red," Hughes pointed a finger at his nerve-wrecked face.

"He's losing it, I'm telling you!"

And as their eyes fell on him as a thousand knives ready to cut him alive, James rose up to his feet and began bolting frenziedly toward the adjacent wall. He paused a few inches shy of the latter, raising his arms at it as though intending destruction with his bare hands.

"Don't do it!" the fourth of them uttered in a nerve-shattering scream.

But James didn't hear, nor did he listen. Instead he stood panting at the wall, both hands raised into fists, puffing like a bruised animal who had just been assaulted by a voracious predator.

"You're going to break your arms!" the fourth one added, licking dry lips.

No sooner said than done, James unleashed his fury on the impervious wall as best he could, fracturing both arms and hands in an eerie shriek bouncing in an atrocious echo across the room and against the four encompassing walls.

"Oh my God…" Hughes sighed as he watched James' body crash down onto the floor as though he had been a prey caught under the massive weight of its marauder, namely the room.

"What? You're feeling empathy now?" Ken grinned as he set eyes on Hughes' ever-frightened face.

"Did you see how hard he actually hit the wall? And he did not make one single scratch on it."

"I'm telling you those walls are unbreakable, simply because there is nothing behind them. You can't tear them down, for you see they are not walls, they are the limit of the universe and behind them that universe ceases to exist."

"What the hell do you know about it, Ken? You've been there to tell, you bloody idiot?"

As he spat his words on him, Ken dove forward, grabbing Hughes by the collar of his snow-white shirt.

"Unless you want to see blood stains on it, I suggest you never call me that again," he threatened, his teeth boasting with a whiteness akin to that of the room.

"Let go of me!" Hughes bellowed, his yelling blending with that of James whose shrieks of fear had been substituted for shrieks of pain. "Let go of me or I'll kill you!"

"Hush!"

"What?"

"Quiet I said!"

The two of them turned to the fourth one, save for James lying in his own drool.

"I heard a noise."

"A noise?"

"Yes…" he answered as he placed his left ear against the cold shell of the wall.

"Where did it come from?"

"From behind the wall, where else?"

"Are you crazy? I told you there is nothing behind."

"I swear I heard it. There is someone behind, I heard steps."

"That's a lot of bull!"

"Come and listen for yourself!"

"I wouldn't bother. You see, I can handle the truth. Not like the three of you. You're just pathetic, trying to see a reason, trying to convince yourselves that there is a meaning, that there is an answer to why we exist here within these partitions. Why can't you just cope with reality and get a hold of yourselves. There is nothing out there! And you, Hughes, you and that patronizing grin for James."

Frowning, Hughes turned around so as to face Ken. In his mind, the loud murmur of silence was mounting in his head, beginning to devour his sanity all the more, as an unquenched beast unable to refrain from greed.

"Perhaps it is you who is afraid," Hughes smirked.

"Afraid?" Ken laughed out loud, his dark virile voice imposing itself above the three others.

"Yes, afraid. Scared, unconfident."

"Of what you mortal fool?"

"Of what's outside. Perhaps you don't dare find out. Perhaps you don't dare listen for fear you will hear."

There was a moment of quietness. Hush soared with roaming silence as though time had come to a standstill. Then silence was infringed by enthralling words.

"Try me."

"What?"

"Try me," Ken repeated, summoning Hughes to succumb to his candid pleonasm.

"Are you challenging me?"

"Let's see which one of us is most afraid here."

"Cut it out, Ken!" the fourth one said.

Hughes stepped forward, walked past James, who was now lying at their feet moaning like a wounded dog whom nobody minded looking at, and paused two inches shy of Ken's face, the latter grinning in wryness.

"I take up the challenge," Hughes uttered, his eyes glaring at Ken's infuriated gaze.

"Wise man. I'm impressed you even do."

"What's the plan? I'll do whatever it takes to show you I'm not afraid."

"Take a look at the wounded dog," Ken replied, his eyes glimmering with self-indulgence, his voice as self-assured as ever.

"What the hell are you talking about?"

"Take a look at the wounded dog I said!" he yelled at the top of his lungs, lifting a finger, aiming at James.

"What about him?"

"Kill him!"

"What?" Hughes exclaimed in sheer horror.

"Put an end to its suffering. The dog has lost its mind."

"What? Have you blown a fuse?"

"If you don't do it, then you have lost the challenge, you'd show you're the one who's afraid."

"What's it got to do with anything, you fool?" Hughes' lips trembled.

Ken turned his back so as to face the wall and began ambling about him, like a shark prior to an attack.

"I believe I'm perceiving an ounce of fear here, Hughes," he uttered sarcastically as he scrutinized, his face ghastly with sweat.

"Enough shilly-shally talk! Get to the point!" Hughes raised his voice, yet not so much in anger as in dread.

"It's quite clear. If you kill him, you'd prove you're not afraid. If you don't, he'll probably die anyway due to his wounds and you'd only prove to be the coward here."

"That is ludicrous!"

"How about *you* kill him, Ken," Hughes retorted in an attempt at reverse psychology, secretly craving Ken would back out.

"Me?"

"Yes, you."

Ken giggled in sarcasm, pulling a wry smile as though he had won the challenge.

"Now I don't comprehend little Hughy. Would you mind enlightening me as to how that would prove you're not afraid rather than proving the opposite?"

"You astonish me, Ken. You really do," Hughes gave his own sarcasm a try. "I'd have thought you were more intelligent than that. I'm rather disappointed."

"Enough! Explain yourself!"

"It's rather simple. I don't have to kill him because I'm aware of the consequences. I know there is a world behind these walls and that if I commit a murder, I'd get judged for that sooner or later. Whereas you, Ken, you don't believe there is anything beyond these walls. Or so you allege. Hence, for you there really should be nothing to fear. No consequences, no witnesses threatening to denounce you to the authorities, because you don't believe there are any authorities out there, Ken, now do you?"

"Shut your mouth!"

"Unless of course, you do believe there is a world out there after all. Perhaps, I'm afraid to say, you're only boasting around to have us believe you're the only one capable of coping with the thought that we're completely alone in this room."

"I don't believe there is anything out there! And I can handle it!"

"Well if you don't, Ken, prove it, kill the dog as you said it yourself. Prove that you don't believe in consequences, in a world out of this one. Prove that you're not afraid!" Hughes shoved with determination, perfectly confident that Ken would now admit defeat.

But Ken's answer wasn't so much satisfactory as it was devastating.

"Very well," he said, smirking all the more in sarcasm as he haughtily gazed at his foe.

His words took Hughes unawares, his heart thumping fast, unsure as to whether Ken was bluffing, yet too proud to call it a day.

"I'll show you I'm not afraid. I'll show you I don't believe in anything out there and I'll kill him to prove you wrong. But that means you lose, Hughes."

Without lingering, Ken began heading toward James at a slow pace, walking with determination as he folded up his sleeves.

Panic-stricken, Hughes cast a sideways glance at the fourth one, in the hope that he would put an end to that ludicrous game of theirs and beg them to stop.

Yet he did not. Instead, he stood watching as Ken strolled to his deeds and the more his footsteps echoed on the floor, running across the room like Doom's Day bells, the faster Hughes' heart beat, having him gasp for more air than there actually seemed to be.

Again, his eyes wandered to the fourth one, craving in silence that he would not hold his peace, that he would speak, that he would spit out his bloody words of wisdom as he seemed to be doing each time things got out of hand. Only this time he wouldn't, for this time he stood watching as the human that he was, as the fourth one of their futile breed and time was his witness. He stood contemplating as a spectator thirsting after blood, striving to quench that primitive instinct deeply engraved in his mind, namely that of death.

Hughes licked dry lips, too proud to betray his ego.

"Aren't you going to say something?" he murmured at the fourth one, his teeth nearly shattering, but his serenity scared him so much that there were no words.

"Why would I?" he sighed flatly, as if the least bothered by the imminence of things.

"He's going to k…he's going to k–"

"Kill him, yes I know, and you know it. That makes two of us."

"But… we can't let him–"

"Of course we can! I feel it's God's will, for you see, I think this room is God's shrine and James is soiling it, he's soiling the shrine of God by believing there is another world out there, by believing there is an outside other than that created by God, namely this room," he recited as though he had been reading right from the holy scriptures.

"No!"

"Yes, don't worry, Hughes, we're just acting in the name of God, the creator of this place. I feel it. I know it. We have to stop James before he manages to brainwash the others by thinking in those terms. Look at him, look how he's lying there, pathetically on the floor, like a fallen angel who has betrayed his kingdom–"

"Shut your mouth!" Hughes yelled, reaching out an arm in James's direction, as if overwhelmed by sin.

At his cry, Ken turned around, his smirk curling at the corners of his mouth, nodding as if it were time to put an end to James' alleged suffering, taking a strong grip at James' throat and squeezing all that he could in His sublime name, in the name of his God, one confined within the short-sightedness of these walls.

"No!" Hughes screamed, at last letting go of his ego, yet in vain, for Ken was already choking him so hard as to see his face turn white, the whiteness of death, the whiteness of oblivion, the whiteness of these walls.

Ken's grin vanished as he turned to glance at Hughes, and his face put on a mask of seriousness, one of victory as the words came out of his mouth.

"You lose Hughy, I win."

Hughes turned toward the fourth of them, "You know something?" His lips trembled, "I think I'm just starting to despise the colour white."

"Don't."

"How so?"

"It's the colour that God has chosen for his world, for this room."

"What can you possibly know about God, you murderer? You've barely touched these walls! How can you possibly know what's beyond and what's not?" he retorted.

"Oh my dear. That's blasphemy. I dare you to repeat those words again, here in the very space of this r–"

"This room is empty! Just like your God, empty to the core, static and impassive as your very heart! You know nothing about the outside, what lies beyond these walls! You just assume something so as to save yourself from the notion of void. Because that's where we are, in a room filled with void! A room lost in time and space!"

"No."

"You said you heard a noise! You admitted that you heard footsteps. In other words, you said yourself, there is something beyond these walls!"

"No, there is God, that was his footsteps."

"How do you know? You don't even remember what your name is!"

"Of course I do."

"Then tell me!"

Ken turned on his heels, starting at a slow pace toward them, James' carcass now as impervious as Ken's unveiling visage.

"Why should I?"

"Liar!"

"I have no name."

"What?"

"I told you I have no name, I wasn't given any."

"So you're telling me you're God now?"

"Of course not."

"Then what is it? Speak liar, speak!"

Ken was nearing now, at a dangerously close distance, having taken an appetite for his deeds, his evil grin revealing ever-sharpening teeth.

"There is no need in speaking, Hughes," the unnamed said.

"Ken! He's telling me he's God, what a blasphemy Ken!"

"A blasphemy?" he whispered as he approached from behind the fourth one, who was as impervious and unaffected as ever.

There was another sound from beyond the walls, now very discernible, very clear.

"How can you be so sure of everything, we've only been here for a few hours."

"Speak for yourself."

"What do you mean?"

Ken had quickened his pace now, to all appearances dashing toward number four, at the jeopardizing distance of four feet.

"I mean that perhaps you've been here shorter than I have," the fourth of them replied, sheltered by the empty gaze of his, one without conviction or sorrow.

Having said that, he tucked his right hand into his left pocket, digging out a double-edged knife, the blade of which reflected his empty gaze and that of Hughes of course, who put on a horrified look as his eyes met with the lethal object.

"What are you doing with this?" he asked, his voice shuddering like a child.

Without an answer, the fourth one hastily turned around so as to face Ken, and by means of one studied, tedious movement, cut his throat wide open as though he had been nothing more than a wigwagging fish gasping for water.

Blood splattered upon the walls, soiling their virgin white in a redness as vivid as that of death.

A shriek ran across the room.

That of Hughes. Not that of Ken's, for no sooner had the blade brushed his skin than he had succumbed to the weight of his body, crashing to the floor with a splatter of blood and panting for air in a vain struggle to survive.

Before Hughes' eyes, the fourth one turned around, all but affected, his hands stained, as though he had only done his deeds, as though it had been nothing else than yet another tainted crime.

"I had to," he said flatly, as Hughes read him in horror, as speechless as filled with dread, mouth agape.

"Why?" was all that Hughes managed to utter.

"Because you see, he was loosing his mind, just like James, and we cannot allow that to happen nowadays."

"We?" Hughes' voice quavered as that of a wounded soldier.

"Our post-modern society."

"What are you saying? What society? There is only you and me left, only you and me trapped in this room,

bound to exist, and I don't even know your name."
Tears ran down his cheek.

"Not quite."

"Are there others?"

"Yes."

"Where?"

"Behind these walls."

Hughes grunted, only he didn't know whether he
grunted out of fear or out of relief.

"But you told me–"

"I know what I told you. That was not the truth."

"Then what is?"

"You're just part of an experiment," he retorted as the
walls suddenly gaped open, withdrawing as the fourth
one began ambling out.

"An experiment?" Hughes yelled, "What's going on
here?"

Soon, a few men dressed in white coats started
storming in from each edge-opening of the walls,
scribbling and scrawling as they inspected the room.

"Follow me," one of them said to Hughes, the latter
looking as if he had hit the earth with a bump.

"Where?"

"You're going back to the chamber."

"The chamber?"

"Yes the chamber."

"What are you saying?"

"Don't worry," the man in the white coat said as he
grabbed him by the arm, "It'll soon come back to you.
Once the drugs loose their effect, you'll regain your
memory."

They dragged him through the exit, which revealed an
entire room with machinery and computer-like screens,

the dashboards of which blinked in an array of colours. And just as he passed the fourth one, now also wearing a white coat, he heard him say;

"Now we have enough data and evidence to establish the outcome of human behavior, when exposed to primitive situations such as the lack of knowledge, how their main driving force comes to destroy one another to survive."

"Wait!" Hughes screamed as he aimed his gaze at his former comrade.

"Yes?"

"What year is it?"

"2077."

"Where are they taking me?"

"To the chamber."

"Why?" Hughes shrieked. "Why?"

"Because you believed in God, all of you, and that is against our government. It constitutes a potential risk for religion, and nowadays, our planet cannot afford a new religious wave. It would inevitably lead to a fourth world war, and we all know how destructive the third one was. It nearly wiped out the whole planet. Take him away!"

No sooner said than done, two men in white coats shoved him toward a room at the far end of the upper corridor, only it wasn't so much white as it was black, and as the sight of the door got closer, Hughes started to remember, flotsam and jetsam of the past, fragments of the feeble life he'd once had.

"Yes… I think I'm beginning to remember now," he grunted, "I remember this place… I do… you're taking me to the chamber, but what for… what's with the chamber anyway?"

And as reminiscences of the past dawned on him like a shriek from nowhere, he uttered in a scream;

"I know the chamber, it's the gas chamber, it's the gas chamber!"

***

Secluded from knowledge and the presence of God. Induced by unawareness and oblivion.

They began to hate one another and fight as the lost race that they were, not so very unlike the four of them. Only the race in question is not trapped in a box, nor is it lost in a sealed white room in the year 2077, without the slightest idea where they come from.

No, that race is lost in the middle of space, on a globe afar in the midst of darkness and infinity, and in the midst of no answer.

That globe, a sphere whose inhabitants slay and eradicate out of intolerance and frustration with no clues left for understanding.

"Where are we? Are we alone? Is there a world outside our own, there beyond the stars? Where do we come from? Where is God?"

A breed deprived of answers, building up religions, wars and temples of worship.

Prisoners on death-row trapped on a planet oppressed by a lethal lack of knowledge.

Some call it hell, some call it Earth, an ultimate punishment banning from the entrance to the presence of the almighty God. And lives taken out of prejudice, just like they did, the four of them, dying to know, dying to know…

FEAR OF THE DARK   *Erik Jayce Landberg*

ROOM SERVICE

FEAR OF THE DARK   *Erik Jayce Landberg*

ROOM SERVICE

In her dreams, she had longed for it for so long. Ever since she saw him step out of that shiny, black, almost mystical cab in London two years ago, when Stephen was passing through for his annual business trip. She had longed for it to happen so strongly, every night of her life, and finally fiction had turned into reality and become true, feeding her most secreted fantasies.

Together they had walked up along the aisle toward the altar, before a self-regarding priest, swearing each other happiness for life and all eternity, in good times and in bad. Yet at that point in time, they knew so little.

She was British, he was American, and hadn't it been for the company he worked for, which occasionally sent him to Europe to investigate the potentials of an ever-growing sales market, they would probably never have met in the first place.

"Love at first sight," she would always say when asked how they fell in love. Indeed, for her it was as though she had been struck by lightning. One as raw and fierce as a thunderclap unleashing an emotional wave so tough that for a moment, she had almost lost her breath.

Yet for him, things were slightly different. He wasn't so much of the emotional type, as the impassive one. Instead he embraced the reflection of Johanna's emotive spontaneity; fierce, raw, sometimes abrasive.

He was a stubborn business man, born to conquer at any cost, regardless of the consequences, the ends justifying the means, and in her, perhaps he had seen those qualities, the fierceness, the enflamed strength mirroring in her eyes, reflecting the projection of what his self-centred, egocentric mind wanted to see, namely the reflection of himself.

They had met in London. Haughtily, Stephen had left the cab, bolting at a resolved trot toward the hotel's gates where Johanna used to drop by most of the time for an after work drink.

She would never forget that moment, because as she had once confided in her best friend in the past, she was determined never to fall in love again.

Satirically, that evening was one of the times when she sat down with Maria, her long-time college friend, rehashing the same litanies as to how she felt disappointed with men and obsessively harping on that same fixed idea that she was better off on her own. She had only had the time to get halfway through the sentence when her wandering gaze grudgingly met with Stephen's. The latter self-blue, imposing, nearly daunting, for at that moment, for her it had felt like a thunderclap, roaring out of nowhere and tearing the time continuum as though it had been nothing more than a ridiculous scrawl on a piece of paper.

In her heart, love had bellowed, calling from afar in a lingering cry and longing to quench its thirst, the thirst of blindness, for that's what she was, blind as a bat in the dark.

As of that moment in time, her perspective had changed, for never again would she bring to light those everlasting complaints about the opposite sex. It was as though Stephen's self-centred eyes had mesmerized her altruistic mind and erased her plagued memory.

Now, several years later, they were married, alive and kicking and en route to the infamous Hotel on East 66th Street, to celebrate their two years of marriage and, in a sense, embark on a second honeymoon. So he had taken her away from her sheltering London to the isle where he came from. The *"center" of the world* as he liked to refer to Manhattan, feeding his egocentrism ever-more so as to quench his hunger for admiration.

***

They were standing a few inches shy of the red carpet, waiting for the porter to pick up their bags, and as they stood there, her gaze wandered toward the endless horns and noises of the ever-crowded, busy avenue, marvelling at the pulse of the city, one he had praised with such perpetual enthusiasm that she had finally felt compelled to nod, give in and follow him there for what *time was about to tell* would turn to be their most important trip.

"Where is he?!" he bellowed, letting through an ounce of anger she was not meant to see.

"Take it easy, Honey. I'm sure he will be here in less than a minute."

"Am I supposed to carry my bags myself? I mean, I'm paying for this trip, ain't I?"

"Of course, Honey. Don't get so flustered, you know it's not worth it, and besides it's bad for your health. You shouldn't stress over small things like that," she was used to replying each time Stephen got carried away by his otherwise inhibited antagonism.

"I'm not stressed!" he struggled to reply calmly, but his tone of voice betrayed more than he knew.

"Oh there he comes, Honey!" she said the way you would address a five-year old child with the aim of quieting him down.

As she spoke, a young porter dressed in a red cap and a matching shirt approached in a hurry, outwardly eager to grab Stephen's luggage.

"Can I help you, sir?"

"Well it's about time don't you think? I've been waiting unnecessarily for more than five whole minutes! My time is worth a lot of money."

"I'm so sor–"

"I was starting to wonder whether I was supposed to carry my own luggage, which of course I wouldn't have done! Do we understand each other?"

The porter responded with an unaffected shrug, all too used to the bluster and audacity of that boasting businessman type that Stephen sadly belonged to.

"Take it easy, Honey, it's not his fault," Johanna said, gently gripping his foolish black suit by the upper arm.

Unwittingly, they both followed the inviting red carpet leading to the reception of the hotel, one perhaps about to reveal something totally different from what they had expected.

***

"Stephen Royce," he uttered flatly, casting a quick glance at his Rolex so as to underline that he was indeed a very busy, not least important man, whose time was billed by the hour.

"I beg your pardon, sir?" the receptionist asked as though pretending he didn't understand.

"Stephen Royce, what are you, deaf?"

"Certainly not, sir. Are you looking for a Mr. Royce?" he pursued, emphasizing the man's ever-growing impatience.

"No I am not! That's my name! Do you want me to spell it for you or something?"

"Take it easy, Honey," Johanna whispered, tightening the grip on his arm.

"No need to, sir. Allow me to say that that's a very fancy name," he uttered in his wry British accent while pulling a tongue in cheek grin.

"Not that I care! Now would you be so kind as to type my name in your computer?"

"Do you have a reservation, sir?" the receptionist responded as impassive as self-assured.

"Yes I have a reservation! What do you think? That I'm standing here chatting with you for fun? Jesus, what an incompetence! First the porter and now this!"

"Oh no, sir, I'm sure a man of your importance would never lower himself to that level."

"You got that right!" he giggled boastingly while straightening his tie. "Now would you speed up the process here, my wife and I had a long trip from London and we're not in a chatty mood, and suppose that we were, that wouldn't be with you," he whispered the last sentence, throwing a mocking glance at Johanna who he was still trying to impress, regardless of two long years of matrimony.

"Let's see…"

"What now?"

"Well, it appears there is no apparent reservation for a Mr. Royce."

"Of course there is! I had my secretary book it personally, now just get me the goddamn room!"

"Honey… not so loud–"

"No Johanna, he is trying to fool around with me and I won't allow it!" he whispered loudly, snarling in anger.

The receptionist remained as impervious as ever, thumbing through a bunch of vouchers, seemingly so as to ascertain the fact.

"I'm afraid not, sir. There is no reservation for a Mr. Royce. Are you sure your secretary didn't book in someone else's name?"

"Now why would she do that? Just check in your computer again!"

"There is no need to, sir, I just did."

"That's it! I'm fed up with the service at this mediocre hotel! I want to speak to the manager right now! Get him promptly!" he retorted, now forgetting the whole lot about impressing his wife.

"That is not feasible," he returned, ever pokerfaced.

"What?" he bellowed as if he had just been insulted, his tone of voice filling all the more with anger.

"Take it easy, Honey, let's just go to another hotel!" she murmured worried.

"Well, that is not feasible because I happen to be the manager in question," he grinned politely, yet his grin was filled with sarcasm, one dark and studied.

"I can't believe it! What a bunch of fools! Okay, listen to me! You don't find any reservation because obviously, your incompetent staff didn't bother to type it in your goddamn computer, which means you have the obligation to compensate the customer and above all find him another room!"

"I'm afraid there is no other vacant room either, sir," he uttered with composure, his sardonic smirk yet visible, vividly screaming at the corner of his mouth and teasing poor Mr. Royce all the more.

"Get me a room now!"

"Sir, the hotel is overbooked, there really is nothing I can do to help."

"I can't believe–"

"If you care to look for yourself, please go ahead, sir," he interrupted passively as he smoothly thrust the computer screen toward Stephen's ever-reddening face. Grudgingly yet determinedly, he cast a glance at the displaying room numbers and their respective 'booked' info sign.

Stephen glared in attentiveness, feeling his body tense all the more, until an uncontrolled moment when he finally cracked and started shouting like only a business fool could.

"Stephen, calm down," she said serenely as though she had grown all too used to her husband's temperament.

Slowly but surely, he struggled to abide to the smooth tone of his wife's words and nearly regained his composure

"Look," he began, looking daggers at the receptionist whom, despite Stephen's menacing tone, didn't seem bothered in the least.

"Yes sir?" the receptionist couldn't have answered in a more blasé and insensitive tone.

As he spoke, the latter's eyebrows shrugged, colouring his face with haughtiness and conceit.

"If you don't solve the problem promptly–"

"Stephen wait a minute!" she interrupted out of the blue, casting a dutiful glance at the computer screen.

"What?"

"There's a vacant room right there. Take a look!" she pointed a finger at the bottom end of the screen, and had it not been for her conscientious and attentive ways, it would probably have gone unnoticed.

"Room 4514?" Stephen uttered in astonishment as he alertly peered at the screen, for the hotel embodied only seven hundred rooms, no more, no less.

"Oh, I'm sorry but I really can't give you that one," the receptionist hastily replied as his facial expression began to let go of its vanity.

"It reads right here, next to the room number; 'unoccupied'!" Stephen retorted.

"Yes but see, that one is always unoccupied, sir."

"That's bull! Now this one is vacant and my wife and I intend to stay there tonight, period!"

"I have to be totally honest with you, I cannot give you that room. It's impossible." The haughty look on his face had now totally withered.

"Why not? Don't tell me the room belongs to the owner of this hotel or anything? Cause' in that case, ask him to get the hell out and drive to one of the local Motel-Inns along the freeway. I've booked a room here and I intend to get it!"

"It is not that, sir."

"No? Then what is it? Speak!"

"You can't sleep in this room just simply because it is haunted."

"What?" Stephen exclaimed in a slight shriek followed by an unrestrained giggle.

"No one has slept there for forty-five years."

"Are you kidding me? Your goddamn rooms are haunted?"

"Please lower your voice, sir. I wouldn't want to alarm the other hotel guests."

"Is this supposed to be a hidden camera show or something? Cause' you're really starting to piss me off!"

"No hidden camera, sir. This is as true as it can get."

"Oh c'mon! What kind of an excuse is that? Haunted? Can't you come up with a better idea? This is totally pathetic, just gimme the goddamn key!"

"Well throughout the years, it has turned out that every guest who's been staying in this room has disappeared without a trace. This is fully documented, everything can be followed up in the police records as well as in ours."

Stephen's eyebrows frowned, casting a probing glance at Johanna, as if to indicate that the receptionist either must have lost it, or else was pulling his leg. Suffice it to say that the last alternative would certainly make Stephen infuriated, and in his eyes, that was exactly what was occurring

"I want you to show us to the room, because I ain't the type who believe in ghosts."

"I'm afraid I wouldn't recommend that."

"Don't you have a cleaner who makes the room everyday? You don't just leave it to gather dust now do you?"

"We do have one but–"

"So if anyone who enters the room disappears without a trace, how come the cleaner doesn't?" Stephen interrupted in nonchalance.

"Simply because the room doesn't seem to affect the hotel staff, only the guests, only newlywed couples to be precise," he answered, his glare dwelling as serious as ever.

"Sir, everyone who's ever entered this room has never been found again. Now before you take any hasty decision, let me give you the phone number of Mr. Ed, he's been in the room, let me call him for you."

"I thought you just told me that anyone who's ever resided in the room has disappeared without a trace. Now you're going to call that anyone? Do you realize how pathetic you sound?"

"I said that, yes. Everyone has disappeared save for one guest that is."

"One guest?"

"Mr. Ed."

Stephen's patience was coming to an end. One could tell from the infuriated gaze of his eyes, emphasized by his ever-frowning eyebrows. They were black, thick, unwilling to listen, unwilling to learn, devoured by an ever-growing stubbornness for which there seemed to be no cure.

"What happened?" Johanna asked in her smooth voice,

proving to be more inclined to listen and absorb.

"He reappeared from the room forty-five years later. When he did, his wife had just died of age. The eerie thing is that, according to the tale, if one is to believe in what he told the police that is, the spouse must die in order to release the spell for the one trapped inside."

"What?" Stephen exclaimed, putting on a disgusted look which momentarily disfigured his otherwise handsome, yet severe, visage.

"I guess that what I'm trying to say is, only if your spouse dies can you come out again, at least so it seems, taking into account the uncanny experience of his."

"What a bunch of nonsense!"

"I wouldn't be so sure about that, sir."

"I've heard enough!" Stephen uttered, fiercely slamming his hand upon the counter. "Now I demand to be given that room. Give me room 4514!"

All of a sudden, almost unexpectedly, the receptionist's visage underwent a drastic change, putting on a severe look, immediately letting go of his haughtiness. His glare blackened, swiftly sowing doubts in Johanna's mind.

"Honey, perhaps we should think twice about it before taking the room–" she said but only got half through the sentence, conceitedly interrupted by her husband's ever-loudening voice.

"Don't be silly Johanna! What kind of an excuse is that!"

"But Stephen, however true or false this story is, it doesn't sound anywhere close to nice. We'd better go to another hotel."

"No!" he retorted, ruthlessly disengaging from her as she intended to hug his arm.

"Listen to your wife!" the receptionist exclaimed, now leaping over the word *sir,* as though the situation had become critical and there was no time left for courtesy.

"What did you say?" Stephen yelled, frowning eyes, out of himself.

"Don't go inside that room! It's haunted to the core, it will devour you slowly, like a vampire in the night!"

The receptionist's gaze had turned into a serious and menacing glare, as he gravely spoke those uncanny and exasperating words. Exasperating, for they were ringing in Stephen's head, ringing loud, like Doom's Day bells.

"Enough! Let me talk to the manager! I'll get you fired on the spot!"

"I'm the manager," he replied, his voice now regaining its former courteous tone, courteous yet filled with irony, "however, if your intention is to get me fired, I'll be more than happy to give you the room."

He leaned forward, opened a drawer and maliciously held him out a dusty key with the number one, zero, three engraved on it. The last one had too much grime upon it, which made it impossible to decipher.

"Dear, maybe we should go elsewhere, there are plenty of hotels in Manhattan."

"No, I'll take it!" he answered, looking daggers at the receptionist while pulling a wry smile as though to indicate he had won the argument, the same sardonic smile he would pull each time he had it his way at the office, and each time he would close a deal knowing that he had just ripped the other party off their hard earned cash. "How much does it cost?" he pursued, his veins throbbing with self-confidence.

"Oh no sir, if you allow me, this room is for free, not that you will ever be able to pay for it anyway."

"What?"

"You'll understand in time."

"Enough! Come on darling, let's head upstairs."

"You go and check it first. Meanwhile, I'll wait in the lobby." Her voice was quavering, wryly betraying her suspicions, not least her fear that room 4514 might indeed be possessed.

"As you wish!"

He ambled toward the stairway, climbing up the steps one by one, the red carpet, scintillating under his advance and seemingly turning all the more red as he strolled.

***

His hand reached for the handle which was covered with dust, under a thick layer revealing narrow streaks, as if somebody had brushed their fingers upon it, but just briefly, fast enough to open it and withdraw them just as quickly, for after all, there was no need for the cleaner to linger on in a place like that.

The door opened on an outwardly normal room, a double-bed covered in red sheets, red wall-to-wall carpet with matching drawn curtains. Through them, a few rays of sunlight penetrated as if they had been Venetian blinds, yet they weren't.

Inside, a smell of lacquer reminiscent of old furniture varnish roamed about the place, entailing a sense of comfort and ease.

"What a bunch of fools!" he snorted as he threw the key on the bed, seemingly turning redder as he closed the door behind him.

Before his eyes, a painting portraying a married couple smiling as they were standing outside a church, hung on the wall as impervious as death itself.

"Pretty," he chuckled as he decisively placed his luggage onto the Rococo secretary next to the drawn curtains.

"Can you believe what kind of sick people there are out there?" he laughed anew, as self-confident as ever. The self-confidence of a fool.

In a swift gesture, he threw the suitcase open, dug out some sort of a towel with aftershave and headed for the bathroom at a shambling trot, walking with arrogance as if to affirm himself and his ever-growing masculinity.

He reached for the light switch, and as luminosity weightily dove down from the ceiling, he peered deeply inside the glass, not quite pondering. In his eyes, the latter seemed somewhat awkward, in that something unusual emanated from it, yet he couldn't quite establish what. Instead, he leaned forward, shut his eyes and began rinsing his face abundantly as though washing off some sort of a burden, one yet unbeknownst to him.

When he rose, grabbing the towel, his eyes met with the differing mirror anew, and as they peered again, there was something odd about the reflection cast back at him.

"What's with this room?" he whispered to himself as he ponderingly stared before him.

In an attempt to cleanse it, he applied the towel to his face and as he withdrew it to hang it back on the wall, he jumped back appallingly, as if his eyes had come across something deviant. Still holding on to the towel, he leaned forward again, his eyes wide open as though a ghost had just flown by. He bowed toward the mirror without so much as the blink of an eye, his heart thumping at a slightly faster pace than usual.

"How odd," he thought aloud, "when I gaze into the mirror, I don't seem to recognize... I could swear the wall was–"

He bowed a bit more, now squinting as he peered, and all of a sudden, just as his eyes wandered within the reflection of the wall behind him, he ceased to breathe all at once.

"The wall in the mirror is blue!" he exclaimed as he hastily turned around to check the colour of the one behind him. "How come the reflection is blue when the real wall is white–" he didn't have the time to finish the sentence, when to his amazement, his gaze uncovered a wall as blue as the deepest sky.

He took one step backward, his eyebrows frowning as he wondered. He stopped. Pausing like that for nearly a minute at the most, silent as a shark, perceptive as a fox, then came the traditional conclusion of a fool.

"Nah, I must have been mistaken, the wall must have been blue all the time, I don't know where I got that from, a white wall?" he giggled off as fast as he was used to discharging begging bums in the subway en route to work.

Satisfied, he got out of the washroom, walking at a shambling trot, for all of a sudden he felt tired, a bit weary, the weariness of a leader, wilful, obstinate, unwilling to listen, disinclined to see. After all, the wall had been white all along, until he had laid eyes on it, that is.

Once again, his eyes met with the painting, the one with the smiling couple outside the church, only now they weren't smiling and the church had turned from white to black, but to Stephen's eyes, that went totally unnoticed. Instead, he strolled past the painting, seemingly heading for the bed.

"I'm just gonna take a brief nap," he whispered to himself as he lied down on the sheets, jadedly sinking his weary head into the comfort of the white silken pillow.

Before his eyelids went down, he took a glance at the window, thinking of opening the curtains so as not to sleep too long, but just as he realized that the curtains weren't drawn, nor there for that matter, weariness took hold of him, shoving him toward a sleep as deep and black as the dead of night personified. Grudgingly, he shut his eyes, drifting slowly into a dreamless slumber, timeless as infinity, black as nothingness.

Just as he fell asleep, gloom began to soar all about him, entailing the end of light.

Suddenly, a sound! One loud and obscure. One so obvious that even the deepest of sleeps couldn't spare Stephen from hearing it. In the twinkle of an eye, it woke him up as surely as he had fallen asleep.

His eyelids loosened up, only to open on perfect darkness, almost unbearable.

Out of the blue, a noise once again.

"What the–?" Stephen exclaimed yet didn't have the time to finish his sentence before another one eerily sounded across the room.

"How long have I slept? Why is it dark?" he questioned as his eyes were drawn to the window on his right.

He stared in the dark, striving to see, squinting with all he could, but before his eyes, darkness was gaping widely, refraining him from seeing, not that there was anything to see.

Embraced by an uneasy sensation for which there were no words, Stephen started a frenzied chase for the small lamp on the nightstand. With a thudding heart and in frantic panic, he finally stroked the light switch, pressing it without lingering. To his chagrin no rays were shed.

Another one of these strange noises throbbed across the room, as though to taunt him all the more. Suddenly, it felt as though something was hovering just inches away from his horrified face.

He sat up in bed, desperately pressing the light switch, yet to no avail. Now he jumped off the sheets, landing with a grunt, his back on the red wall-to-wall carpet, only from then on, it didn't seem so much red as it did black.

He crawled on all fours, with stapled breath, his heart thumping as never before, in a quest for light, in a quest for deliverance, for blackness was on him like a plague, unbearable, devouring, infiltrating his mind like an ever-growing sickness taunting from the dark.

Now he heard yet another blare, oh so close, much too close, puffing at his terrified face, as if something else had taken possession of the room, as if he was intruding and disturbing its roaming peace.

"What was that?" he screamed interiorly, like a motherless child, lost in time, not daring. "There's something in here," his lips shivered, not able to abide to the words, "What was th–"

The lights went on, out of the blue, shafting from nowhere it seemed.

He looked about him with a ghastly face, his eyes nearly rolling out of their sockets, as he glared from right to left. He gazed all he could, panting his lungs out until he finally burst out in laughter, for there was nothing there, nothing to gaze at, nothing strange at all. He glanced at the ceiling – nothing abnormal – at the wall, at the floor – nothing strange, – at the painting, at the window – nothing str–, or so he thought, for almost instantaneously, his smile disappeared, vanishing as hastily as a sigh in the night, – *the window* – he exhaled.

Slowly, he stood up from all fours, walking slowly toward the arisen mystery, throbbing heart, quavering hands. His lips felt dry, as dry as an autumn leaf drifting at the mercy of the winds. He held out a hand, so as to ascertain that he wasn't dreaming.

"Why is it so black?" he whispered, as yet oblivious of the fact that the curtains were no longer there.

He touched the glass, it felt cold and impersonal, strumming the palm of his hand across its surface as though it had been a piece of gold or a gemstone.

He stared right into it, the glass seemed blacker than nothingness itself, harder and thicker than a rock.

He stared, striving to peer through it, but all reflection was gone, including his very own.

"What the hell is going on here?" he thought, his fear now substituted for an ounce of anger. "Oh I see," his eyes wrinkled as he frowned, "this must be one of their stupid pranks. I must be on one of those ridiculous hidden camera shows!"

Silence roamed proud, invulnerable, as though contradicting his theory.

"What a pathetic bunch of fools!" he exclaimed loudly, only to notice that his voice wasn't as loud as he had wished.

Behind him, the nightstand lured from the other side of the bed.

He dashed toward the phone and lifted it off the hook.

"Room service!" he ordered, sweat running down his throbbing temples.

At the other end of the line an unspeakable hush soared.

"Room service!" he roared.

Back from the phone, silence stung his ears. It seemed to grin at him ever more, as his face grimaced into an ugly cramp, and just as he was about to hang up he swore he heard a voice.

"Hello? HELLO?" he bellowed.

"Sir, how can I assist you?" a charming feminine voice lured like a mermaid.

"I wish to talk to room service! Is this room service please?" his voice quavered. He uttered the words *wish* and *please* as though the Stockholm Syndrome had finally got the best of him.

"To get through to room service, please dial three, four, six," the beautiful voice rejoined.

"What?"

"Three, four, six. Please dial three, four, six. Please dial three, f–"

No sooner had he hung up than he lifted the phone off its hook just as quickly.

"Three, four–" he panted for air as his fingers began dialling.

"Si–".

He paused. His breath was short. Very short.

"It can't be? What is this?"

He began dialling again, his eyes frowning upon the numbers as though it had been too difficult a task."

"Three, four, si–" he could no longer speak the words properly.

"Six! Where's the six? There is no six!"

Before his eyes and, to his dread and chagrin, the numbers on the phone read *one, two, three, four, five, seven, eight, nine, star*. He wiped the sweat off his eyes. Again, his face turned into another one of those ugly cramps, as though he had wanted to weep. Yet unable to shed tears.

He turned around, peering and dissecting the room in what seemed as an awaken state of R.E.M. His gaze wandered along the ceiling. It chased the walls, the furniture, the window–

"The window!" he said out loud before bolting back so fast that the he left the phone off the hook.

In an endeavour to open the pane, he grabbed the handle, taking a good grip with both hands. Then, pulling eagerly toward him, the tension loosened before he knew it and the window gave in, opening on what seemed to be absolute blackness.

Stephen leaned forward through the window, peering out at the night, striving to see, striving to sense, smell, hear, but before his eyes nothingness soared conceitedly, unveiling nothing else but a black throng of emptied space. Eeriness was imminent. It gaped at him from a dark abyss, the ways of which seemed endless and indefinite.

"How can it be?" he giggled, yet not out of amusement.

He turned around in desperation, panic-stricken, glaring at the room door with his eyes nearly jumping out of their sockets, "I gotta get the hell outta here!" he thought, starting with determination for the one and only exit.

In the twinkle of an eye, he stood shivering at the door, hyperventilating in a desperate quest for the handle, only to discover, to his chagrin, that it had been locked, as if sealed from reality.

He pressed it once or twice reflexively yet not expecting much, so as to ascertain all the confusion hadn't made him sink into misconception.

Now, he's in the bathroom, desperately searching for a screwdriver or some other tool, one that would help him unseal the gate to reality. Out of the blue it dawned on him. Why would there be a screwdriver hidden in this bathroom, the mirror of which seemed to cast back a totally different reflection? Unless of course it was meant to be. Unless all of this was nothing more than a miserable act of fate, one wry and deceptive, one out to condemn and rejoice at his very downfall.

But Stephen had never been much of the "I believe in fate" type. In his mind, that was only for weak folks, people who hadn't a grip on life, who were unlucky enough not to know the difference between nonsense and reality. For in his mind, how could one believe in such drivel?

Now, all of a sudden, he was one of them. He was one of those fools who couldn't tell fate from coincidence, right from wrong, real from unreal. He was sealed in a room apparently gifted with a life of its own, a room not willing to let him go that easily, because for all there was to know, perhaps he had something to learn, or perhaps the world didn't want him anymore.

Not able to find the tool, he bolted out of the washroom, panting for air, looking right and left as if he were being chased. Eventually, his eyes met with a drawer at the far end of the room, next to the bed's left corner, in the nightstand under the silk lamp.

He ran like only a fool could, throwing himself on it, his heart thudding ever more.

"There's got to be one in the drawer!" he exclaimed. "There's got to be one hidden in there!" he screamed, eventually bursting out in a horrendous laughter, one shoving him to the brink of madness.

With quavering hands, he pulled toward him. The wood was old and stiff but eventually, the drawer gave in and unveiled its contents with outstanding audacity.

It was as if it was all meant to be, for at the far end inside the drawer lay a screwdriver, nothing else aside, only a screwdriver. And with both hands tight, he grabbed it hurriedly, hastily giving in to its lure. As he did, a strange smile formed at the corned of his mouth, one entailing so much more than just rejoicing, for all to judge, he didn't even pause to wonder, to question, not for the slightest of seconds, why in the whole world would a screwdriver so outwardly be lying in the nightstand drawer.

Then, his lips smiling all the more, he turned around toward the door, its whiteness screaming at him from the other side of the bed as if to dare him. He leaped over the latter, chortling madly as he neared, for as of now, only a fine line separated him from lunacy.

"I'm finally getting out of here!" he screamed, both hands quavering as he stood at the door.

Hysterical laughter followed, not so honest as it was disturbing.

In a moment of eagerness, he dropped the screwdriver on the wall-to-wall carpet, promptly diving after it such as a hungry dog diving after its drowning master.

"I'm finally getting out of this r–"

He backed off, his eyelids wide open, to a point where one would almost expect both eyes to drop out. His mouth was gaping as though he was no longer able to close it. Drooling out of dread, he gasped for air, yet to no avail it seemed, for as he was about to use the tool, he realized with sheer dismay that there was nothing to use it against. The door stood before his panic-stricken gaze, white, impervious, challenging him all the more with its cleansed whiteness, one so vivid and sharp that it almost stung his eyes.

The handle was gone and so was the lock. It was as if neither had ever been there. No trace whatsoever, no holes, no peeling in the paint. The surface was as smooth as water and it screamed at him in an unbearable shriek. It screamed in his head with horrendous hatred, one devouring every inch of his brain, blurring his vision with a majestic red colour, that of blood, for inside his head he was bleeding, bleeding at flow.

It screamed so loud that he almost turned deaf, and slowly succumbing to its dire weight, he fell down to his knees with blaring strength. His mouth opened, striving to utter the slightest sound if any, but out of his throat only came a pitiful moan.

Panic-stricken, his eyes wandered up to the wall, meeting with the painting portraying the newlyweds, only now it portrayed nothing but an antonym to a wedding, one as sombre and dark as death itself; the couple's very funeral. And as he understood that blackness was about to swallow and digest him, he closed his eyes, holding back tears of fears.

He dwelled like that for several minutes and when he opened them again, with the hope that he'd had a bad dream, he realized with horror that the door was gone.

Before his eyes lay a wall cold as ice, apathetic and static. It was closing in on him like a devilish spell, the shaft of which would soon shove everything to an end.

Inundated, he tried to scream the name of his wife but the words stuck in his throat. Now he was nodding, as if he had known all along, as if it was time, and as much as he didn't want it to be, deep inside he knew it was inevitable. And slowly, his attempted shrieks were subdued by silence, his lips giving in to its very burden, for as much as he strove to call for Johanna, he could no longer hear his own voice.

The more he screamed, the more his vision became blurred, surrendering to the overpowering weight of darkness wryly falling all around him and choking his screams.

Soon blackness had won and all that was left was a black thump of emptiness and silence dissolving his very soul. He could no longer hear, no longer see, nor feel anything but pain. From then on he never felt thirst, nor hunger, and taunted by the burden of his own thoughts he dwelled like that for what felt like an infinity and eternity.

And when the latter had passed him by, the door opened on thirty-seven lost years, revealing a light that stung his eyes. He got up to his feet, and trembling as a frail flower he aimed at the doorway, staring at a thirty-seven year older receptionist, and as Stephen whispered the name of his beloved, the former shook his head in a cramp, staring down with horror at his feet, afraid to meet with Stephen's gaze.

TAKEN

FEAR OF THE DARK   *Erik Jayce Landberg*

TAKEN

I open my eyes, yet all I see is void. Blackness surrounds me. I must have slept, I can't recall. I must have come to from the void.

Where am I? Where did I come from? How did I end up here? I don't know. I have no recollection of yesterday. I have no memory of the past.

The air is stiff, cold, a sense of uneasiness fills the room. I'm gasping, striving to breathe, the air is too thick, I'm having trouble inhaling.

I look about me, unable to see, unable to hear. There is not a sound, not a clue. Darkness encompasses me, burdening my thoughts. I'm quivering, feeling so frail.

What is this place? I'm all-alone. I don't remember, anything at all.

My heart is thudding at a fast pace now, I can feel it. Something's wrong, I have a sensation I don't belong. I squint, to no avail, for the room is plunged into darkness, one gaping at me from a cloaked void.

It roams about in eeriness, as an invisible shade wryly shrouding light. I think I'm lying, I'm uncertain. A shudder runs across my body, and as much as I try to, I cannot move. Underneath my back, I can sense metal, as cold as ice, as hard as rock. It feels foreign, otherworldly, not of the kind I know.

Fright embraces me.

Perhaps I'm in hell, perhaps I have died. Dread overwhelms my body, taking me aback. I want to be aware, I want to comprehend. Is this a nightmarish dream, a tale from beyond? The place instils vagueness, a dreadful one, one without an end, as though boundless, infinite. Yet, I'm uncertain as to whether it is fear, for whatever it is, it is vast, it breathes nothingness.

Gloom dwarfs its presence, I can feel it come, an uncanny sense of impending doom, overlooking nothingness with infinity.

I cough. I can't help it. My lungs feel damp, as though they have been immersed in water. I cough again. Some sort of fluid runs down my chin. I can feel its warmth caressing my skin. I must have coughed blood, yet I feel no pain. Somehow, it's like I have been drugged, for all I can do is think. Aside from rolling my eyes from right to left, it seems as if my physical capabilities have been subdued, restrained, compelled to abide.

The uncanny feeling which I am downcast to, embraces me. Why? Why must I abide, and most importantly, whom must I abide to?

Suddenly, it feels as if I am no longer alone. A mysterious feeling of reluctance submerges my mind. I begin to shiver out of fright. Although my brain doesn't remember, my subconscious does.

I am not alone. There is something else here in the dark. Something atrocious and unspeakable. My eyes are stinging, they are filled with tears. Now I know I don't belong. This mustn't happen, this cannot be happening! I am somewhere else, somewhere where I shouldn't be. It seems like an other world, one thoroughly unknown to me. My home feels so far away, as if it no longer exists, as if it never had.

Perhaps I am dead. I must be dead. There is no other explanation at hand. This ought to be the afterlife. And if it is, I don't want to be deceased.

What did I ever do to deserve this? Is this what they call hell? Is this the ultimate punishment for having lived a life paved with sins?

"Oh God, I don't want to be here, in hell." I think in silence but in my head the sentence screams.

I should have listened. I should have followed the holy scriptures, whatever they were. Can it be undone? Will I be given a second chance to relive my sinful life? This must be hell. This is hell. It is written in the scriptures.

"Far away from the presence of God, from his sheltering hand. Far away from knowledge in a sheer unknown, one not ready to unveil, not now, not ever."

I'd like to wake up now! I've had enough of this. I've learned my lesson well. As of now, I will no longer sin. Were I to be given the chance, I would live a righteous life amongst the others. But I'm alone. There are no others that I can make up to. I am alone facing the pit of my fears, coping with something as atrocious as death, and yet I don't know what.

My mouth opens. My lips struggle, they crave to move. I'd like to scream. I'd like to shout for help, but I can't. My mind is mesmerized, caught in a web, my thoughts drifting awry, flotsam and jetsam.

I'm having flashbacks now. Recollections of the past, snapshots disturbingly unveiling an unspeakable truth. I close my eyes, in an endeavour to make them disappear, but it's like casting pearls before the swine. They're taunting me, short pictures flashing through my brain, reminiscences of what has happened to me. They're atrocious, horrendous. I want to scream, I want to disappear from here for I cannot cope any longer. I'm not ready yet. I'm not ready to uncover the truth. I'd rather not know. I'd rather lie here forever immersed in gloom and never know. I want to dwell in ignorance for what you don't know cannot hurt you.

All at once, the images disappear. To my relief, they vanish, gradually abandoning my brain. My heart is thudding, leaping fast. My lungs thirst for air. My body coughs. The cold metal on which I am lying stings, seemingly cutting underneath me in a painful sacrament, like the sharpness of a titanium knife.

As of now, I will ignore them, deny them, those atrocious images sardonically numbing my brain. I will do my utmost not to remember, to forget, for what I saw is unbearable, the world they unveiled is far too fearsome to cope with. I crave for amnesia, surrendering to the sheltering gloom about, the latter offering peacefulness and quietude, far away from the unveiling unknown. My body longs to be embraced by its throbbing sense of safety, one sadly anchored in make-believe. But I don't mind, ready to live in pretence.

My body shivers, yet not owing to coldness. It quavers out of sheer fright, one absolute and nerve-wracking. It blends with gloom as a ghost lingering by, tactfully crawling somewhere there on the floor, around a shrouded corner in the dark.

Now the images are gone, as if forgotten. I can no longer refer to them. Yet their taste remains, as sour as an otherworldly tart wine. My psyche is trapped under their influence, enslaved by their bluntness.

For a moment, I don't dare open my eyes, lest they would return and encompass my mind. I'm lying in silence, paying heed to the sound of my own breath, at the mercy of a piercing gloom, one glaring from beyond what I don't understand, what I don't see, glaring from beyond my sheer ignorance.

I gasp for air but this air is otherworldly, different, as if I had been dragged far away from home, far away from where I belong. A strange sensation enraptures me, soaring above as a recollection of the past. It is a sensation of elevation, weightlessness, as though somehow, I have flown through the air, so as to end up here amidst a cluster of ignorance emphasized, weighed by gloom.

I hesitate. My eyelids remain sealed, closing out the encompassing darkness embracing the icy room. The sound of my breath faintly bounces in a slight echo, one almost indiscernible, indicating that the room walls may be made of steel. Steel is not good. Steel is a bad sign. It is reminiscent of a surgery room, or even worse, an advanced torture room. I grunt. I actually hear myself moaning in fear, reluctant at the prospect of what is about to come, what is lying ahead of me. My grunt runs across the room, rebounding in an eerie echo against the walls. They are of metal. I want to weep. The metal underneath my back seems even colder now, even more lethal.

I concentrate. I strive not to recall, not to remember. The sensation of weightlessness is mounting, shrieking to come alive. I am counteracting it, striving my utmost to dwell in ignorance, for in as much as I am deceiving myself, ignorance is bliss.

I hesitate. A voice within myself whispers. I need to see. It inundates me with an overwhelming feeling of compliance, nearly compelling me to abide. It wants me to open my eyes and see. It wants me to remember. Submerged by its persuasive vigor, my mouth opens, ready to shout, ready to cry for help, yet all I manage is a faint groan as mundane as any.

At last, I give in to its sourceless craft. In a moment of apprehension, my eyelids loosen, pushing my eyes to open on a hovering darkness, the luster of which is blinding me.

With a staggering glare, the images all come back to me now, one by one, divulging one memory after another and taunting me with horrendousness. Flashbacks are running through my brain in a nightmarish journey of confusion.

No! I am not dead! This is not hell! This is far worse!

I'm beginning to remember. I'm beginning to recall. This cannot be happening! This is not possible!

All the rules of rationality are defied and put at stake. I must be dreaming, yet deep inside I know I'm not. If I were, I would have awoken by now, out of fright, out of instinct.

It dawns on me, whether I like it or not, unleashing its uncanny truth, its formidable recollection of the facts. There is no use in fighting against it, for now I remember, now I recall, a horrendous occurrence, poisoning my body and each of its members.

No, I am not alone, here in this secluded room made of steel. There are others, horrific others.

I scream. I yell at the top of my lungs in an endeavour to die, to pass out before I see, before I witness their appalling faces once again.

I scream but nothing happens. I am still here, alone in this room surrounded by gloom. I attempt another shriek but my vocal cords have dried out, compelling me to cease. With a leaping heart, I lie, striving to catch my breath, struggling not to suffocate, strangled by fear.

About me, silence dwells disturbingly like quietude prior to a storm. Its venomous omnipresence lingers on, as though impervious. At last, my heartbeat slows down gradually, until I manage to regain composure. I listen, afraid at the prospect of hearing a clue, let alone a sound. In an attempt to fall asleep, I try to remain immobile, craving that I will wake up in a normal world.

I lie listening, attentive to the surrendering dark, preparing to hear.

There is a presence, here with me. I can sense faint movements. It comes from the floor. It brushes against it, as if something is moving slowly, crawling toward me. My heart begins to leap again. I lend my ears to the mute sound of air. The stroke is exceedingly faint yet I can sense it. Something is sharing the room with me.

I cannot move, nor do I dare. I'm attached, tied up to this bed of steel, held in confinement. My right eye sheds a tear, one of fright, one of horror. It runs down my cheek to finally reach my upper lip, dry as a rock. It tastes of bitterness, nearly of death. My heart struggles to leap faster yet to no avail. It lacks energy.

Deeper and deeper, my mind slowly sinks into a state of half-awareness, my subconscious longing for evanescence. I want to vanish, I want to wither into a sheltering sleep, one made of a lack of knowledge and unawareness.

At last, my body succumbs to the weight of fear, and as my eyelids close beneath a burdening weariness, darkness turns into nothingness. My body fades. Everything blackens.

***

I'm coming to. I must have slept a dreamless sleep. Perhaps I am back home now, at least I hope. But I'm not. Icy metal still stings my back. I quiver, as yet unable to move, tied to the table I am lying on.

I can't move but I can sense something in the room. It's like a presence. I'm not alone. Something's alive, an entity, something I don't know of. I'm afraid. I'm not ready for this. I feel it, it is close to me.

My eyelids are sealed, yet light is penetrating them. I don't dare look, I don't dare open them.

Now I hear footsteps, roaming all around me. They're moving fast, there are several of them, more than a few entities all around, otherworldly creatures lost in greed. I grunt, shiver in dread. They want something from me, their cause is spiteful. I can sense their greed.

I weep. My eyes shed tears of sheer fear. I sense them all around, viciously sharing the room. Although I'm afraid to see, I want to, I need to see to believe. In a moment of truth, I open my eyes with reluctance, but they are shrouded by a veil, refraining me from seeing anything but penetrating light. I peer through it with a leaping heart, yet all I can see are silhouettes, hasty movements and uncanny activity.

I hear sounds, voices. They are talking now. Oddly enough, their language is very similar to mine. Although some meanings are blurred I can understand. I can hear their strange voices. They are whispering, they want to harm me. They need to they say.

They are hostile, angry, I have a feeling they want to eradicate me. I don't know how to communicate, I'd like to say I am not a foe, I'd like to say so many things, but there is something upon my mouth, a shroud refraining me from uttering the slightest sound.

All of a sudden it all becomes clear to me. All these images confirm my deepest fears. I have been abducted by alien beings, taken onboard one of their crafts. I understand everything they say, for I have studied them for years. I have been out chasing them in the woods, watching, learning in thirst of knowledge. I have been obsessed with them, yet this time I regret it, this time I went much too far, I crossed the line. I went too close, they found me, they caught me observing them in secret, hidden behind gnarly undergrowth. I failed, they captured me, they brought me by force to a distant place, a place unknown, the one where I am, right here, right now.

I remember flying, above woods and forests, lakes and ponds. I remember the sky, black as the dead of night, their awful visages surrounding me, their otherworldly eyes looking daggers at me.

I quiver in apprehension. My body quavers like a leaf. Suddenly, I sense a movement, this time much closer to me. I feel so frail, I want to scream and unleash my dread, but I can't, I'm petrified.

The shroud upon my eyes is withdrawn hastily. Light intensifies through my eyelids. I keep them shut in bleak horror. They're moving fast all around me, as though preparing something atrocious.

Yet, as much as I try to, I cannot withstand. My eyelids open.

My mouth screams. They look awful, beyond words. I am panic-stricken, unable to breathe. Their eyes are repulsing, bleak and evil. Their skin colour is odd, not like mine. Their gazes are filled with hostility, glaring at me with despitefulness, as though they found me repulsing, not to say disgusting.

One of them leans forward above me. He induces horror. He smells abnormal. Upon his face, there is hair spread out all over. I loose control, plagued by spasms. I crave to go home, disappear from this secluded place.

What they say comes as a scourge. They're talking about harming me.

I can hear their words clear, emanating from the oddness of their little voices. They bounce in my head;

"We need to perform an autopsy."

"Yes, but he is still alive."

"What do we do?"

"Kill him?"

"We should have done it inside the craft right after we found him."

Oh God, I want to say no, but I can't, I cannot speak their language, only understand. I'm scared stiff.

"What is his gender?"

"He must be a male."

"We need to perform an autopsy now."

"How do we kill him?"

"We will do it while he is alive. It will be interesting to see how he reacts to pain."

My heart is leaping fast. I want to wake up now. This is only a dream. It must be a dream! It must be!

"Remove the shroud from its mouth. I wonder if he reacts to pain the way we do."

One life form leans forward and touches me. I can feel its skin against mine. It feels viscous, filthy, almost obscene. He pats my face as though to study and establish the nature of my DNA. Then, in an unexpected move, he withdraws the shroud from my mouth quickly, almost painfully.

"Hurt him!"

Another being comes closer. In what looks like the palm of his hand, he carries a strange object, apparently of glossy metal. It reflects light sharply, lethally.

I yell at the top of my lungs, loosing control. I scream but I cannot utter a single word, my lips paralysed by dread.

The creature seems to cleanse the object with some sort of liquid, the nature of which I cannot determine. Now it approaches, looking daggers at me with nothing but despitefulness in its eyes. It is going to hurt me, it is going to torture me with that strange instrument.

In my head I shout, but my lips don't abide. He looks awful, angry. His face is ghastly.

"Cut him!"

"Where?"

"Cut off his ears."

It leans above my head. I see the blade, the lethal blade.

"Somebody save me!" I shriek so loud in my mind that it almost echoes in my head.

The knife reaches my skin. I can feel its touch, cold, raw, despiteful.

"Do it now!"

"Cut him deep!"

"I want to see how he reacts to pain."

If only I could talk! If only I could utter a sound and communicate! I would ask them to stop. I would confirm that I am intelligent too, just as they are. Then, perhaps they would stop. Perhaps they would cease their distasteful sins and understand that my life is precious, that I am not an animal, that I am worth much more than that. Then I'm certain they would spare me.

Slowly, the blade cuts down through my skin. I feel blood rush across my temples. Pain embraces me with fury. It unleashes a burning sensation of abandon. I am lost, awry. I am going to die!

"Cut him all the way. Cut off his left ear."

"No! Leave me alone! Let me be!" I yell, yet only in my head for my mouth is paralysed.

The blade feels halfway through my ear now and it must have cut off a nerve for I no longer feel any pain. All I sense is dread, pure, furious dread peering at me in an evil glare, the nature of which is alien, not of this world.

I can see its gaze. The creature's eyes glint as it cuts deeper and deeper. They are filled with disgust, and yet I think I can glimpse an ounce of enjoyment in them. They glimmer in the dire reflection of the blade.

"He doesn't seem to react. Cut the whole ear off!"

"No!!!" I scream with a grunt.

"Stop it!"

"He can utter sounds."

"It sounded like our language."

"It sounded as if he yelled the word 'no'."

"How is it possible?"

"It is not. Cut him."

"Leave me alone you horrible creatures!!!" I yell at the top of my lungs.

"What was that?"

"I could not understand."

"It sounded as if he uttered a sentence."

"He is trying to communicate."

"He is not. Kill him."

"We have to perform an autopsy."

"We will carry out one while he is alive. I want to see whether he can feel fear."

One by one, the entities leave the room, plunging it back into perfect darkness, as if it had become an abyss. My heart is thumping, blood still running down my temples and my cheekbone. Again, silence roams about the room. Yet it is a fallacious one. It is a silence lingering with impending doom and a fatality of demise.

I shut my eyes. I squint inside myself, within the steep depths hollow in my mind. And as I strive to awaken, to leave this world of nightmarish unreality, fear enraptures me. It is a fear hard to describe, for which there are no words. It is one despiteful and fierce, for all of a sudden, I see clear. I realize with sheer horror that I am not going to live to tell the tale, for this is not a dream. This is as real as it can get, embraced by an ever-growing dread, it is a fear of the dark.

I open my unveiled mouth. I shriek. I scream. I yell at the top of my lungs until they begin to lack air. It echoes across the room, bouncing on each metal wall, as if they were yelling at one another. My lips are dry, fissured, splintered, yet the physical pain has been substituted for a mere psychosomatic one, confining my brain all the more. I feel like weeping, yet I no longer have any tears. My eyes are all dried out. Every vessel of my body widens, as if it were going to explode. I'm dying here, all alone, in a place elsewhere, far away from home. I'm dying out of dread, craving that I would be spared from seeing, spared from lying under their vicious knives. For soon they will come back. The alien beings will return with all that it entails and I crave I will not be there to witness it, I crave I will be gone.

Oh God, how I regret. How I wish I hadn't been stalking them, studying them, there, in the forest, night after night, week after week, hidden behind the umbrage of a shrub, or even that of gnarly undergrowth. I got too close. I observed them, with all that it implies. I shouldn't have.

I feel weak now. Exhausted. As if I have lived too long a life, as if it is time to let go of it. I want to open my eyes, but fatigue is overwhelming me. Little by little, my thoughts are substituted for images, recollections of the past divulging their horrendous visages, their evil glimmering eyes filled with scorn. I can sense how they spurn me, the way they stare at me.

They are filled with hatred and abhorrence, as if in their eyes, I am repugnant. I can see how their pupils glimmer in anger. They are hostile, emotionless, cold.

I would like to open my eyes now, for I don't think I can't take it anymore. I don't think I can handle these images flashing through my brain. I only wish I could wither away far from here and substitute the state of pain I am about to undergo for one of evanescence and nirvana. Yet deep inside, I know I cannot. I'm trapped. I'm on their sacred ground, and God only knows what lies ahead.

I will die now. I was so unaware, so naïve, thinking that they might have emotions, sentiments, not least intelligence. But they seem deprived of any common sense, let alone any ability to feel compassion or empathy. They are like predators taking enjoyment in torturing their prey, rejoicing at the prospect of destructing whatever is different, for perhaps, who knows, deep inside they are afraid of difference and otherness. Perhaps, that might be their only fear, an undisputed, threatening one.

The silence in the room is mounting in a lethal scream. In my ears it rings as loud as war, for soon the alien creatures will be here, in a matter of hours, perhaps minutes. Soon they will want to see me suffer under soaring lights and glimmering knives, breeding nothing but prejudices and hatred.

Nevertheless, I lie still, giving in to the hands of fate and abandoning myself to a destiny undoable. My blood is starting to dry out now, and as my heart starts to beat slower, a sensation of unwitting acceptance enraptures my body, compelling it to surrender and confide in the idea of demise.

Suddenly, I have grown to accept and cope with it. It's eventual. Soon they will return and slaughter me as the wicked entities that they are, entities devoured by ravenousness. Bred by intolerance and taunted by haughtiness, their greed will blind them all the more into murder, without so much as the slightest feeling of regret.

I breathe slowly. My lids are ajar now, gazing up at the ceiling, the metal surface of which mirrors my silhouette in a taunting reflection. I smile to myself, yet it is a wry smile that I pull, one of grief, for deep inside I know this is the last one I will ever witness, aside perhaps from theirs, the entities', grinning in anger behind an ever-blackening evilness.

I shut my eyes again, in an endeavour to prepare myself, and in the hope that I will not fear when they return. Yet I know I will, and in a subliminal attempt to forget, my thoughts begin to drift awry, leading me to landscapes of meadows and hills, mountains and horizons, pictures and reminiscences of home.

Suddenly, a sound. It came from behind me.

I open my eyes, gazing about my head without so much as the bat of an eyelid. My heart is thumping, my pores sweating out whatever water there is left in my body.

A creak. I am not alone.

There is something else in here, something sharing the smiting presence of horror and dread.

I grunt, for there is another movement behind me, and this time much closer, as though something had budged, something alive, something otherworldly. I can smell its odour, one reminiscent of cinnamon. It feels as if I am being watched. The whole room is taunting me in sheer horrendousness, staring at me with anger and gauntness.

Petrified, my gaze wanders up to the ceiling, seeking a reflection behind mine, one that would divulge the horrendous visage of the budging *thing*. I roll my eyes frenziedly, up and down, in a sheer state of panic, yet all I see is the pathetic reflection of my own body, lying, moored to what appears to be an autopsy bed made of icy metal.

I lick my dry lips. There is another movement followed by yet another creak. Perhaps they are back, perhaps it's time to shut my eyes and succumb to the lethal weight of their knives. How can it be? I didn't see them come. How did they ever enter the room?

Now there is an awful sound. It echoes across, adding to the dreadful ambiance. It is the sound of tinkling metal, as if something is handling surgery tools.

"Oh my God... they are back... they are already back..." I gasp for air as the very thought is choking me.

Panic-stricken, I glance *skyward*, only to witness the dire reflection of an alien entity. It is standing only inches behind me, handling what appears to be a double-edged knife, the blade of which seems sharper than death itself.

I try to scream, but there is too little of their air in my lungs to even utter a moan. The tinkling sound is growing all the more loud, confining my head with the reflection of a glimmering, ever-sharpening blade. One as lethal as the pain it is going to cause.

"No... I'm not ready for this... I'm not ready... please God, make them disappear, make them vanish away from here... away from my sight!" I scream internally.

The entity's glimmering eyes wander up to the ceiling too, as if it had heard me shriek inside my head, as if it had heard the very thought of my prayer and that of my wish. They stare at me, divulging an atrocious alien face, corroded by eons, light-years from here. It is a face of otherness, and as much of time as it is one of space. Its gaze mesmerizes me, breeding a middle ground between real and unreal.

I pant for air, my chest inhaling and exhaling in a shatteringly painful quest for oxygen. My heart thumps in frenzy as though it is about stop. Struck by fear, I look away in denial, yet still able to glimpse the silhouette's alien reflection in the side of my vision.

The tinkling sound renews, eerily emphasizing the prospect of my demise. Not any demise, one paved with a dark fate of throbbing and suffering. In an attempt to deny the course of things, I shut my eyes, frowning everything I can, striving to awaken, striving to leave this eerie world of seamless unreality.

Now, another creak echoes behind my head and across the room with piercing loudness. It is followed by the disturbing sound of spinning wheels, turning harmony into discord, as though the entity was approaching with a despiteful thread, shoving nothing else but the wicked reflection of a surgery trolley. My eyes dwell shut, lest I would have to see, lest I would have to watch as that evil grin forms at the corner of its mouth, only seconds shy of proceeding to slaughter.

I can hear footsteps now, bouncing on the metal floor, as if to signal that the end is near.

"Please help me God... please..." I pray as I sigh uncontrollably, struggling to breathe such thin air.

The squealing sound ceases. The being is standing at the side of the autopsy bed, as silent and inert as hushness itself. It breathes heavily as though weighed by a plaguing sentiment of fatigue. Although my eyes are shut, I know it is there, only inches from me, standing at the side of the surgery trolley, and about to carry out so vicious and murderous an act. I can see it from within, shrouded by shut eyelids, veiled by the comforting darkness soaring within, its homicidal visage drooling at the prospect of smelling blood.

There is a movement. I can hear it as a metal instrument is misplaced on the trolley. My heart thumps all the more strongly, shoving blood through my vessels and up to my temples, conveying it to leak out of the open wound behind my ear. It runs abundantly, alongside my cheekbone toward my upper lip, entailing a flavour of impending doom, one tasting of death and demise. Panting for air, my lungs are compelled to swallow drops of the vital fluid. It chokes me as a submerging sea of lamentations, spewing out its venomous warmth and bringing me all the more close to annihilation. All of a sudden, the final curtain feels close at hand, drowning me whole into the vastness of its ever-blackening umbrages. Its swoops down on my body like the wrath from a god plagued by a sinful world.

I sob, throbbing and coughing at the taste of my own blood. The being utters a sound, something I cannot quite understand. It leans above me, with bleak, flickering eyes, carrying something in his palm, something metallic and lethal, evilly gleaming under the white rays of light shed by something moored to the ceiling. I grunt, frowning ever more, awaiting the final coup de grace by which the being would sink its mortal blade into my flesh, craving for my life to cease before the pain becomes unbearable. Fear devours me. Its insatiable embrace submerges demise, and with a shriek as abominable as the imminent fate I'm coping with, my eyes frenziedly open before a seemingly hovering alien visage, the glare of which deters like a squirt of venom. At the same moment, the being takes a step backwards as if somehow, my shriek had caught it unawares. In its right palm, the double-edged knife glares as an otherworldly beam of twilight for which there are no words. Mutely, it holds it in the air, about halfway between its face and mine, my pathetic life only held by a thread.

I gaze at it with despitefulness, throbbing at the pace of my thudding heart. All of a sudden, an awkwardness sinks over the moment, skimming across the room like death brushing against life in a lethal gust.

Without grace, it gazes back at me, its glare darkening all the more, as though striving to grasp the nature of my facial expression. The being looks awful, corroded and altered by whatever created it, and God only knows who did. Its visage weighs in favour of a female one, bleak and repulsing, radiating a sinful karma.

It leans its head slightly to the side, as though studying me. My breath battles against the air, disturbingly moist and cold. For a moment, it looks as if the being is frowning, revealing a glare so frightening that it nearly unleashes devastation.

I shriek again, at the top of my lungs, until the air dies out and my throat can take no more. Unbiased, the creature dwells over me, outwardly impervious to my outburst. It frowns ever more, unveiling glimmering austere pupils. My mouth opens, I lick my lips.

"Please don't kill me…" I whisper in sheer exhaustion, plagued by helplessness.

The being looks at me, still viciously holding the metal knife in its fist. Its mouth opens slightly, revealing a viscous liquid inside, one repelling and outlandish.

It grunts, a puff of air skims across my face. Its breath smells bad, of death. Its fist loosens up, then firmly its grip tightens onto the blade again.

"Please… let me go… let me live…" I manage to utter in a tone of voice succumbing to that of desperation.

The creature glares at me thoughtfully, utters yet another grunt, then raises the knife up in the air, as though preparing itself to strike.

"No! Please! I won't tell that I've seen you, I won't tell that you exist!"

As yet impervious, the alien entity pulls a severe frown, its eyes glittering in an uncanny glare, and all of a sudden, the metal blade swoops downward, hastily diving toward my bulk.

I scream. My eyelids shut, my field of vision blackening out, as though immersed by a lightning made of gloom. In the blink of an eye, everything darkens as if struck by a thunderclap. Silence sinks down from beyond, roaring as a beast untamed. Blackness encompasses me, embracing my body with wry awkwardness. I lie pointlessly on the metal bed, uncertain as to why I am still able to think and reason without the curse of physical pain.

In an endeavour to seek awareness, my eyelids open, thirsting after knowledge. They open on an uncanny visage, eerily staring down at me with stapled breath, as though in pity.

With an ever-thumping heart, I look about me only to see that the knife has sunk down only inches away from my hand and wrist, and to my astonishment cut off the cord formerly wrapped around my arm. As I gaze, its glimmering blade mirrors my eyes in a blinding ray of light. They are panic-stricken, thunderstruck, and although dragged to the limits of mortal endurance, unable to weep.

Slowly, my eyes wander up toward the eerie creature, seeking to meet with its gaze, in quest of understanding, and for the very first time, I think I can discern an ounce of empathy in its otherwise bleak glittering pupils. They are solemn, woeful, outwardly weighed by lament. I glare at them quizzically, yet in reluctance, lest I have been misled, lest I have mistaken its expression for a forthcoming and affable one.

The being dwells impassive, as the different life form that it embraces. It keeps staring at me, taking on an ever-growing sombre look, then out of the blue, reaches out both its scrawny arms so as to grab the cord that is imprisoning my right wrist, and unties it.

With stapled breath, I give it a reluctant look, one pondering upon the outcome of its action, not least its truthfulness and candour. For a moment I don't dare move, although I know it expects me to. Fearful at the idea that this may actually be a deceptive, ill-omened gesture from its side, I remain wholly immobile.

Then unexpectedly, the creature ventures downward past the trolley to the bottom of the autopsy bed. There, by means of its agile skinny fingers, it begins untying both of my legs, taking the whole thing one step farther.

My heart starts thumping, beating at an ever-increasing pace. Not only don't I dare move an inch, but my muscles also hurt. They feel strained and bruised, as if they had been beaten and assaulted. I have been lying here for too long, craving minute after minute, hour after hour that this will turn out to be nothing else but a dream, praying to God that they will release me and let me return home. I have been longing for that moment to occur all along, but now that the occasion has presented itself, I am embraced by a sentiment of fear, one breeding paralysis, one compelling me toward a sheer state of standstill. My mind is mesmerized, panic-stricken, afraid of what will happen when I decide to make a move.

Meanwhile, the creature dwells at the bottom of the autopsy bed, standing only inches from my legs. It keeps peering at me, perfectly impervious, save for the mournful expression colouring its otherwise repulsive and revolting outer shell.

I gaze back, my body quavering, intimidated by its otherworldly presence. My lungs pant for air, my body as yet unwilling to move. Then, in one of the most uncanny voices there is, the being opens its viscous mouth, uttering a loud scream causing a shudder to run across my spine.

Scared out of my wits, I look back, uncertain as to what to expect next, unsure as to whether its behavior should be interpreted as an act of hostility or as one of fury.

All at once, as appalling as it is, its facial expression undergoes a sudden change, putting on a foreboding frown and uttering yet another eerie shriek, so as to all appearances, scare me off. Without so much as a thought, my whole body responds in reflex by hastily moving to the side, gliding alongside the edge of the autopsy bed and fatefully falling down onto the icy metal floor in a harsh, callous thump.

The floor is cold, unforgiving. With stapled breath, I struggle to stand up, but too strained, my weary muscles succumb to the encumbering weight of my body which is becoming all the more frail. I crawl upon the icy metal surface, craving to live, with the being at my back, walking behind, as though compelling me to flee. I edge toward the door. It looks immense and inhospitable. The life form is still behind me, shoving me toward the exit and even though it looks burdened, there is still an ounce of empathy and mercy in its bleak repelling eyes, as if it were helping me flee, helping me live.

At last I reach the door, cold, made of metal. After much effort, somehow I manage to rise to my knees, almost to my feet. They hurt badly, as though they had been subject to extensive surgery.

At a great pace, the being approaches the door, and in a violent studied gesture, throws it open so as to let me out. Gradually, the gate veers ajar, then gapes at the unknown, the nature of which is a totally different world, one sinister and unforeseen. I catch a last glimpse of the creature behind me, still unsure as to whether its intent is to help or destruct. It is glaring down at me, yet not so much in despitefulness as in pity.

Without a thought, I bolt off through the gate, reeling through a corridor also made of otherworldly metal. My heart is thumping, my lungs nearly suffocating. It's dark, chilly. The puff of my breath skims against the air in an icy film, reminiscent of mist. Underneath my feet I can feel the humid floor, moist and damp. I run and run but the narrow corridor seems all the more endless. Its burden is perpetual, taunting my brain. There is no light, no clue for direction. I flee frenziedly, surrounded by darkness, one veiling the outcome of a lost saga, the very outcome of my fate.

Suddenly, it dawns on me, this is nothing like a ship. I must have been mistaken all along. It cannot be, for it is much too long a corridor. I must be somewhere else, an alien place far away from where I belong, most likely light years from home.

All of a sudden, I can feel how exhaustion embraces me. Against my will, my steps are slowing down as if compelled to surrender. I cope with fatigue, determined to live, determined to get out of this eerie place, but the truth is that my legs are betraying me, no longer capable of carrying my weight. I fall down onto the floor, unable to carry on running, let alone stagger toward the prospects of a taunting unknown.

Thus, overwhelmed by an imminent lack of hope, my knees bend helplessly, succumbing to an inevitable demise. My whole body goes crashing down against the rough metal surface of the floor. I gasp for air, but it seems to grow thinner, trapping me in a maze of darkness and pain. I groan, seemingly encompassed by nothingness personified.

"What is this place?" I ask myself aloud, but this time, the voice doesn't echo, nor does it bounce upon the walls.

To all appearances, the corridor stretches endlessly through a cluster of blackness and dusk, gaping in wryness at a lingering void, the essence of which breeds desperation and oblivion.

My hands search the cold surface of the floor, in quest of a clue, a hint, yet to no avail, for all there is to it is gloom, a dark burdening gloom, pulling a wry smile as it watches me go under. As for the narrow corridor walls, they too breed nothing else but coldness and a lingering smell of death.

My heart thuds all the more fast now, fearful at the prospect of what lies ahead, there at the far end of the corridor, one veiled by the mighty hands of an ever-darkening gloom.

An awkwardness falls upon the instant, burdening silence with a disagreeable sensation of impending doom. I'm on the floor, as silent as nothingness, waiting for something to rise, there hidden in the dark, something for which there are no words. And deep inside, I know it is unavoidable, for they have chosen me, they have captured me and taken me here to a place indefinite, far away from the world as I know it. And what else am I doing if not fooling myself, confident that there is a way out, a way to return and flee from this sickness. But how would that be, taking into account that I may be light years from home?

There's a sound now, an eerie sound, coming from the other side of the hall. It burdens silence with thoroughness, its essence is as loud as battle. I lie silent, lending my ears to its nature, striving to fathom out what it is made of. It seems to grow ever-louder as if nearing, approaching at a fast pace like a shriek mounting from the gloom. Its presence is imminent, offering nothing but a bleak promise of downfall.

There are two sounds now, the other one emanating from the other side of the corridor, closing in all the more so as to encircle me. I'm lost, trapped, left at the fate of ruin, and the more my heart thuds, the closer they get, their heavy footsteps bouncing upon an eerie, icy floor, blending with the rhythm of my heartbeat, following at the rhythm of dread.

I can hear voices now. I pant for air, my lungs longing to breathe, craving to inhale life and exhale fear. They are out to chase and capture me. They are shoving me toward the end of my rope, leaving me without the shadow of a chance.

"We ought to get him."

"It is crucial that he remains inside."

"Don't let him sneak out."

Out? Is there a way out? Far away from here? Far away from this maze of gloom?

Without a split second of a thought, I jump to my feet, flabbergasted that I did so for my brain is no longer in control of my legs. They are the ones who are leading now, compelling me to bolt in a desperate and frenzied quest for a fleeing path, an exit.

I run all I can, suddenly sensing as a squirt of energy submerges my veins and shoving me to succumb to the deceptive illusion shed by hope. I dart toward the voices ahead of me, fleeing from those at my back in trust that my eyes will see, if anything, a ray of light, a clue for salvation. I crave but my eyes don't see, for all there is to it is a thick throng of gloom gaping at a hovering black void before my eyes.

Nevertheless, my legs sprint all the more, my body surrounded by sheer darkness. They are dashing as fast as my heart is thumping, as though to outstrip it.

"He's running."

"We need to stop him or he will make it to the outside."

"Judging from the sound of his footsteps, he must be only a short distance ahead."

"Turn on the lights so that we can discern him."

No sooner said than done, the ceiling sheds what seems like a thousand rays or more, glaring at my blinded my eyes.

The entire hall lights up, revealing a sombre colour corroding the walls which seem to grow narrower as I bolt. Slowly, my pupils are adjusting to the light, and in a moment of bleak horror, my gaze meets with theirs, grave, dark, weighed by voracity and resentment. They stare at me from behind their wicked expressions, standing there, only a short distance away.

I pause abruptly, then turn around to look around me. There are others behind, coming from the other side of the corridor. Their faces are pale, their skin colour tanned by fury.

I'm trapped like a mouse, marooned on the brink of the unknown.

"Catch him."

"Don't let him flee."

Catching me unawares, they start running toward my shivering body, coming from both sides, closing in as two narrowing walls about to crush me alive. They are moving fast, at a daunting pace.

They scream.

"Don't let him get to the outside."

"Catch him before he does."

If they say so, then there must be a way out! Right here right now, here in the middle of this corridor! There is an exit right where I am standing, but where? God, tell me where!

Panic-stricken, my hands start brushing the surface of the wall to the sound of their nearing footsteps. My lungs are lacking air, nearly suffocating under the pressure of their advance. To my chagrin, there isn't anything, nothing under my palm, nothing that would enable me to open a gate and dash out like a gust of wind. It's only seconds shy to them confining me, I need to find the gate.

Then, out of the blue it strikes me like a miracle sent from above. A puff of air from underneath my feet brushes against my legs. Hurriedly, my eyes wander to the ground only to discover some sort of locked opening. In the wink of an eye, my body dives down, my trembling hands taking a firm grip on the handle and violently throwing the gate open.

As the opening closes above my head, I can hear their thumping steps blending with screaming voices, otherworldly, eerie voices.

"He found it, he's underneath the ground,"
"He's going to make it to the outside."

Before my eyes, there is a cavity, a small access strip or air duct leading to the outside. I can see a beam of light penetrating it at its far end. Without a thought, I throw myself into it, crawling all I can toward the source of light, with the creatures at my back.

The cavity is shaped like a small tunnel, extremely thin and narrow. I'm striving, coping with its ever-constricting edges. I'm halfway through now. I mustn't fail, my life depends on it.

Behind me, there's a loud thump. I can hear it run across and echo through the air duct I'm in. They must have opened the gate now. They must be inside, right at my back, about to embark through the tunnel. I would like to turn around and have a glance about me but I can't, there is no time, there is no place either.

I pant for air, struggling to crawl myself to the pulsating beam of light ahead of me, striving to stay on course and praying not to lose faith.

There are eerie sounds behind me now. They are inside, perhaps only ten yards behind me. I creep ever faster, gasping all the more for air. I cough, my vision is getting blurry. Yet I'm almost there. I mustn't lose faith. Only a few more yards and I am out. I pray as I crawl. I pray for strength to be shed from above. I pray that I will be spared from ever seeing them again, their evil, pale visages, their daggering eyes filled with spitefulness. I pray ever more, as hard as I can, and suddenly I am there, at the other end of the tunnel, amazed at what my eyes are witnessing, at what my vision is unveiling.

Before them, through the opening, I see a sky, blue and innocent, gazing back at me like a crystal ball full of promises. I see the horizon and an orange yellowish sun. It is dusk, or is it dawn? Hopefully daylight will be substituted for night time. Soon darkness will swoop down like a thunderclap, flashing through the sky and giving birth to an aftermath of gloom and shadows. Gloom is good, for in it I will hide, in it I will veil from the weighty reach of their gazes.

I glance below the darkening sky. There is sand everywhere, a sea of dust and grime bordering the scope for miles and miles. There are mountains beyond, retrieved and veiled by a rounding horizon.

My hands reach for the grating. I'm on the verge of opening it and getting out. But all of a sudden my heart beats faster, forcing my lungs to inhale more air than there actually is to breathe. It thuds faster and faster for there are other things out there, eerie things, horrendous things. There are machines, otherworldly machines, things my eyes have not seen before, things better left unseen. There are moving silhouettes too, beings, moving life forms. My mouth opens, I shriek, I yell at the top of my lungs, embraced by a sheer sentiment of horror. I shriek all the more loud until my vision narrows, slowly darkening out and then, out of the blue, a thump at the back of my head. Everything turns black.

***

My eyelids feel heavy, weighed and burdened by an overwhelming sentiment of fatigue. I'm striving to unlock them, I'm struggling to come to. I cough, the air is stiff, cold, a sense of uneasiness fills the room. I'm gasping, striving to breathe, the air is too thick, I'm having trouble inhaling.

I think I'm lying, I'm uncertain. A shudder runs across my body, and as much as I try to, I cannot move. Underneath my back, I can sense metal, as cold as ice, as hard as rock. It feels foreign, otherworldly, not of the kind I know.

Fright embraces me. My heart begins to thud. An eerie sensation of deja-vu squeezes me from head to toe. I think I've been here once before. I think I know where I am, helplessly lying on an autopsy table in the middle of an icy alien room.

I can hear voices, all over the place, voices not of this world, the tone of which is grave, sombre, alien. With a thumping heart I open my eyes. They are everywhere, surrounding me from every corner imaginable, their bleak aliens visages unveiled by the light, their eyes scintillating with evilness, their darkening gaze staring at me in disgust, their little hands firmly holding lethal silver tools mirroring my panic-stricken face.

Out of fear, I try to speak out but my vocal cords are gone. I try to talk but I no longer have a tongue. I yell in my head, I yell so loud that I nearly feel pain reach my ears. They're talking about harming me, destructing me.

I pray to God that these creatures will spare my life, that they will see beyond their prejudices, beyond the thin barrier or appearances. I pray until I am shoved toward the brink of psychological exhaustion and my mind can take no more, succumbing to the overwhelming sensation of fatigue and slipping into a state of half-awakening. The aliens' voices bounce in my mind and confine my head in a perpetual maze of words.

"We need to put an end to his life."

"We cannot do that."

"We don't have any choice. It is crucial that it is done now."

"We haven't even received authorization to do that."

"At this point, it is no longer relevant."

"It is relevant, we were supposed to carry out an autopsy for scientific purposes."

"We no longer will. Our requirement at present is to kill him."

"We are not authorized to do that."

"I am willing to take responsibility for that. It is essential that he dies, he represents a danger for us."

"Why do you presume such a thing? We haven't even been able to communicate with him."

"I know because he is different, he is a different life form."

"Is that a sufficient reason?"

"In my eyes it is. Look how different he looks, it is repulsing."

"I won't allow that you kill him for no reason."

"We will kill him anyway! We can't afford another one of those controversial incidents!"

"How do you mean? What incidents?"

"We can't afford to see him flee from this area, nor can we afford incidents like those that have occurred in the past."

"What?"

"I'm talking about the Rosewell incident and all the others that followed!"

"That was a long time ago–"

"We should have killed him in the aircraft, after we found him. I say we should have killed him before we *flew him here to Area Fifty-One. We can't afford to see these kind of news and discoveries reach the public eye once more. As the "Majestic Twelve" that we are, it is our mission to ascertain that these sorts of incidents never get out and reach the press! God only knows what would happen if it did again!"*

"I understand that but he is not necessarily a menacing life form."

"He isn't?"

"No."

"Well, how do you explain that there has been such numerous reports of alleged sightings of him and his kind all around the surrounding states?"

"Are sightings a sufficient danger?"

"Thank God we got there in time to capture him before he got to any human being. We can't afford any more reports of human abductions. My only regret is that we failed to capture the other beings while we were there."

"Human abductions haven't even been proven as far as I am concerned. In my eyes, they are only the fruit of human prejudices."

"It is not for you to be the judge of that."

"Nor is it for you to be the judge of his life or death. As a creature of God, he is also entitled to live!"

"You're calling this a creature of God? Have you completely lost your mind? Take a look at his appearance for Christ's sake!"

"I don't know, but that's the point, we don't know whether he is or not, and thus, we don't have the right to put an end to his life! That's why I released him from the autopsy table–"

"There is no place for moral issues here, as to you having helped him flee, that clearly constitutes a grave legal infringement of the regulations set by the government of the United States as regards all classified activity within the 'Majestic Twelve', and as a consequence, the result of that will be an internal trial and of course a sentence."

"To be candid, at this point, I couldn't care less. I still think it is wrong to kill an entity no matter how repulsing or dangerous that entity may appear to be. For God's sake, this is a form of racism! It is that way of thinking that got us into approving of slavery in the past!"

"We are awaiting orders from above. The president will be calling soon from the White House."

"It is wrong to kill him with or without authorization!"

"Major?"

"Yes?"

"We just received a phone call."

"Is it the red phone?"

"Yes."

"Put it online."

"Yes... I understand Mr. President, yes... of course Mr. President. We will see to it that it is done. Madison?"

"Yes?"

"You know what you need to do?"

"We're awaiting order, Sir."

"Very good. We just got a call from above."

"What are the orders, Sir?

"The orders are very clear and come from the highest chap himself."

"I'll obey the orders, Sir."
"Very well."
"What are the orders?"
"Kill it."

FEAR OF THE DARK   *Erik Jayce Landberg*

FEAR OF THE DARK

FEAR OF THE DARK   *Erik Jayce Landberg*

FEAR OF THE DARK

The snow lay upon the road as impervious as non-existence. Its white shimmering surface reflected the reddish shaft cast by a round glowing moon, soaring in the winter night sky above the neighbourhood.

It was cold, late December, and the winds howled athwart as if they knew of something that nighttime was oblivious to. They hollered, skimming above the white powdery surface in a choked shriek, one as eerie and twisted as the encompassing gloom itself.

On the outward, darkness seemed silent, peaceful, but its exemption instilled a sentiment of foreboding, one screaming from the abyss, mounting from the depths of night in a desperate urge to manifest itself.

A thick layer of snow covered the trees, above which a dark Scandinavian sky hovered unbiased. The night was black as evanescence. It lingered by like a ghost, imminent by its presence, yet absent to the eye.

There, lurking in the dark, outside the sheltering walls closing out the cold and its wailing winds, something crawled, something yet unknown to the inhabitants dwelling within those walls. For they slept, the sleep of the just, the sleep of those who did not dream, for their weariness was as their knowledge, eaten by the lack of understanding.

And the more they slept, the more it breathed there, surrounded by blackness, as if it didn't exist, for in their minds, it didn't.

"What was that?"

"Nothing, go back to sleep," she said.

He turned on his side, pulling the sheets with him, for they were on the verge of falling down. The sound of wintry winds rocked him and, though he struggled to remain awake, fatigue danced before his eyes.

"Didn't you hear the n–" he mumbled just enough to fall back asleep.

"No Honey, probably the wind."

Even though plunged into obscurity, the room felt clear, illuminated by a lingering twilight which pierced through the windows above the electric candles reflecting in the glass. Inside, silence breathed all across, instilling peacefulness and serenity. But outside, the mild snowstorm had it its way, exhaling at the night as though whispering a dazzling spell. Just as it did, so did Robert, waking up with a choked jump only to find himself sitting in bed, there in the half glowing twilight of the room, striving to come back to his senses, senses he had left in his sleep.

"Now did you hear?" His heart was thumping as he held back his breath to listen.

"Yes, what was that?" Valerie sat up in bed too, her hair uncombed, her eyes half-opened, her mind half-aware.

"I'm not sure, Honey, but it sure sounded loud."

"Oh geez, it must be the barn again. Someone has got to fix that damn door," she whispered.

"Maybe I ought to have a look."

"Don't bother. You'll have a look at it tomorrow. What's the point in doing it now if the door's broken anyway?"

"You're probably right. I'm going downstairs for a glass of milk. Go back to sleep, Honey."

"Right," she yawned, running her hand through her tangled hair before crawling back under the sheets.

Robert glanced at the alarm clock on the nightstand. Two a.m. sharp. He reached underneath the bed for his slippers and started toward the stairs.

"One of these days, I'm'na fix the damn barn once and for all," he murmured as he walked down the steps. "Yeah, yeah one of these days..." he whispered.

The stairs pointed down in a spiral, descending through total darkness towards the kitchen door. Upstairs there was no light switch and Robert had no choice but to descend in the dark, until he reached the ground floor and its wide encompassing gloom. He walked unsteadily, weighed by fatigue. The wind whistled faintly through the air ducts and Robert could almost swear it was whistling to the pace of his footsteps.

"Almost there," he sighed, "Almost in the kitch–"

There was a sound. It didn't sound like anything he had heard in that house before. It echoed through the stairway like something drifting in from the outside. It came from the barn. It came uninvited.

Robert stopped halfway downstairs, and as he stood there in the dark squinting all he could in the hope of shedding some light on it, darkness gaped candidly. It swirled about him in a silent dance, the pace of which led in the faint twilight. A hush fell on that moment as though a quieting spell had been cast.

"I gotta get that glass of milk," Robert wanted to say but his lips didn't obey.

He put his right foot in front of his left and began walking down the rest of the steps, paying heed not to skip any for they were hard to see, there in this throng of black.

At last, he was there, ready to press down the handle of the kitchen door but the door was already ajar.

"How odd, I could swear I had closed it last night before going to bed," he mumbled before waving it out of the way, already stepping inside.

Without thinking he opened the refrigerator, the light painting his face in a yellow shaft. As he bowed in search of the beverage, his eyes glimmered, as though he had opened a safe glowing back at him with dazzling gold. Sitting down at the table, he poured the milk into his glass, emptying the milk carton, warts and all, and peered out the window at the barn. It was covered in snow nearly as white as the milk he was about to bring to his mouth.

He gazed but he didn't see, for outside it crept, there between the shades of a sheltering dark, longing for something to quench its lust. And the more he gazed, the less he saw, and the less he saw the more it crept, slithering like an unwanted creep in the abyss of the night.

Robert held the glass firmly, as though he was afraid to drop it. Perhaps an instinctive reflex dwelling deep in his subconscious, one not as unaware as he was.

He leaned forward, preparing to raise the glass to his mouth, and just as it was on the verge of brushing his lips, another sound voiced with loudness. Caught unawares, Robert's hand let go of the glass. It crashed down onto the kitchen floor into a thousand pieces of splintered glass glimmering in the twilight. Embraced by fright, he jumped off his chair with a moan.

"Valerie?" he called, but the only answer was the burdening and deafening sound of silence.

"Is that you?" he persisted.

But it wasn't her. No, it was something else, something made of divergence and dissimilarity, and somehow, Robert understood, although he didn't quite know yet. This time the sound he had heard was far too loud to have come from the barn, or from outside the house for that matter. It was clear it came from inside the house.

"Valerie?"

Robert licked dry lips and shivered, as though the cold had come in from the outside, as invasive as a thief. Before his eyes, gloom roamed like a beast untamed, and the more he gazed about him, the less he saw.

All of a sudden, footsteps were heard from upstairs, disturbing the distressful quiet hanging in the air.

"Damn!"

He bolted, leaping forward.

"Valerie, answer me!"

He paused by the flight of steps in front of the kitchen door, peering into the dark like a blind fool. Upstairs, something was definitely lurking, and the more he thought about it the more his body shivered, inundated by the tart smell of darkness.

And then a shadow, flying by like an elusive breeze.

A door slam.

A scream.

"Valerie!" he yelled, his mind surrounded by the bitter scent of dread.

He ran up the stairs, his slippers brushing against the red wall-to-wall carpet, red as blood. He slipped, fell, rose, fell again, his heart thumping all the more.

Even though it was all happening so fast, everything in his brain ran in slow motion. A grudging eeriness dawned on him, restraining him from seeing clear.

Now he stood barefoot, halfway between downstairs and upstairs, gasping for air. In the tumult of his mind, he had lost his slippers and the roughness of the wall-to-wall carpet had almost burned his feet. Robert stared at the bedroom door ajar, screaming in the dark as if made of flesh and blood.

He licked his dry lips.

"Someone's in that room," he thought as he began to climb the remaining steps, those too screaming at him in a blood-red pitch. Darkness added to that scream and as soon as he reached the doorway, a shudder caught his spine. His lips whispered her name again, unsure of what he'd see once he pushed that door open.

All of a sudden, a faint noise came from beyond it, as if something were brushing against sheets. With a trembling hand, he fought back his fear and shoved the handle. The door opened with an eerie creak that nearly made his ears bleed.

"Valerie?" he attempted to say but his throat was too dry.

A streak of twilight pierced through the blinds and at its core stood a shadow, shrouding the light not quite like an eclipse. It stung his eyes like the blades of a thousand knives and without so much as a thought, Robert uttered in a scream, "Who are you?"

"It's me," the shadow replied, "no one else but me."

Robert's eyes widened.

"Valerie?"

"Yes dear?"

"I thought a burglar had entered the house."

"A burglar?"

"Yes, I mean all the noise up here, you know–"

"It was probably me."

"Did you hear the door slam?"

"Not really. I had the water running in the bathroom."

"Probably the damn barn again."

"Probably," she replied, and as she spoke the word, a faded noise came from inside the closet on the right side of the bed. A noise so faint that neither Valerie nor Robert heard it, but it was there, as omniscient as the embracing gloom and its shimmering twilight.

***

"...the wave of testimonies seems to continue. Over a hundred people have and are still contacting local police authorities, having allegedly witnessed an abnormal light phenomena around the county throughout the past week. Scientists claim that it is probably nothing else than an aurora borealis even though the likelihood of it happening this far down the country is close to none. In the meantime, government officials have shown a complete lack of interest in the matter. Our reporter Michael Persson has been talking to people where the phenomena has allegedly occurred and here is what they said–"

"Valerie? What time is it?" Robert yawned as he struggled to get his eyes accustomed to the light.

"I think it's around ten or so."

"Would you mind turning the TV off, I can't stand voices this early in the morning."

"Sure, Honey."

She got up and walked past the nightstand toward the other end of the room to grab the remote control.

"I had the most peculiar dream last night," she said while pressing the button.

"Really?" Robert answered as he struggled to sit up in bed, his eyes yet burdened by the bothersome weight of fatigue.

"I dreamt about the barn, that there was someone there."

"Why would there be anyone in the barn?" Robert answered, now beginning to wake up.

"I know. It's silly."

"Let's go down and have some breakfast," he said, "I'm starving."

Robert opened the fridge door to reach for the milk, then realized that he had poured the last of it into the broken glass, the pieces of which were still lying scattered across the kitchen floor. An embarrassing memory of last night. A dark souvenir.

"Damn it! We're out of milk," he uttered.

"Oh, no we're not, Honey. I put the milk carton on the table. It's right behind you."

Robert continued to look in the fridge, searching for the one he had used last night and emptied out.

"Where's the empty pack?" he asked in astonishment.

"I told you. Right there on the table, Honey, and it's not empty, it's quite full."

Robert turned around and laid eyes on that candid white box, there screaming on the table as though an artifact that couldn't be.

"How can it be full? I emptied it out last night."

"I dunno," she retorted flatly as she took a plate from the shelf, making sure not to step on the ever sharpening pieces of glass.

For a moment, Robert simply stood there frowning at the box, his mouth agape. As he laid eyes on its white uneven shell, he realized with apprehension that it was indeed the one he had used, the one he had intended to drink, but whose taste never reached his lips, choosing to crash down onto the floor instead, like the betrayer that it was.

And now it was betraying him all the more, seemingly looking daggers at him from its paper shell, one impossibly containing milk.

"What happened on the floor by the way?" Valerie asked as her eyes fell on the scattered glass.

Robert didn't answer, nor did he hear the question for that matter, all too focused on that snow-white piece of swill, the colour of which seemed to sting Robert's eyes even more.

"You ought to clean that up before one of us steps on that shit and gets hurt," she sighed.

Intrigued, he headed past the fridge toward the table, as though somehow, he knew it wasn't milk. There he turned around, not quite panting as he stood facing a wall, as impervious as a rock.

"Do you want me to pour you some, Honey?" Valerie asked.

He didn't respond. Instead, he stood silent with his feet firmly on the floor, awaiting with reluctance as of that moment in time.

He heard her grab the milk carton, sigh as she felt its weight and uttered, "It seems full Honey."

The glass tinkled as she lifted it off the table. Robert bit his lip, his eyelids still closed, frowning in dread at the prospect of what was going to occur.

Then, silence was raped by a horrendous shriek, that of Valerie. It rang in Robert's head like Doom's Day bells. They were summoning him to turn around.

"Oh my God!" she bellowed.

Robert's eyes dwelled sealed, closing out whatever horrendous sight Valerie had set eyes upon.

"This is not milk Robert! This is not milk!"

"Then what the fuck is it?" he yelled back.

"This is blood! This is fucking blood!"

As she swore, Robert's gaze wandered down to her trembling hands.

"You've just poured blood into the glass!"

Whatever he had poured seemed to coagulate within the goblet's walls and in a twinkle of an eye, he let go of the glass. It landed on the kitchen table with a deaf thump.

"Valerie," he said, his forehead ghastly with sweat, "This must be some kind of a bad joke."

Decisively, yet not without some reluctance, she seized the milk carton only to discover the whole pack was filled with vivid red.

"Are you sure this is blood?" he asked.

"I don't know. It seems to coagulate, doesn't it?" Her voice quavered like a trembling leaf.

"It seems quite fresh–"

"Okay. Let's calm down. Let's not jump to conclusions. This might only be a joke. Only a very bad one."

"Who's blood is it?"

"We ought to take a closer look."

"I'm not sure I want to."

"We have to, Robert. Or do you just want to put it back in the fridge?"

"Hell no!"

As their eyes glanced with horror at the arisen mystery, Robert caught a glimpse of something floating on the surface of the liquid.

"What is this?" he said.

"What?"

"That."

He pointed his index at a gray substance close to the surface.

"There's something in there. We need to extract it."

"Go ahead, do it! I'm not putting my fingers in there."

"Do it!" she begged?

"Aright! Aright! Stop yelling already!"

His heart pounding, he seized the glass between his hands, stared briefly at the object and gave Valerie a disgusted sideways glance.

She glanced back and nodded.

Biting his upper lip, he plunged two fingers into the coagulating fluid and extracted whatever eerie substance it contained.

Thick clumps of half-dried blood dripped onto the table and the floor, staining them with an insatiable colour, the taint of which screamed at their eyes.

"It feels like wet cotton," he uttered in dismay.

"What is it?"

"Valerie, the blood is still warm," he whispered in the frailest voice she had ever heard from him.

"Dear Lord! How come it's warm? It was in the fridge!"

"Whatever happened here happened just a few moments ago," he continued.

She stared with repulsion.

"The window is open. Someone came in and put it in there!" His voice worsened.

"Robert, what is that, cotton?"

He brought it up to his nose and inhaled its nauseating stench.

No sooner had he started than his nostrils gave in, shoving him to a revelation that almost made his heart stop.

"Oh my…" he began, his lips unable to finish the sentence.

"What, Robert?" Valerie exclaimed in reluctance.

"Valerie," he continued as he fingered the alleged cotton.

"What, Robert, what?

"Where is the dog, Valerie?"

She frowned. Her eyes widened as he spoke, and she collapsed in an outburst of sobs and moans.

"This is not cotton, Valerie. This is not cotton…"

"Then what are you saying?" she cried, tears dashing down her cheek, wetting her lips.

He turned toward her, the expression on his face more dumbfounded than aghast.

"This is fur," he added as his hands let go of it.

She took one step backwards, and then bolted out of the kitchen, her footsteps hitting the cold, blank tiles.

"Bruiser?" she yelled once.

Then twice.

"Where are you? Come here Bruiser! Come here!"

But as her ears expected the barking that would usually follow her summons, silence hung over the moment as a sign of fatality.

Just as her mouth opened afresh to call out the carnassial's name, Robert interrupted.

"He's not in the house, Valerie."

"What?" she looked at him, a frail ounce of hope piercing in her eyes, as if Robert had finally found the dog, found it safe and sound.

"Where is he then?" she questioned hesitatingly.

As his eyes wandered out through the window, he set eyes on the snow. The unyielding snow and the barn, the barn door ajar. Ajar like a wicked invitation to follow, as a summon to enter its ever-widening darkness, one screaming at them from the gloomy entrails of the barn.

Without a word, he nodded, inviting her to follow his gaze, a gaze now all the more saddening as the impervious snow bore dire stains of blood. Blood leading to the door, to the ajar door, to the gloom that it embraced.

"He's in the barn."

"Who did this to us, Robert?" she screamed. "Who would do this to us?"

Walking across the backyard, Robert headed toward the agape door, his breath puffing at the cold and the snow cracking underneath calculated yet hesitant steps.

He had left his wife behind. Valerie was panting at the kitchen window as she followed her husband's course. He didn't want her to see the atrociousness of what surely lay inside, and whatever horrendous sight awaited there in the sheltering gloom of the barn, he most certainly didn't want to share it with his wife.

With bated breath, he paused shy of the door, and his eyes met with splinters of fur and dried-out pieces of skin. They lay spread out on the snow as the wind stroked through the straws like autumn leaves.

He bit his lip, then shoved the door out of his way. Gloom smiled at him with infuriating ardour, blinding his vision as he advanced.

Quickly he found himself at the core of the room, unable to watch, unable to see.

In his right hand, a flashlight. One about to share, one about to disclose his deepest fears.

He held it to his heart for a brief moment. Then he plucked the courage and pressed the switch.

Suddenly darkness was raped by the presence of light, inundating the scene with unwelcome lucidity. Nevertheless, his lids remained closed, as yet unprepared to uncover whatever there was to uncover. And as he stood there, part of a scene he wasn't able to see, there was a noise.

At first, he remained silent, attentive to its texture, waiting for it to sound afresh.

Yet it didn't.

Instead, the muted noise was substituted for a mere complex one.

The sound of fluid. Then a smack, as if someone or something was feeding.

His eyes as yet sealed. His lips felt damp against the cold air encompassing him.

The noises grew louder. By now, he knew he wasn't alone. He also knew that whatever shared his presence wasn't human. No human would ever feed with such barbarian appetite.

"It must be a wolf," was the first thought that dawned on him. But as he recalled the milk in the fridge, the blood in the pack, he suddenly understood that it couldn't be further from the truth.

He opened his mouth.

"Who's there?" he barely managed to ask, his vocal chords nearly deserting him.

There was no reply, save for that smacking sound, that perpetual smacking sound.

He raised his voice.

"Who's there, goddamit?! Answer!"

The sound stopped. Then, before he even had the time to think, a puff of air.

The animal in the room had ceased feeding and the sound of its breath was now ringing in Robert's ears with dreadful revelation.

If the smacking sound hadn't been human, the sound of its breath was nothing by comparison.

Robert stood silent as death, as though a prey before a predator, and as his lids strove to dwell closed, the animal let out a shriek never heard before. It filled the barn with insatiable horror, and as Robert's legs bent under the burdening weight of fear, his eyes opened so widely as to catch a glimpse of whatever was sharing presence with him.

"Oh dear God!" he bellowed as his left hand inadvertently let go of the flashlight.

It broke in splinters of breaking glass as it hit the floor, and no sooner did it occur than darkness inundated the barn with foul and soiled obscurity.

"God, what was that? God, what was that thing?" Robert craved to know as he raised his voice to the heavens.

Down on the floor and with gloom embracing every inch around him, he could still hear the irregular breath of the beast, puffing against the cold, surrounding gloom, devouring silence. Then without warning, it rose in the dark and fled out, breaking a window at the rear. It dashed out of sight *(had there been any light)* across the snow and into the night.

With tears in his eyes, he began to crawl like an insect on the wooden floor, madly aiming at the exit, scraping his face in a frantic struggle to survive.

And if he had crawled like a creep, he also fled like one, seizing the door handle with the weakness of a coward. For wasn't it exactly what he was after all? A disaster-prone coward ruined by damnation, running for his life, stumbling and falling on the snow as he left the barn without looking back, without looking back even once.

***

The following night bore the vices of the previous. Cold, empty, yet not devoid of dread. Valerie couldn't sleep well. Nor could Robert. For out there, under cover of darkness, something still lurked. Something hungry and untamed. Something feeding on dogs and rats, and God knew what else.

As they slept the sleep of torment, the gray Scandinavian firmament soared above them like a malediction from another world. Another world light-years away, so far yet so close, intruding on theirs. Intruding with greed and hunger, with death and blood, downfall and demise. For what they were about to encounter, had never been encountered before.

***

"...*Government's explanation as to the alleged light phenomena and the few reported mutilation cases around the county this week is that there is absolutely no connection. Officials like to maintain their view on the subject by claiming that of all the mutilation reports, none could actually be established or proved.*

'As long as no pictures or facts have reached our offices, the mutilations have not occurred as far as I am concerned' says mayor Chris Lundgren although UFO activists claim there has been some sort of internal cover-up as regards to the matter. Rumours also have it that some citizens might have been threatened by government officials were they to disclose testimonies or pictures providing evidence–"

"Valerie?"

A moan.

"Valerie?"

"What?" she answered.

"Wake up, please. Wake up!"

"What is it?"

"Who turned on the TV again?"

"I didn't. You must have done it."

"No, I did not!"

She wiped her eyes.

"Robert!"

He didn't answer.

"Robert! Tell me!"

"No, I told you. I didn't turn it on. Something's weird."

"I'm not talking about the television, Robert."

Silence again.

"You know what I'm talking about. Tell me!"

"I... no, I don't know."

"What did you see in the barn yesterday?"

"Nothing, Valerie, nothing."

She sat up in bed, shoving off the sheets.

"Oh come on! You must have seen something! You should've seen your face when you came back running like a fool in the snow. I thought someone was after you."

"I told you, it was dark. I couldn't see anything in there."

"Robert, look at me! Something happened in there! I heard a shriek last night!"

"No."

"Look at me!"

She pulled him toward her.

"He stared at her with horror, as though she had been a ghost, as though he was trying to deny what he saw.

Perhaps he was denying it.

"Oh my God, you look terrified!"

"No, no. I just didn't sleep well that's all," he grunted then rolled back on his side, turning his back to her.

"Robert, I'm your wife and I insist you tell me what you saw in there! What was there in the barn? Did you find Bruiser?"

Her question defied silence and lost, for Robert didn't so much as groan.

"You saw him, didn't you?" she muttered behind his neck, frowning, "He's in there in the barn, isn't he?"

Robert tucked himself underneath the sheets as though to seek shelter from her candid question. Then came the words, heavy and burdensome.

"Bruiser's dead, Val."

Her face went slack.

"What?"

"He's dead, okay? The dog is dead."

She lay back on the bed without so much as a sound.

"Who did it?" she said, striving to hold back the tears mounting in her throat.

Again, there was no answer. Her eyes wandered skyward, as white and cold as the lingering snow in the backyard.

"I asked you a question," she said.

She stared at the unyielding ceiling soaring above her like a spiteful cloud veiling the room.

"Val," he began. "Don't."

"Why not?"

"Asking too many questions wouldn't serve any purpose. It wouldn't lead anywhere, believe me," he murmured as if to welcome stillness and serenity.

"Never mind," she answered, yet not with the serenity he had hoped for. "I'm'na find out by myself."

Robert turned around, the sheltering sheets floating down onto the floor like a heavy feather.

"What? What do you mean?"

"I'm going to the barn," she snapped as she put on her slippers, rising from the bed with the determination of a soldier marching out to certain battle. Only that battle was already lost. So knew Robert and so knew the creep out there, the bloody wicked creep that had sunk its greedy teeth into their beloved pet.

Robert rose out of bed and grabbed her by the shoulder.

"Don't!" he said.

"Robert! You're not telling me all there is. I'm going out there to find out!"

"Don't, Valerie! Don't do it!"

"Why shouldn't I? Tell me, Robert! Why shouldn't I? Is the dog still in there?"

"Yes… he's in there but–" he stammered, tears filling his dreadful eyes.

"Then let me see it!"

"You don't understand, Val. There is not much left of it to see."

"What?"

"It's been devoured. The dog has been devoured."

She paused by a chair at the corner of the bed and sat down.

"Was it a wolf?" she asked, her eyes staring blankly in front of her, as though there was nothing but emptiness before them.

Robert bowed his head, unable to answer.

"There are no wolves around here, now are there?" she said.

He shook his head.

"But it must have been a wolf. What else, Val?" he tried to smile but failed.

"What about the milk in the fridge. Or should I say the blood? Was that a wolf too, Robert?"

Her gaze was now as empty as ever.

"It was a wolf Val. It was a wolf. But it's over now. It's over–"

She rose from her chair.

"I'm going into the barn."

"No don't–"

"Why not? I want to see the disaster with my own eyes to believe it."

"Valerie, don't go in there!" he searched for the right words. "The wolf… the wolf might still be out there–"

"Wolves only stay long enough to feed on their prey, Robert. Only so long."

He stared at her in desperation, unable to come up with a reasonable answer.

"It wasn't a wolf, was it, Robby?"

She reached out to him and ran her fingers through his hair, like a mother. Like a mother and a wife.

"It was something else, now wasn't it?" she murmured.

"Is that why you didn't want to tell me? Is that why you're so afraid?"

Her gaze was thoughtful.

"What is it that you saw in there, Robby?"

He stared at her on the verge of tears. Longing to confide in her. Longing to get rid of that vision burdening his head with blood and torn flesh.

"What is it that you saw in there?" she repeated so as to force an answer.

"I saw a–"

"Yes?"

"I saw an–"

His confession was interrupted by the doorbell. It rang loud.

"Who can it be?" he said, wiping his eyes.

"It's pretty early. I don't know."

"It must be the police or something. No doubt they're coming about the dog."

"But we haven't called the police, Robert, have we?"

"No," he said flatly as he tightened his dressing gown, walking down along the stairs toward the door.

Valerie followed slowly holding on to the banister tightly, as tight as Robert had tightened his garment.

"Be careful, Robby!" she exclaimed but his hand was already on the handle, cold and hostile.

She could hear a voice in her head, screaming to be heard.

Don't open the door. Don't open the door.

Robert hesitated as he glimpsed through the peephole at the unyielding silhouette outside.

"Perhaps we'd better not–" she began.

"What's that on your chin?" Robert said.

"How do you mean?" She brushed her skin in search of an anomaly.

"And there on your upper lip? What's that?"

The bell rang anew, this time twice as loud, it seemed.

"Blood…" she answered as she withdrew her hand from her face.

Her eyes were wide open, glimmering as though in sheer horror.

The bell.

"Don't open!" she said, reaching out a hand but Robert was already turning the handle.

A bright unyielding sheen penetrated the hall as gusts of cold followed invasively. There was a shadow in the way, veiling the light, and as the door opened still wider, Robert exclaimed in astonishment;

"Hans?"

"Who is it?" Valerie's voice shivered.

"The farmer," Robert answered.

He stiffened slightly as he spoke the next words.

"What are you doing standing here with that in your hands, Hans?"

Save for puffing nostrils, Hans remained silent, eyes wide-open, shotgun in both hands, fingers longing for the trigger.

"What's going on?"

Valerie attempted to step forward but Robert poked her right back.

"Stay there!" he ordered

"Put your shotgun down, Hans. What's the matter?"

The neighbour's frozen lips gaped to speak, revealing chattering teeth.

"What's the matter? You seem all shook up," he said as though they had been unaware of something absolutely atrocious. "Haven't you heard?" he continued, bellowing the words.

"No!"

"Haven't you heard the news, Robert? Haven't you heard the goddam news?"

"No, what?"

Hans grinned terribly, revealing more frozen fissures in his lips, as if he had been up all night long, all night long searching.

"Why are you smiling?" Robert asked nervously.

"They're here, Robert!" he screamed. "They're here, all over the woods and the county. They're among us!"

"What the hell are you talking about?"

"Shut up!"

Hans' grip on the shotgun suddenly tightened.

"Hans, what's going on?" Valerie asked, tears in her throat.

"Hush, Honey. Let me handle this."

"Someone emptied my milk container and put blood in it. You don't happen to know something about it, Robert? Now do you?"

"I… I'm, not sure what you want me to s–"

"My horse is dead, Robert! It's dead right to its guts! In fact there are no guts left!"

"What?" Robert exclaimed.

"It's been devoured, eaten, feasted on!"

"By a wolf?" Robert's throat suddenly felt very dry.

"I took samples and had the blood analyzed. It belongs to my horse!"

Hans' hands began trembling all the more, as if he were losing control, letting fury take him over like a disease.

He continued; "A wolf doesn't replace milk with blood Robert. No the wolves didn't do that. *They* did it! They're giving us some kind of warning!"

"What?"

"Don't you understand?" His voice quavered ever more. "Milk represents birth, life! Blood represents death!"

"Okay, okay. Please calm down!"

"Now, what's your opinion on the matter, Robby? I'd be very glad to *HEAR* it!" he emphasized the word.

"I'm very sorry, Hans. I'm very sorry. I'm sure they'll find the animal who's done that."

"The animal? I think I might already have found it."

"Really?" he asked.

"I think I know in which house the *animal*, as you're referring to it, is hiding!"

Silence soared above the lingering snow like a calm before a storm.

"Really? Where?" Robert shivered.

"Where's your dog, Robby?"

"What?"

"Where's your fucking dog? Where's Bruiser?"

Again silence. As loud as war. As heavy and burdening as a plague.

"He's upstairs, I think. Sleeping in front of the TV."

"Oh, how neat! Sleeping in front of the TV you say, huh?"

"Well yes, Hans–"

"While every other animal is being devoured by them?"

"Them?"

"Call for your dog, Robert! I wanna hear him bark."

"Hans, this is ridiculous. Where do you want to go with all this?"

"He can't bark now can he?"

Robert didn't answer.

"He's sleeping, right? So he can't bark right?"

"Right," was the only answer Robert came up with.

"But he's not sleeping upstairs, now is he?"

Again silence.

"He's sleeping in fucking hell because he's dead!"

As he uttered the last word, Hans' shotgun trembled in his hands, demanding an answer.

"How do you know?" Robert snapped.

"Let's just say I got suspicious and paid a little visit to your barn, pal. No funny sight up there, I gotta tell you. Pretty nasty if you ask me."

"I don't know who did that, Hans. I don't know what to say," Robert uttered in nervousness.

"I don't agree with you, Robby!" Hans' grip on the trigger tightened. "I think you have a pretty good idea where they are hiding."

"They? What the hell are you talking about?"

"Haven't you heard the news, Robby? How could it go unnoticed?"

"No, I haven't!" he said, anger piercing his voice.

"Everybody is talking about them! Everybody in the neighbourhood. It's all over the news, Robby. They're everywhere!"

"Who is everywhere? I don't understand! Explain yourself, will you!"

"Again, I'm surprised to hear how little you know. Or should I say; how much you know?"

"I have no idea what you're talking–"

"The aliens! The goddam aliens, Robby! They're demons from the sky. They're everywhere! They've invaded the county, feeding on whatever crosses their way."

Robert burst out in laughter, but inside he didn't.

"You're pathetic, Hans."

"Some say they take the form of the humans they have eaten and then melt in the neighbourhood."

"Aliens taking the shape of humans? Are you kidding me?"

"You should know whether I am kidding you, Robby, don't you? They're not only aliens! I told you! They're demons! They hate life! They love blood! The milk is a little prank of theirs!"

Robert stared at him in complete astonishment then shook his head.

"See, me and the neighbours began to get a little suspicious when neither you nor your wife took any interest in this. You didn't even react! Nothing! A normal reaction after what happened to your fucking dog would've been to come and talk to me. Yet you didn't! I've been your neighbour for more than four years now and you didn't!"

"I… I haven't left the house, Hans. Really–"

"Bullshit! I saw you! I saw you go to the barn from my window. You went in there and–"

Silence dawned on them like a coup de grace out of nowhere.

"And then?" Robert asked, his breath puffing against the cold air.

"You're not really Robby," Hans countered.

Robert stood in the doorway, reading Hans' infuriated visage as he put on a vicious look, one not as intimidating as it was threatening.

"And then what?" Robert said.

"And then you ate it," Hans' finger caressing the trigger as he spoke the words.

"What?" Robert shouted, his voice running across the snow and echoing throughout the cold.

"And then you ate your fucking dog, Robby!" Hans bellowed.

"For God's sake! Are you completely crazy?"

"You're one of them, Robby. You're one of them and so is your wife."

"Leave my wife out of this! Valerie, go upstairs. I'm 'na sort this out, okay?"

He gave her a look, as if to say everything would be solved in no time. But she didn't listen. Instead she got closer behind him, grabbing his arm so tightly that it almost hurt.

"Hans, you're overacting. You're not thinking clearly right now. Please put the gun down!"

"You're not Robby, you demon freak from outer space! You're not Robby! You fed on him! You killed him and you fed on him, you bastard! And now you stole his shape!"

"Get a hold of yourself!" Robert yelled, his heart thudding like a mad hammer.

"I'm telling you! You ain't foolin' me! I know what you're up to and I'm sending you right back where you belong!"

No sooner had he spat the words than he seized the gun with both hands, aiming at Valerie's forehead, ghastly with sweat.

"Don't!" Robert bellowed, "She's got nothing to do with this!"

"Oh is that so?" Hans' hands were quavering. "Then please enlighten me! What's that on her chin?"

"What?"

"What's that on her fucking chin?"

Robert turned.

"What's that on her chin!?"

Robert stammered. "I… I don't know–"

"You don't know?"

"Valerie… what's below your lip?"

"You don't know? I'll tell you what it is you damned freak! It's blood! She's been feeding on my horse!"

"Now calm down, Hans!"

"You fucking aliens have been feeding on my horse and now you're gonna pay for the feast!"

"You don't really think we're aliens, Hans?" he smirked.

"I don't know what the fuck you are! But you sure ain't from this planet!"

"You can't be serious!"

"Take a closer look at my face! Does it look like I ain't serious?"

"Come on, Hans! We've been neighbours for years! What's gotten into you?

"I saw you! I saw you walk into that barn, Robby, or whatever your name is now."

"You're losing your mind buddy! Put the gun down!" Robert urged, but Hans stood frozen in time, stroking the trigger with ever-closer intimacy.

"I'm not the only one, Robert! I'm not the only victim. There are others. The whole neighbourhood was struck."

"What are you talking about?"

"It's a plague! I'm telling you! A fucking plague!"

"Please go home buddy. We'll talk about this when you come to your senses!"

"There's been rumours of abductions and, and–" he stammered, ghastly with sweat, freezing almost all at once as it hit the cold wind.

"And what?" Robert panted.

"And mutilations. Mutilations all over the place."

Hans' voice weakened. His gun lowered momentarily as a wave of fatigue seemed to overwhelm him from head to toe.

"That's nonsense! You can't believe this shit!"

"Haven't you heard the sounds?"

"The sounds?"

"Those eerie sounds at night. They're inside our houses, hiding in dark corners, closets, beneath beds. And then, when we least expect it, they strike out of the blue. They sink their voracious teeth into our fleshes, into our women and children!"

The gun went up again,

"As a matter of fact I have," he replied.

"Aha! You see, you've heard them too, you hypocrite!"

"Yeah! Does that make me an alien demon?"

"I don't know!"

Hans' eyes filled with tears.

"If I had been a monster, I'd have told you I haven't heard those sounds!"

"I don't know! I'm confused! Your wife's got blood on her chin! She's been feeding!"

"No!"

"She's been fucking feeding!"

"No! We found blood in the milk too! Blood in the milk Hans! There was no milk left! Only my dog's blood and I don't know who put it there! I don't know who did this to us. A bad joke Hans! A really bad joke!"

"And you want me to believe that! Can't you space freaks come up with anything smarter? I thought you're supposed to be more advanced and intelligent!"

"We're not! We're your neighbours!"

"We're your neighbours!" Valerie recurred as she bolted forward.

"Valerie, no!"

"Step back, wicked demon!"

"But Hans, it's me Val!"

"Step back or I'll shoot you! Perhaps I'll shoot you anyway!"

Deaf to the words, she bolted toward him with open arms, "It's me. Val."

"Die you goddam space animal! Die!" he bellowed, squeezing the trigger as best he could and firing one lethal shot at Robert's wife.

Valerie went crashing onto the floor in a deaf snowy thud, as if she had died before hitting the ground.

"Val!"

Robert kneeled down beside her, embracing her as she struggled to breathe. The white snow around her didn't remain white for long, for soon it sponged the blood running down her inert chest and arms.

"Get an ambulance Hans! She's dying!"

Overwhelmed with tears, the *sniper* fell to his knees.

"Oh God, what have I done!" he grunted as he let go of the still smoking weapon, fossilizing the encircling snow.

"Get an ambulance, for Christ's sake!"

"I'm sorry, Robert. I'm so sorry!" he wept as Valerie's lids closed out the frozen air once and for all.

"The blood, Hans... The blood came from the milk! She must have drunk out of the pack–"

"How was I supposed to know?" he cried, tears inundating his ever-widening blood-red gaze.

***

Once again, the beast had struck. There, under a cold and empty hovering sky. It had hid from the reach of their eyes as a vicious predator deprived of empathy yet overwhelmed by hunger.

It had lurked in the snow, behind doors ajar, shy of a bedroom closet unveiling noises that shouldn't be there. It had crawled in the barn like a shape, his eyes had encountered but whose nature he did not dare reveal. For the face he had recognized in it had scared his guts to death. Sometimes as the years passed by, he would still dream in the shaft of an unbiased twilight. The beast would pop up in his mind, whispering from upstairs with the voice of a witch;

It's only me, Robby, it's only me.

By no means did it have the shape of an alien, nor that of a demon lurking in the dark or allegedly feeding in the barn. No the beast he had seen was something utterly different. Something far more scary. Something deeply anchored within his cultural heritage and that of his fellow men. It had a wholly different name, one as dark and greedy as the sound of it.

Blood-thirst. Blood-thirst from the darkest core of our breed. That of human nature. That of a wife.

GOSSIP ON A PARK BENCH

FEAR OF THE DARK   *Erik Jayce Landberg*

GOSSIP ON A PARK BENCH

It's nine in the morning. For Jonathan Johnston, the traffic jam never seems to dissolve. He's sitting in his car with a firm grip on the steering wheel, staring through the windshield with thoroughness, as the obstructed avenue only appears to grow all the more thick. Inside his Mercedes, there's a smell of leather, a smell he has grown to like over the years. One reminiscent of his seemingly rocket-like career, for in the five years he has spent working for the corporation, there hasn't seemed to be so much downs as there has been sheer ups.

There is also a smell of lit cigar, actually a cigarillo, innocently smoking in the silver ashtray reflecting the leather seat. Yet Jonathan doesn't smoke, nor does he drink for that matter, at least not ever since he got out of the rehab clinic in Tucson six years ago. No, Jonathan has left all the little bad habits of his behind, and now that he is one of the most prominent members of the ever-growing corporation, he only enjoys the smell, neither more nor less. It provides him with a sense of self-confidence, makes him feel important. Not that he isn't, but the blending odors of leather and cigarillo really help approve of his value.

The radio is on, just like every morning en route to work. Soon there will be today's news broadcasts followed by this week's weather prognosis. Jonathan couldn't care less about the news or the weather, for after all, what difference does a radiant sunny day make when you're compelled to sit behind closed office walls heeding you from the radiant outside world? No, what he really cares about are financial chart broadcasts about to be revealed. Like every morning, he expects them with a blend of eagerness and anxiety. For that is the news that really makes a difference, that is the one who determines whether it is going to be a good or bad day, not least on a personal level. Not a bloody forecast predicting a beautiful sunny day or a whole gory week of it.

The traffic is growing, to all appearances sinking down into a state of perpetual chaos, the prospects of which are only likely to worsen. Sometimes, when it gets like this, Jonathan thinks about veering through Forty-Second Street, for he knows that it is always a good shortcut. Though, he doesn't like driving there through the slum, because of the bums, because of the hate-filled gazes that he gets.

Yet sometimes he does, embarking on an ordeal too unpleasant to speak of, for somehow deep inside there are feelings hollow in his mind, sentiments inducing a sort of bad conscience that he'd rather not think of. They are used to swooping down on him like a predator out of the blue, only he knows when it will occur, he knows when those wicked emotions will begin to taunt and devour his soul, torment his mind, for somewhere at the back of his head, he is aware that had it not been for that seemingly endless rehab which he underwent roughly six years ago, he would most certainly have ended up there on Forty-Second street amidst the bums, staring at all the shiny German cars hastily driving by and the three-piece suit dressed fools inside of them, wryly concealing their tormented faces, there behind a sheltering windshield.

Only, today the only fool they are staring at is him, and only him, more than any other it seems. Against all odds he knows fate would like him to be one amongst them, one looking in from the outside, wondering how it feels to be driving there on the inside. Yet he is not and sometimes it aches deeply, like a knife blade cutting through ever more, and made of silver just like his pathetic Mercedes ashtray, the one cradling a self-smoking cigar seemingly glaring at him as if in iniquitous temptation.

Not that he is not grateful, nor that he isn't thankful for his well earned success, but now he also knows something else. A luxury those who dwell outside will never know and sometimes he just wishes he didn't. He wished he wasn't blessed with the knowledge of how it feels to be one of those fools cowardly driving through with the sole goal of avoiding that thick and damp traffic jam.

However, Jonathan doesn't have any choice today. Whether he likes it or not, his secretary has scheduled three essential appointments with significant officials, three of which he can't afford to miss, for the corporation depends on them. It depends on his punctuality and input to his detriment and chagrin.

Hence, in order to avoid the burdening and bothersome jam, Jonathan reluctantly veers to the right, embarking on an outside journey as much as on an interior one, for when it all comes down to it, Forty-Second street presents nothing else but a daggering ordeal, one unfathomable, thrusting weighty memories to the surface.

He drives thoroughly, paying heed to the bordering sidewalk, past the bar where he, just like the others, used to be a devoted regular. He drives but he doesn't see, he just stares. The cigar is still smoking and Jonathan gets pleasure from its smell, for it closes out another odor, one much less enjoyable, namely the smell of reality outside his sheltering Mercedes.

Now he's at the junction, waiting for the traffic lights to turn green. How he hates that perpetual red color endlessly looking back at him through the windshield. How he despises its never-ending glow.

The radio is still on, humming like a motor, or at least so it seems. He reaches for the volume knob, turning it clockwise in the hope of choking out the shouts of the street and its bums, roaming outside, at the gray encompassing crossroad, shouting at poor Jonathan Johnston all but words of wisdom. Only he is not so poor, at least not financially, yet deep inside, hollow in the darkest abyss of his soul, Jonathan has never felt so deprived, not even six years ago when he was striving to make ends meet.

Thus, nervously, he sits there, surrounded by a sheltering stench of leather. One recalling against his will, grudgingly remembering that he no longer is what he used to be, that he has now reached another level, the privileged one of sumptuousness and wealth.

Strangely, sometimes he envies them. Their liberty, their freedom and simplicity. He gazes at them in secrecy, he watches shrouded by a tanned windshield, admiring the lives they're leading and somehow wishing he was elsewhere. A different place, far away from the corporation, far away from his fining, empoisoning duties.

Now, to his great relief, the light turns green. It is a welcoming light, one longed for, one delivering and inducing reprieve, allowing him to leave the wicked reddish one behind as he hits the gas with fervor. And before he knows it, in the twinkle of an eye, he is en route past the worn-down crossroad, toward a brand new day, one offering nothing but great prospects of achievement and cash flow, one about to erase this incommodious little tribulation of his, namely the all in all taunting Forty-Second street.

***

With grace he parks the car. A few turns of the wheel and he is all set, right there at place hundred and forty-two, right next to hundred and forty-three, the spot reserved for the CEO's glossy Hummer. In a considered gesture, he turns the engine off, puts out his still smoking cigarillo and steps out of his shiny Benz.

"Yet another Monday," he sighs to himself as he starts heading for the skyscraper's entrance.

"What did you say?" a voice utters from behind.

As Jonathan turns around, he is surprised to see Mr. Kreamer walking a few steps behind him. He had just stepped out of his well-earned Hummer and carries a black briefcase, as glossy as the car itself.

"Good morning, Mr. Kreamer!" he responds, almost unwittingly, "How are you doing today? Did you have a nice week-end?"

"Johnston, there's no time for weekends! I've told you that several times now. All one's spare time needs to be committed to Kreamer Inc. Nothing else," the CEO bellows not quite abrasively.

"Of course sir! I was just pulling your leg–" Jonathan jests.

"Good!"

As they stand waiting for the elevator, Kreamer gives him a little tap on the shoulder and adds;

"You know, I may ask a lot from my employees, but on the other hand I remunerate them a lot as well. Don't you agree?"

"Of course sir, what's a few weekends in one's lifetime uh?" he grins politely, but deep inside he feels like ripping Kreamer's head apart.

He responds with a sardonic little giggle as if amused by Jonathan's daring sarcasm.

"You know Johnston, today is a big day, today you and I are gonna see to it that the company earns more money than it did on Friday!"

"Yes sir, we will…"

Kreamer is always saying that, every working day of the week, with the joyfulness of a circus clown about to unwrap a colorful present, and as though he was saying something new each time, as though he had come up with a brand new strategy to motivate his world-weary, jaded employees.

There's a small ringing sound. The elevator doors open as if welcoming today's working labor into the gates of hell. Behind them, the same doors close on a free world outside, imprisoning them within walls made of glass and seemingly reaching for the heavens with sky-scraping audacity.

"How's the wife?" Kreamer asks as he vigorously presses the twenty-third floor button, eager to see the day begin and the cash flow in.

"She's fine," he nods politely although he hasn't been able to spend a single evening with her for at least a week or so due to required overtime hours.

"You have a wonderful wife, Johnston. Stick to her like a tube of glue, for you know, not every spouse is willing to oversee romantic weekends in favor of her husband's professional career."

"Right... by the way, Mr Kreamer?"

"Yes?"

"I was wondering whether I need to put in an appearence next weekend, for you see, Julia and I have been talking about this trip to the countryside to sort of visit–"

"Johnston!" he utters abrasively.

"Yes...?"

"You need to stop pulling my leg with your hilarious jokes! One of these days, I'm gonna laugh myself to death because of your crazy humor!" Kreamer snorts like another one of those crazy clowns.

"But–"

"You know, if I didn't know you better, I'd really think you were serious," he adds in jest.

As if to shove the banter to an end, the elevator reaches floor twenty-three with a disturbingly sharp ping, the floor highly anticipated by Kreamer Incorporation's CEO, yet vastly dreaded by Jonathan. Before he knows it, the doors open on a brand new working day and to his chagrin, on no prospects of spare time in sight.

"I'll see you after your meetings, in about two hours. Come into my office with the contract signed!"

Somewhere in his mind, Johnston's requests weren't so much meant as a joke as they were meant as an attempt to have Kreamer die of a burst of laughter, and although he knew that he would have to come up with a really good joke to make it happen, that didn't refrain him from fantasizing about the probability of such an outcome.

"Yes sir, I'll see to it that they sign it–"

"Not only sign, Johnston, but sign wholeheartedly!" he taps him on the shoulder in an amicable gesture to the untrained eye, yet in sheer threat in reality.

"Of course," Jonathan answers with a grin, "I would never make them sign half-heartedly."

"I know that, Johnston, I know that! See, now I'm the one pretending and pulling your leg!"

"Right…"

Jonathan feels compelled to express amusement and before entering his office, Kreamer throws him an appreciative look and starts heading approvingly past the reception for the far end of the corridor.

***

Jonathan presses the handle downward. The glossy wooden door opens on a well assorted office, clean and in order. As anticipated, his desk is sparkling, ready to be soiled with grimy files and paperwork. Behind it reposes his office chair, warm and welcoming, made and smelling of leather, just like the interior of his Mercedes. The one fashionably parked next to Kreamer's envied hummer. Upon his writing desk, a silver ashtray, one more symbolic than anything else. One reminiscent of the one cradling his ever-burning cigarillo.

He closes the door behind him. For a moment, he stands silently contemplating the desk. His meeting begins in about fifteen minutes and he has come to withdraw the file from the drawer, so as to extract the contract, craving for it to be signed. Yet somehow, the eagerness is gone, the motivation has disappeared, as if it had never existed, as if it had never been.

He strolls toward the window overlooking the park and gazes down at the tiny benches below, along the narrow broad-leaved trees bordering the paths by the little curved ponds. He watches ponderingly, almost in envy, nearly feeling vemodig toward the past. One all but glamorous, one not enthralling, yet for a moment, he longs to be taken back, almost craves for it. But the weight of reality is too burdening, as imposing and imminent as its presence. It leans in favor of a meeting he does not want to attend, one he'd rather not cope with, but he is called, beckoned, compelled to follow, compelled to abide and relinquish. He has been given no other choice, no other prospect nor fate, but the daunting one of the company, perpetual, continuous, obstructing a sense of freedom now slowly beginning to fade away and wither with the past.

Sitting on one of the benches below, there is an old man. He looks worn-out and deadbeat, as if time had corroded him, not least consumed him. From his window, he glares down in search of his silhouette.

Sometimes Jonathan walks past him, on his lunch break when heading for the closest 7-Eleven to order one of those cheap fast-food menus. Sometimes, his gaze meets with his, empty, blasé, as though the monkey finally got the best of him.

Many times, Jonathan has thought of talking to him, perhaps offering him a buck, but he knows how it feels, he knows what he used to think of all these fools dressed up in their ridiculous three-piece suits approaching to proffer them charity. Now, in spite of being one amongst them, he's the fool, the goddamn bastard stuck in a never-ending utopia, the prospects of which are all but promising, at least when it doesn't breed money, big fat money.

The phone rings, shattering his daydream almost instantaneously. He picks up the earphone.

"Yes?"

"Mr. Johnston, the representatives from Sandstorm are here, the meeting has begun and we're all waiting for you to get started. People are beginning to whisper you know," Jonathan's secretary indicates shyly.

"Right Laura, I'm handling the contract, I'll be there in no time."

Jonathan's gaze withdraws from the glassy window only to wander down to his attaché case, the one sheltering the disturbingly precious contract which Kreamer wants to see anchored. Without so much as a thought, Jonathan grabs his attaché and bolts out of the room as if he was about to miss a train. He runs down the corridor, past the fax and the coffee machine, and before he knows it, he's standing at the door with his right hand on the handle, ready to press it down, ready, yet somehow grudged.

Emanating from behind the doors, he can distinguish murmurs, sighs, voices instilling rumors and questions as to whether Mr. Johnston is going to show up or not, with or without the infamous contract. He can sense the ambiance is tense, for somehow he knows that this might as well be the most important deal of the century for the corporation, and not least for him, whom Kreamer seems to expect a lot from.

In a brief moment, Jonathan inhales, exhales, and in an unwilling, compelled gesture, he presses down the golden handle beneath the lock, throwing the wooden doors open on an oblong, strained conference room, the imminence of which is going to reveal the prospects of a future hard to predict or imagine.

"Mr. Johnston, we've been waiting for you!" a man utters vividly as he stands up to shake Jonathan's hand with vigor and affirmation.

"I'm sorry I had you wait, an important phone call kept me," he makes up so as to not give the wrong impression.

"No problem, the important thing is that you're here now. We at Sandstorm Inc. have really been looking forward to the completion of the contract and our role within the corporation as a future leading actor on the market."

"Likewise, Mr…? Excuse me I guess we haven't been introduced yet…"

"Oh, my fault really. My name is Brown, Whitley Brown, head executive of the international and inland department."

"Head executive of my ass," Jonathan thinks as he manages to compel a fake, approving smirk followed by a nod.

Firmly, Brown grabs his hand anew, as if it weren't done once already, and pulls a somewhat nervy smile as he politely yet keenly shows Jonathan to his seat, shoving him slightly toward the far end of the conference room where an empty, cold seat awaits.

"It's a pleasure meeting you Mr. Brown," Jonathan adds, again grudgingly for all he wishes for now is to be anywhere else on earth but here, any random place including the all but hopeful park bench underneath his twenty-third floor window, where the old bum is taking a nap, right now at this very moment.

As he makes himself at ease, Jonathan looks about him with reluctance. The room is filled with at least eight or so representatives from Sandstorm Inc., all gazes dug down in paperwork and grimacing from time to time as they take a sip of sugar-free coffee, overlooking their overweight bellies. They all seem to wear the identical black suit and the same tie color. Sitting in the middle between them is Whitley Brown, as enthusiastic as ever it seems, eager to get started and return with a deal.

"Gentlemen, if everybody's ready, I suggest we move straight to business," Kurtz begins as everybody straightens in a mutual hush.

In the five years he has worked for the company, Jonathan has never liked Kurtz, neither has he tried to for that matter. In his eyes, he always was and always will be the *besserwisser*, loud-voiced type of guy, perpetually licking up for the boss (in this case Kreamer) and in a constant need to assert himself.

Somehow, the deficient personal chemistry has always seemed to be reciprocal, for Kurtz Hoff has never really felt much for Jonathan either. Somehow he has always presented a threat to him, one breeding concurrence and obstructing brilliant career possibilities.

As to Jonathan, his reasons are slightly different, for they never had anything to do with career or profession, nay, they tended to weigh more toward a personal texture, one of distrust and aversion.

"Very well. Mr. Hoff, we have studied the conditions that you offer thoroughly and find them extremely convenient, almost too convenient if you see what I mean," Brown begins slightly in jest, forcing through a proud but polite snicker.

"It gladdens me to hear you say that and we're confident that the conditions offered will satisfy your company in every field. As to your allusion, we can understand your reaction when you perhaps question our motives for offering you such advantageous conditions. But believe us when we say that there is absolutely no hidden catch," Kurtz answers not a second too late.

"My associates and I have gone through every single point and paragraph stipulated in the contract and can not see any clause or section that would constitute a clear infringement of, the yet to be implemented, new directive that will permit us to launch ourselves into the market."

"That's because there isn't any," Kurtz counters with one of those forged grins Jonathan hates so much.

"Mr Hoff, we haven't read any negative clause at all save perhaps for the pricing issue in *exhibit four, point three*."

No sooner had he said that than Kurtz fervently grabs his spectacle case, pulling out his shiny silver glasses, the reflection of which shows nothing else but the section of the contract spoken of, and lying there screaming on the table.

"I suppose you have omitted to include the pricing in this section?"

A brief silence dawns down on the room yet withdraws just as quickly.

"No, see we haven't omitted it, we have neglected to include it on purpose," Kurtz responds.

"And why is that? If you allow my curiosity?"

"Well simply because there isn't any pricing, nor invoicing as regards to that specific clause, which means that you will not be invoiced by Kreamer Inc. at all," Kurtz smiles nervously.

"That sounds a bit too good to be true, doesn't it?" Brown gazes up as his eyes withdraw from the piece of paper.

"Actually not, and Mr Jonathan Johnston here will be glad to elucidate any query as regards to the issue."

In an unforeseen moment, Jonathan sees how Kurtz arrogantly points his right index finger at him, washing his hands from any subsequent debate, hence putting Jonathan in *a painful* charge of the arisen situation.

For believe it or not, that is exactly how he had meant it to be. Obviously, Kreamer had foreseen the likelihood of such questioning from Sandstorm Inc., and he had been very clear on the fact that should such a situation arise, Jonathan was to be placed in immediately and take over the whole discussion. This was too much of an important deal to let it go down the gutter, and when it came to solving burdening problems such as contract issues, Kreamer had only faith in Jonathan, a fact adding to Kurtz's ever-growing jealousy toward Joe, and at the same time toward himself.

It was crystal clear. It was Jonathan's task to bullshit himself out of the situation and return safe and sound to Kreamer's office with the contract harbored.

Those were also the tasks he hated the most. Sometimes more than life itself. More than his shameful times of yore when he was worth no more than that elderly lazy bum lying on the park bench beneath his glassy office. For as of now, Joe would have to lie, he would have to fool Sandstorm Inc. big time and rip them off on their hard-earned goddamn cash. For that clause screaming there in the contract like a beast craving to be freed, that clause was meant to be, that clause was deceitful in every imaginable way. So knew Kreamer, and so knew Jonathan.

What didn't come across as clear and understandable from the cluster of words constituting the fraudulent section, was that although it was stipulated that Sandstorm Inc. was not going to be invoiced by Kreamer Inc. in any way regarding offered services, another greedy company would. Another third party which had entered into a deal with Kreamer's corporation; namely that of invoicing Sandstorm for every free service rendered by Kreamer's. For mind you, there was nothing written about not being invoiced by another party.

And if everything went according to plan, the fraud was to go unnoticed by Mr. Brown and his associates. At least it was Jonathan's dirty deeds to see to it that it would.

"You will not be invoiced by Kreamer Inc. at all," Kurtz had exclaimed so untruthfully.

"That's right, not by Kreamer Inc.," Jonathan thinks, *"but by another one. One which in its turn will be invoiced by Kreamer."*

"Not by Kreamer," is what he is thinking, but what he says is nothing else but an antonym; "No invoicing

whatsoever, Mr. Brown," he utters grudgingly, his forehead shining with sweat and clumsily revealing an ounce of discomfort as he speaks.

"That's outstanding, Mr. Johnston, really outstanding, and may I ask you how your corporation intends to pull in an income without invoicing us?"

With no hesitation, yet not without burdening reluctance, Joe sets his tongue in motion, speaking faster than his brain is possibly able to think, speaking faster yet brilliantly, not to say, stunningly.

"It's really simple. See, what we intend to do is market ourselves for free, which means that we offer you these specific services at no cost and eventually and hopefully, our trademark will gain a name which, in its turn, will allow us to catch the interest of a wide variety of affiliates from which we will gain advertising money for each placed ad," Jonathan utters as he unwittingly rubs his nose, for that's what Jonathan does, each time he tells a lie or each time he used to hide his bottle of Scotch from his wife when she was about to bust him.

A brief moment of silence sinks down on the wooden conference room, instilling the essence of an unstable atmosphere, one as uncertain as tomorrow's market forecasts Jonathan is used to listening to, each morning in his fat Mercedes Benz en route to work.

Then on a whim, Brown withdraws his greasy spectacles from his eyes, bringing the tail of the frame to his mouth and putting on the most thoughtful look Jonathan's eyes have ever witnessed. He dwells like that for half a minute or so, sucking on the tail as if in pensiveness, compelling poor Kurtz to hold his breath, in wait of Brown's answer, his heart thudding all the more as the seconds leap forward.

Then, out of the blue, Brown's lips let go of the greasy spectacle frame, only to pull an approving smile, one shamefully soiled by naivety and inexperience, two attributes, before which the sharks at Kreamer Inc. are used to drooling.

"Well Mr. Johnston, if you put it that way, I guess my associates and I will see no objection to signing the contract," Brown smiles like a fool smiling before demise.

"It gladdens, us Mr. Brown, it gladdens us," Jonathan tries to nod as truthfully as he can, for hollow deep in his mind, what he really would like to say to Mr. Brown is; *"It makes me want to puke my guts out."*

"I tell you what, whyn't you let my colleagues and I have a brief discussion in private for a minute or two, just for the formality of things, and we'll give you our approval in about five minutes?"

"Very well," Kurtz nods in greed, "We'll leave you alone so that you can clear anything out, we'll be back in about five minutes."

"Thank you Mr. Hoff."

As if the deal was closed, each and everyone of Kreamer's guys begin to leave the room one by one, marching out in victory with a filthy wry smile at the corner of their mouths, the conference gates closing behind their filthy backs.

"You did very well Johnston! Kreamer is gonna be proud of us," Kurtz throws at Joe while giving him a harsh tap on the shoulder, one almost too harsh for Jonathan's taste.

"I couldn't care less Hoff. Whyn't you go and get yourself a cup of coffee while I stand here waiting by myself?"

"Oh c'mon, Johnston! Don't you think it's about time you and I became partners? I mean, don't you think our mutual careers would suffer a greedy boost were we just to join forces and impress Kreamer?"

"I ain't a shark like you, Hoff."

"Oh really? Is that so? I see that you have rather high thoughts of yourself, Johnston. It's quite amusing really, taking into account what a great job you did in there. You lie just as good as a preacher! Your mom must be proud," he chuckles, while wiping off whatever imaginary grime covers his costume jacket.

"Whyn't you just cut me some slack, Kurtz, I'm in no mood for this today."

"You're doing great for a guy with no mood!" he laughs as he mockingly throws a scornful glance at the other Kreamer sharks roaming in circles outside the conference room.

Before Jonathan is given the time to think of an answer, the gates open again, unveiling an ever-smiling Mr. Brown, standing firmly in the doorway, and waving a silver pen so as to indicate that the contract is now signed.

***

"Johnston."

"Yes, sir?"

"You know you're impressing me don't you?"

"I guess so… I don't know."

"You don't know?" A twisted smile forms at the corner of his lips as he, with fervor, takes a deep sip off his cup.

"Let me tell you something, Johnston," he adds with the grin of a shark, "what you did in there, in the conference room, shows what a real man you are, and–

"But sir–"

"...don't ever forget that Johnston. You know, just between us, somehow you and I are quite alike in that we're both winners. Do you understand what I'm saying, Johnston?"

For a moment, Jonathan's gaze drops down to the floor which was constituted by a horrible green wall-to-wall carpet, stretching throughout Kreamer's entire office. Then, on a whim, his lips abide to his thoughts.

"What about Kurtz?"

"What about him?"

"Is he a winner too?"

To the question, Kreamer utters a deep, weary sigh, lets go of his cup and slams it upon his shiny wooden desk, causing a squirt of coffee to land on and stain his dark green silken tie, the same awful green as that of the goddamn carpet encompassing him. Then his voice raises as he heatedly speaks his mind.

"I told you Johnston! You gotta stop those goddamn jokes! Try to be serious for a moment. I'm trying to discuss your future here at the heart of the corporation."

A brief silence follows as he strokes his wet tie, yet only a very brief one, for shortly after, his eyes wander back with the disturbing aim of meeting with Jonathan's. "I tell you what. This goes for a reward, and not any reward!"

"I appreciate the thought sir but–"

"Don't you dare interrupt me Johnston! How many times have I told you not to interrupt me when I'm speaking?" He puts on a frowning look.

"I'm sorry, Mr. Kreamer–"

"No time for sorrys! Listen, this contract is going to earn Kreamer Inc. a large of amount of money, more than you could ever think of. Hence, I'd like you to become my right arm. I want you to become my assistant. In other words vice president."

Out of the blue, silence dawns on the instant like a million bombs unleashed.

"Well say something, Johnston, don't sit there speechless as a fish!"

"I… I don't know what to say sir, really."

"Well what? Aren't you happy?"

"Yes of course I am, Mr. Kreamer, of course I am. It's just that, it all comes so fast–"

"Well if this is your happy face, God knows I don't wanna see it at your dog's funeral!"

"I appreciate it, sir, I really do."

But Jonathan does not. On the contrary, his mind starts to feel weighty, burdened by a scornful conscience from which there is no escape. His eyes are weary, gleaming slightly as they try to repress tears, ones of scourge, for his mind is plagued by an ever-darkening vision of a future in which he cannot picture himself. One blurry and giving in to mists of dark, for somewhere in the confined depths of his mind, he knows he doesn't belong,. Not here at the heart of the ever-growing corporation, not here nor elsewhere.

***

With a heavy heart, Jonathan strolls back to his office, his spirit burdened by an ever-aching conscience. His lips are dry, dusty. They thirst for water, something to drink, a bottle of Scotch, a bottle of goddamn Scotch, and for the first time in six years, a thirst like never before.

He pauses shy of the door, presses the handle down and throws it open with an ounce of discomfort embracing his mind. Throngs of sunrays pierce through the door left ajar, compelling him to squint as they blind him mercilessly.

He staggers in, walks toward his desk and sinks down in his leather chair. An awkwardness lingers on, for this time the smell doesn't comfort him in the least. Quite the contrary, to his astonishment it repulses him and deep inside Jonathan thinks he knows why. It repulses him, simply because it reminds him of himself, of his shiny Mercedes parked next to Kreamer's Hummer, of all those fools driving by Forty-Second Street with the bums looking at them, looking at *him*, Jonathan Johnston, the biggest fool by far, he thinks.

His heart begins to thud, obsessively longing for a refill to a last drink he took six years ago.

He opens the drawer, digging out a snapshot of him and his wife with the Eiffel Tower in the background. It was taken during their honeymoon in Paris, reminiscent of the lives they once shared. Until he was recruited by the company. Until he started selling his time and soul for money. Until he became an industry prostitute.

In a snappy movement, he throws the photograph flat on the desk, sighs deeply, then reaches for another item deep in the drawer.

A bottle of Scotch. One untouched, half-empty, half-full, and today it is his call to determine whether life is to be regarded as half full or as half empty, and something at the back of his head tells him in obstinacy everything weighs in favor of the latter.

On the desk, the picture of his wife screams as if refraining him from doing it, but the urge is too intense, his lips too dry.

With a troubled mind, he rises from his leather chair, reeling past the desk, his hand firmly holding on to the spirit bottle. He stops shy of the window glass, peering out at the sun with thoroughness, his eyes on a quest for something, a clue, a hint, anything.

He peers yet sees nothing but a crowded park and a sunny Monday sky shedding down what suddenly feels like a million sunrays at least. His face finds itself wholly covered by their soothing warmth, yet not a single one brings him comfort, not one miserable ray of light.

In an effortless movement, he raises the bottle to his mouth, his lips now thirsting ever more, thirsting for an unlawful knowledge, namely that of drunkenness.

Holding the bottle one inch from his mouth, he stands before the window, his face disturbingly reflected in it. It is a face of despair, one of desolation. He stands hesitating as if he had come to a halt, to a life junction. He falters, and the more he does, the more his lips seem to grow dryer, as if shoving him to death row.

Now his hand is quavering, as though he had made up his mind, as though he was determined to go through with it and swallow that venomous squirt of poison flavoring the horrendous bottle gleaming in the sunlight.

Thus, in both a decisive and thoughtless gesture, he gazes in desolation at his own reflection as he is on the point to drink, the glass mirroring his mediocre face. He stares knowingly, aware that he is nothing else but one of those fools, one of those three-piece suit fools boastingly driving their Mercedes through the narrow metropolitan middle ground, the one between rich and poor, light and dark, life and death.

In a thoughtless gesture, he's about to gulp down the infamous liquid, his hand quavering slightly as his lips long to be wet, when suddenly the phone rings on his desk, shoving all his plans to a halt, at least for now.

He turns around hastily, hurries toward the desk and answers while putting the bottle back where it belongs.

"This is Kurtz," a voice utters as he lifts the earphone.

"What do you want?"

"I just wanted to say congratulations, that's all. Mr. Kreamer has just told us that you've been promoted to vice president," he answers joyfully, but his rusty voice betrays his jealousy.

"I see. Are you going to start kissing up to me now that I am vice president, Kurtz?"

"What... It's not like that at all..."

"It's not?"

"Well no... I just wanted to be friendly. I'm surprised you take it that way."

"Oh come on! You haven't been friendly in a thousand years, Kurtz."

"But–"

Before Mr. Kurtz Hoff has a chance to answer, Jonathan hangs up on him so as to close him out of his office once and for all, and while shutting the wooden drawer in which the bottle of Scotch now rests in peace, he takes a glance at his watch. It's lunch time.

He rises from his leather chair thankfully, for even though he has grown to despise Kurtz more each day, deep inside he knows that he was saved by the bell, that

Kurtz saved his life by way of that phone call. And as much as he would like to deny it, somehow, somewhere, he feels grateful toward him.

Jonathan starts for the window and pauses to peer out as if called, beckoned. The park is crowded, busy, yet to Jonathan it appears devoid of life.

He gazes down at the seemingly open space, his eyes wandering down in quest of something, someone, the bench, the mighty park bench.

It's lunchtime, definitely lunch break and this time Joe will dare, this time Joe will approach it with all that it takes, for sometimes the bum's eyes wander skyward, looking at the skyscraper, not least at the third window from the left, the one on the twenty-third floor, the one sheltering good old Jonathan.

***

Overwhelmed by a strapped feeling of determination, he dashes down the stairs leading to the exit gaping at the park. He darts, leaping two or four steps at a time, and before he knows it, he's standing there, at the skyscraper's feet, a warm wind howling though that sunny day, brushing against his face like the ever-green foliage in the surrounding trees.

As he begins to amble toward the park, his footsteps burden silence.

He saunters past the kiosk, walking somewhat unsteadily as his eyes catch a glimpse of the bench and its occupant.

Now, just like a thousand times before, his gaze meets with that of the bum, who was worn-out, both filthy and beardy at the same time.

Just like a thousand times before.

Yet this time, he will not walk past him, he will not ignore and pretend he didn't see him as he continues toward the cafeteria across the street. No this time, Joe is determined not to act like a fool, even though he is aware of the fact that he is one.

He plucks up the courage and deviates from his daily itinerary by veering to the left, for left is where the park bench is.

"Excuse me," he says, his voice quavering a bit as the bum let his filthy eyes wander up toward him.

But the only answer he gets is a scrutinizing look, one from a bum frowning upon his three-piece suit and his conformingly straightened silken tie.

"Do you mind if I join you and sit down on this bench for a minute?"

For a moment, the bum glares at him imperviously, his face as abstract as a slapdash painting. Then, out of the blue, a tender smile forms behind his grey beard, revealing teeth nearly as black as Jonathan's leather briefcase.

"Why would a man like you choose the same bench as a man like me?" he questions ever-smiling.

"Well, why not? It's a beautiful day, isn't it?" Jonathan inhales almost haughtily as if longing for the smell of fresh air.

"It all depends on who the onlooker is," the bum replies in an elderly, hoarse voice, one seemingly corroded by the course of time and mankind.

"That is so true."

"I bet that every day must be a beautiful day for you," he chuckles as he struggles to dig out a hip flask from his grimy jacket.

"Don't be so sure, everything's not always as it seems you know."

"Well if you look at me it is," he laughs while swallowing his wine in gulps.

Jonathan looks at him pitifully, almost ashamed to wear a suit in his presence.

"Ah… listen… can I offer you a few bucks? I'd like you to buy yourself a sandw–"

"I never accept charity!" the bum exclaims proudly, putting on an approving smile as though it was the best thing he had ever said.

"I see…" Jonathan smiles back.

"Yup!"

"Can I at least buy you a sandwich, if you don't accept any money?"

"Told you! I never take anything I'm offered!"

"I see… very well," Joe shrugs, running his hand through his hair as if not knowing what to say next.

"Want some?" the bum asks while merrily agitating the hip flask of his.

"Nah… I don't… I don't drink you see."

"You don't drink? You're missing something, I can assure you!"

"No, not anymore," Jonathan coughs.

The bum takes a deep sip of the bottle, consequently wiping the wine drying in his beard.

"It's a Saint-Émilion!" he jests.

"Is that so?"

"Shaatauw Matzoooeeee," the bum struggles to pronounce the best he can.

"Chateau Mazouet?"

"Yeah that's right! My French is not what it used to be you know," he laughs before adding; "Vintage 2000!"

"I know this wine, my wife is used to drinking it. It's one of her favorite."

"And one of mine! Hard to believe that two people from such different backgrounds can have so much in common, don't you think? I mean, we like the same goddamn wine!"

"Right…" Joe pulls a forced smile, "You shouldn't drink that stuff you know, it's not healthy."

"Not healthy?" he laughs almost hysterically, as if thunderstruck by a sudden wave of madness. "Do I look to you as if there's still any health left in me at all?"

"You shouldn't, it's likely to kill you one of these days."

"Kill me? Who the hell cares anyway? Right now, it's one of the only things that is keeping me alive. Must be hard to understand for someone like you I guess, we don't come from the same cradle."

"Oh don't be so sure, we do have much more in common than meets the eye."

"Haha, you're a funny lad! Aren't ya? I've never talked to funny business men before," he says then slurps at the flask.

"How did you ever lay hands on such a bottle of wine anyway? It's not one of the cheapest sorts you know!"

"Of course I know! Whatcha think? That I'm one of these goddamn fools that came down to earth with a bump? I stole it, that's what I did!"

"You know, I've been seeing you on this bench almost every day."

"Yeah me too!"

"You too?"

"You work on the twenty-third floor, third window from the left."

"How do you know that?"

"I've seen you. I've been watching you from this bench. You were standing, peering out from behind the glass."

"Yeah…"

"You often seem so goddamn sad if you ask me!"

"Do I?"

"Yup!"

"I wasn't aware–"

"Especially today. You seem very sad today," the bum affirms with a piercing gaze.

"Maybe so."

"You must have had a really bad day, huh? The guys at the firm must have beaten the hell out of your mind."

"Actually not. Actually it couldn't be better…" Joe answers with an ounce of pensiveness in his voice.

"You look pretty soiled for a guy whose day couldn't be better," the bums utters before taking another thirsty sip of his wine.

"The thing is, it's weird you know 'cause I shouldn't be puzzled."

"What? So the guys are not giving you a hard time?"

"No, I told Kurtz to buzz off today."

"Kurtz? Does he wear a goddamn tie too like you do?" His voice grows all the more hoarse.

"Yes he does, but believe me, that doesn't make him look any better.

"So what is your dilemma? You don't earn enough money to spoil your wife with one of these new Rolex watches or bloody Gucci purses? She's mad at you is that it? She wants to suck more money than you have and you didn't get a raise?"

"Quite the opposite! I just got promoted to vice president of Kreamer Inc."

"You what?" the bum coughs as he wolfs down his wine the wrong way, spitting it out half a second later.

"I'm next to the CEO and Kurtz hates my guts for that."

"See what you did? You made me waste my Shaatauw… Shataw–"

"Chateau Mazouet," Joe interrupts, thrusting him back on the right track as vividly as a thunderclap.

"Whatever… you made me waste my goddamn wine! Why aren't you happy? You should be happy, you're almost CEO!" he exclaims with a grunt.

"I know I should."

"I will never be able to understand you rich people. You're always so sad and miserable, complaining all the time."

"I haven't always been rich you know. There was a time when things didn't look so bright for me."

"You mean *a time* as in *the time* for me now?"

"I'm sorry, I didn't mean to–"

"Keep your sorrys for the priest at your church, I ain't no sober preacher."

"You know, believe it or not but once I used to be just like you, sleeping out in the open on a rotten park bench in the middle of the night and sipping on a bottle just like you."

"Yeah right!" the bum grins in jest. "You're a funny lad, really funny. I've never met such an amusing business man!"

"Yes, you told me that. You know, it's odd, but sometimes I wish I could turn back time, return to the one that I was. Sometimes I just admire people like you, almost envy them, people who are unconventional, not choked by the system, free to do as they please when they please."

"Me free? What are you crazy, or something?" the bum bellows in astonishment.

"Why?"

"That's the dumbest thing I've heard, and God knows I've heard and seen many things squatting on this park bench throughout the years. Besides," he groans, "I'm not the one with a ton of money."

"I know it sounds strange, but not everything is about money in this life."

"Do you call it free not being able to eat when you want because you don't have what it takes to buy a donut? And when you do have it they throw you out anyway because you don't have the looks."

"I understand that, but you're free in terms of other things such as freedom in its purest form. You don't have to bow to anyone, sell your soul, your life, work from nine to five in a place you don't want to be and prostitute your heart, now do you?

"Maybe not, cuz I just steal from them."

"Way to go!" Jonathan taps him gently on the shoulder half-approvingly.

"Lemme tell you something! I haven't always been like this you know."

His voice seems to turn ever hoarse. Jonathan gives him a sideways look as though he was longing for the bum to reveal his past, and at the same time, who knows for sure, Joe's future.

"Really? What happened?"

"Well, believe it or not, but several years ago, I used to be a writer."

"A writer?"

"An author. I wrote thrillers, a bit like the stories Agatha Christie used to write. That was a few years after I jumped out of university."

"You've been to university?" Jonathan exclaims in sheer astonishment.

"Of course I did! I studied literature and arts. But I got tired of it really soon and became fed up with all their rules, how you should write, how they want you to, expect you to. If you wrote in an unconventional manner, they would always give you a bad grade and go; 'You don't follow the rules, Andrew. You don't write like all the mainstream authors out there', and that would always make me throw my guts out."

"Is your name Andrew?"

"Yeah."

"I could never have imagined that you've studied literature, Andrew."

"That's only one of the things I have done in my miserable life. Anyway, I told 'em once that literature is not about abiding to confining rules or restraining them. It's about the opposite, it's about extending the limits and exploring the art of writing."

"It makes sense. What did they say?"

"They told me I was crazy and that no writer had even said anything like that before. So I packed my stuff and left the same day. I moved here to New Porthamn and really had to struggle to make end meets. But I spent my time in coffee-shops writing all the time, fantasizing about crime stories and so forth. I spent so much time there that I began to get really acquainted with the owners. And one day, I received a phone call, one totally unexpected."

"A phone call?"

"Yes. It was from one of the most respected publishing companies in town, and I didn't believe them at first. I didn't think it was possible."

"Why not?"

"Simply because I had never sent any of my manuscripts to anyone. I used to write for myself, only for myself, thinking that no one would appreciate my work anyway, thinking that they're all obsessed with rules and this and that. One of the owners at the coffee-shop knew me, and he liked my stories. He liked them a lot, because sometimes I would forget a few pages there due to my half-drunken state, and he would read them. The following day he would always compliment me and try to convince me to send my stories to a publisher. But I didn't want to, I was categorical. These stories were only for myself. Nobody else!"

"But how did your manuscript end up with them? I don't understand."

"You're not going to believe me. But aside from writing, I also used to be sort of a heavy drinker, and so sometimes, I wasn't really fully sober. One evening at the coffee shop, I wrote and wrote, the most fantastic story I thought I ever could. I spent hours revising it, evening after evening until one night when I just woke up at home, totally unaware of what had happened."

"I don't get it…"

"Later, I found out that I was so drunk that I had passed out writing. So they called for the cops, and they sent a car to drive me home. But the worst thing was that the manuscript was gone. There was no trace of it. It had vanished away like a goddamn ghost in the dead of night."

"Well didn't you return to the coffee-shop to ask?"

"Of course I did, but the owner told me he hadn't seen it and that somebody had probably thrown it in the trash can. I felt miserable about it for weeks. This was the most amazing story ever written!"

"Go ahead."

"Like I told you, one day I get this phone call and they tell me they want to publish my book, that this is one of the most catchy stories they have ever read in their whole career. And I just didn't believe them. I answered that I hadn't sent them any stories and so I asked them to keep away from me, clearly determined to avoid them like the plague."

"And?"

"And what happened you see is that the owner of the coffee-shop, after the cops had taken me home, had found the manuscript on the table where I had been sitting, and knowing that I would never accept to send it in, he did it unbeknownst to me. He did it behind my back."

"And so you became a writer?"

"Yes I did, and I was very grateful that he did so, because I was so goddamn stubborn at the time that I couldn't see all the opportunities before my eyes. I was a complete fool."

"How come I have never heard of your books?" Jonathan asks, not convinced.

"Oh you have dear, you have," he coughs as if he had a frog in his throat. "Have you never heard of '*On a trace*'?"

"'*On a trace*'? You mean the famous criminal novel that came out years ago?"

The bum responds with a nod, a faint nod, colored with a slight ounce of pride.

"No, I don't believe you! Get outta here!" Joe smiles as he strives to accept it as true. "You're the author of that novel?"

"Yes. And of many more!"

He reaches for the flask vividly, lifts it to his mouth and takes a deep sip of it, as though all the talking had dried out of his mouth.

"If you reached such a level of success, what happened? Why did you end up here on this bench?"

"Because I was charged for murder!"

"You what…?" Jonathan exclaims with a shock.

"I was charged for murder, and I've been on the run ever since."

"Are you wanted?"

"Yeah, and it has been like that for at least fourteen years now," he answers unbothered, as if he finally had grown used to the idea.

"Would you care telling me why?" Joe asks, his voice slightly quavering.

"I used to be married. One day, my wife and I wake up in bed. It's early morning and we're at our cabin situated in the northern part of town in Landcaster. We wake up to the sound of breaking glass coming from the ground floor. Terrified, I jump out of bed, put on my dressing gown and dash down the stairs like a madman. Downstairs, there is a silhouette, a man I think, but I cannot discern him clearly because it is early morning and it is still too goddamn dark. I yell at him. I yell at the top of my lungs, scared to death. However, he just stands there, looking back at me as unyielding as the dawn surrounding him. Then he says he is going to kill me, he says he is going to kill me and my wife."

Jonathan looks at the bum stupefied, nearly taken aback, as if mesmerized by the man's chronicle.

"I ask him why. My voice quavers, he's there in the middle of my living room, apparently holding something in his hand. A weapon? A gun? He's there and it cannot be, yet he is. It is as real as you and me and this very bench, right here right now!"

"Did he answer?"

"He tells me I am going to die because he didn't like my story. He didn't enjoy my last novel and how things ended up for the main character. He says he will arrange for me to end up the same way as my character. My wife is behind me, she has come to see what's going on. She's standing on the steps right behind my back. I beg the man not to shoot but it's too late, he's in a trance, he won't listen. And so he fires his gun, aiming at me. But to my chagrin, the bullet doesn't hit me, it hits my wife, killing her on the spot."

"Jesus… you're not kidding me, are you?"

"I wish I was kidding but I am not. The man smiles at me. He smiles the most horrific and horrendous smile I have ever witnessed, and before fleeing through the broken window, he turns toward me and utters these very words; *'Just how it happened in your book, just how you wrote it. You're a murderer!'* I will never forget."

"I'm stunned, I don't know what to say really…" Joe struggles.

"Don't worry about that! It was a long time ago, a very long time ago."

"What happened after that?"

"The man did it exactly like I had written in the book. The main character's wife died under the exact same circumstances. He made it look like the whole scene was literally taken word by word from the book, and it was so obvious that the cops immediately saw the connection, incarcerating and charging me for murder on the spot. I was brought to the New Porthamn P.D. station where I underwent endless police interrogations. No one would listen to me. Their version was that after writing so many criminal stories, I got mad, insane and became unable to differentiate fiction from reality, that I got mad to the point of applying what I wrote and killing my own wife."

"I'm stunned…"

"There was a trial. They had very good lawyers and the jury didn't like me. For some reason, they hated my guts and so the verdict was very clear; *'Guilty to the charge of first degree murder'*. I can still hear it ring it my head."

"This is awful, Andrew… awful," Jonathan grunts.

"Anyway before they had the time to imprison me, I escaped. Somehow I managed to flee from a lifelong sentence, if not death row. The police started chasing me everywhere from my friend's cellar to my parent's house, in upstate New Porthamn. I had to live on the run for years, hiding from them, hiding from my friends and relatives, for they thought I was guilty too. And so here I am, today on this bench gossiping with you," the bum smiles, but it is a sad smile, one of disillusions.

"You have all my sympathy, I can't even imagine having such an experience," Joe confides.

"Thank you. Not many people trust me you know. Most of you three-piece suit wearing guys don't even dare to look at me. For the most part, most of them are very wary."

"Well, I trust you! I do, I think all men are good you know! Save maybe for Kurtz–" he intends to jest but the joke is too thin.

"Perhaps you shouldn't trust me," the bum retorts.

"Why not?"

"Perhaps you shouldn't."

Joe doesn't pay attention to the answer. Instead he tries to revive the mood.

"So you stole the wine?"

"Just like anything else," the bum responds imperviously.

"Anything else? And the jacket? Who offered you the jacket?"

"I told you! I never take anything I'm offered! I only take things I am not offered, I steal them!"

"I can't really blame you. You have to live on the streets, steal food to survive, it's understandable.

"See, the things is, I don't just steal little things such as food or money, I steal other things too, important things."

"Like what?"

"Well," the bum begins, "I just stole a little bit of your time didn't I?"

"Oh only a little really, but everything is relative."

"Perhaps, or is it, Jonathan?"

"What do you mean–" he begins then realizes with a shock, "How do you know my name?"

"I know a lot of things, Jonathan."

Joe gives him an anxious look, as if the bum had begun to frighten him, as if his words were too raw, too straightforward.

"I don't understand, I've never talked to you before! How is it that you know my name?" he exclaims, his voice betraying his nervousness slightly.

"Don't you worry too much about that. I need to leave now. I don't like staying on the same bench for too long. The cops might find me anytime. I'm wanted remember, dead or alive. I have to be on the run constantly."

"What are you talking about? You're here almost everyday," Jonathan grimaces in astonishment.

"No can do," the bum rejoins with a sardonic grin concealed behind his beard.

In a quick jig, he leaps over the bench backward and grabs his worn-out saddlebag.

"Wait!" Joe shouts.

Andrew replies by turning around slowly, the grin still all over his face.

"You didn't tell me about that story you wrote! What made it so fantastic?"

"It is about a businessman meeting a bum by a park bench," he rejoins as he begins to amble away from Joe.

"What?"

"And how he ends up stealing his whole life. Swapping pl–"

The last sentence cannot be heard for he is mumbling.

"Swapping what?"

"The last pages are yet to be written," he raises his rusty voice in farewell as he takes his leave, "But they are close now, they are very close."

By now he is too far away for Joe to hear the words last spoken.

Stunned, Jonathan dwells on the bench, staring at the bum as he lurches away in the blurry distance of the park. There, he remains, thinking for seconds, minutes, hours, pondering upon everything the bum has told him. He remains a long time, watching as newly arisen clouds begin to shroud a sunlight as of now obsolete.

He stays until his thoughts at last shove him toward an irresistible fatigue, one he cannot withstand, and thus, on that very park bench, he falls asleep almost unwittingly, forgetting about returning to work, let alone about his own life.

From nowhere, darkness roams in. He surrenders to the dead of night, sliding within an endless sleep it seems, one peaceful and tender, one having him drift ashore on a sea of dire lamentations, reminiscences of the past, a horrific past. He dreams of his home, his wife, his kids and how lucky and blessed he has been.

All of a sudden, he realizes, he understands there is a meaning. The bum's words made him appreciate. They made him value the life he has now.

He realizes and at the same time he wakes up from his lucid dream. He wakes up from a profound sleep never to be met again and as he opens his eyes on what he thinks will be nighttime, dawn reveals another truth,

As his eyelids unbolt, a thousand rays of light pierces his gaze and blurs his vision. They are all aimed at him, and beyond that blurry sheen, there is cacophony, tumult, a burdening cluster of noise confining his weary head.

"What's going on?" he whispers to himself.

Suddenly, screaming voices make him come to in the twinkle of an eye. He looks about him in sheer confusion. From every corner, sirens, police cars, a chopper and snipers surround him with weapons.

"Put you hands in the air!" one of the voices bellow through a loudspeaker.

Joe dwells on the bench with stapled breath.

"You are under arrest! Surrender now and there will be no one injured!"

"What the hell is going on?" Jonathan screams but the sound of the helicopter hovering above him is too loud for him to be heard.

Wind battles his face, the noise, the light, everything is unbearable.

"Take the bum, dead or alive take him!" the voice screams.

"No! Don't shoot him! He's innocent!" Joe yells at the top of his lungs in a desperate attempt to convince them that they are making a big mistake.

"Take the bum, encircle the bench!"

Panic-stricken, Joe turns around back and forth so as to catch a glimpse of Andrew and the bench he's sitting on. He looks everywhere only to realize there are no other benches around other than the one he's sitting on.

"Don't shoot! He told me everything, it wasn't him, it wasn't him! He's innocent! He's a victim of a set-up!"

"Take him!"

Suddenly, Joe sees two policemen start running toward him with weapons in their hands, and in a twinkle of an eye, it dawns on him like a thunderclap; they are not chasing the bum. For some reason, they are bolting like mad men, ill-omened and determined to shove freedom to an end.

And before they dive on him with handcuffs like two predators blinded by greed, he has just enough time to take a glance at his own clothes. To his astonishment what his eyes witness is no longer the three-piece suit of a Mercedes-driving fool. It is the garments of a bum. A goddamn bum. It is those of Andrew!

Before he knows it, they have swooped down on him, striking his body like a bolt of lightning, and the harsh thump has been painful, almost unbearable.

He's lying on the ground, his face injured by the grazing concrete. He's lying inertly with handcuffs around his throbbing wrists, and all of a sudden they pull him up. They shove him in violence toward the police car, giving him a despiteful look, one blended with contentment, for at last they have caught him, they think. They have caught the bloody murderer, the former crime author whose stories have gone to his head.

And before Jonathan is forced to step inside the black and white vehicle, his gaze wanders up toward the third window from the left on the twenty-third floor. It stretches beyond the glass where several faces are gathered, bloodthirstily looking down at the park square and all the tumult about.

He recognizes the faces. One of them is Kurtz, glaring down with despitefulness in his eyes, and giving him a judging look. And standing next to him is the silhouette of a three-piece suit fool, looking daggers at Jonathan as though he was worth better.

And in a horrendous finding, Jonathan recognizes the suit, but the face doesn't match the suit, for the face is that that of a bum. The face is that of an impostor.

Hastily, Joe's gaze withdraws from the skyscraper, and before grudgingly stepping into the police car, he sees the reflection of another horrendous visage in the windshield. It is the reflection of a face, but that reflection doesn't match either.

Suddenly, up there with a wry grin at the corner of his mouth, peering out from the twenty-third floor and holding an attaché-case in his left hand, he looks stylish. White silken tie, black suit, he watches as they take him away. He watches as his life is being stolen. For had he not stolen a little more than just a bit of his time, as he had said?

REVERIES

FEAR OF THE DARK   *Erik Jayce Landberg*

REVERIES

Cathy Peterson. Age thirty-six. Daughter of Serge and Gertrude Peterson, the latter a former pathological nurse. Occupation, a lawyer's secretary whose ambitions in life were nothing else but to become one. Cathy Peterson and the night. She and a series of phone calls shy of dawn, ones about to change her life, now and forever. Cathy, about to uncover a reality unreal.

Against all odds, the day had begun well. Outside the snow glimmered bright and the air bore the freshness of icy mint. She gazed out through her office window as if for the first time, her eyes meeting with the virgin blue sky hovering above like a diamond veil.

Mr. Clawson was sitting in the office next to hers. Only his had a lot more square meters, not to mention the furniture and the view. Wasn't that natural after all? Mr. Clawson was a lawyer, a damn good one, and that had no price in times like these.

She lingered in her chair, daydreaming about what she was going to buy Gertrude, for tomorrow was her birthday. Not any birthday mind you. Her seventieth one, and that had no price either.

In the long-dragging thirty-six years that Gertrude had been her mother, Cathy had never really come up with a good gift. Not that her mother was hard to please, but she had never thought of that special magic little thing that would catch Gertrude unawares. For gifted with brains beyond the ordinary, her mother seemed to have the nasty ability to read people's minds like an open book.

Cathy was dying to surprise her and knew it would take more than the stroke of a wizard's wand to achieve that. Yet she kept a smile on her lips, for she had thought of that little extra. Something innovative and eccentric. Something Gertrude would never be able to suspect or guess. Something she had now turned into a vicious obsession, as small as the task might be. She had laid eyes on it a week before at Seer's and knew at once that it was the thing to buy. Only she had to wait for the sales to begin and today was the day they would start.

She glanced at her watch, bright, golden, as if suddenly it had become an object of interest. For she was never used to checking the hour, due to a tremendous amount of work. She never had the time.

"Cathy!" a voice ran from the doorway.

"Mr Clawson?" she burst, her daydream bubble bursting all at once.

"Got a new watch?"

"Oh… no I guess I was just–"

"Can I take a look?"

She wasn't sure whether he was just being sarcastic or really meant it in a cheerful way.

"Of course Mr. Clawson but it's not new you know. I've had it for quite some years now."

"Never mind. Did you send that letter I asked you to write yesterday?"

"Oh, you mean the demand letter to Leasepark?"

Clawson nodded quite blankly, somewhat preoccupied by a bunch of documents he was holding in his hands.

"Yes I sent it in the afternoon."

"See to it that you don't transfer any phone calls to me regarding that case. It's quite a bothersome one you see."

"I understand. Should I give a reason?"

"If anyone asks, I'm busy in a meeting, or else on a business trip in Miami."

"I'll take care of it."

"Too many phone calls nowadays, Cathy. Too many phone calls," he sighed as he was standing distant in her doorway, wishing he had chosen any other profession but that one.

"I guess," she smiled gently, quite unsure as to how to react.

"They're like a box of chocolates. Only bad chocolates. You never know what they'll come up with or what surprise they actually conceal. Regardless of how well prepared you are, sometimes they'll just catch you unawares, sneaking in like a serpent from behind."

"A serpent, Mr. Clawson?"

"It's an analogy, Cathy. Sometimes their lawyers counteract with arguments as venomous as poison."

"I'll tell them you're on a trip."

"A trip to Miami Cathy. Miami. We need to have the same version, when push comes to shove," he blinked.

"That goes without saying."

***

Time flies they say, yet today it didn't. Not for Cathy anyway. In her cramped mind, seconds felt like minutes, minutes like hours, hours like days. No matter how much she strove to remain focused on her work, her eyes kept wandering back to her watch, as though fascinated by its mesmerising glance.

Her hands brushed the keyboard with the dexterity of a pianist, and even though she typed fast, time wouldn't pass any quicker.

She paused, sighed. Her gaze ventured out the window, along with her thoughts, carrying her back to what she was going to buy her mother. She found herself daydreaming for a while, until the phone rang and put an end to it, all at once.

"Welcome to Clawson Inc., Cathy Peterson, how can I help you?" she said in the nicest voice she knew, expecting her interlocutor to call about the bothersome file. For after all, Mr. Clawson didn't get but bothersome phone calls nowadays.

"I'm sure you can. The question is, can you help yourself?"

"I beg you pardon?"

"You heard me well."

"Who's speaking please?"

"What difference does it make. The facts are the same."

"The facts," she coughed a bit. "If you're looking for Mr. Clawson, I'm afraid he won't be available for at least a week or so. He's in Miami at the Florida's annual congress for–"

"No he's not."

"I don't understand…" She thought of what to say.

"No one has asked you to understand."

"Are you calling from Leasepark?"

"Do you think I am?"

"I… I don't know," she replied, her voice quavered a bit, taken unawares.

"There are other things that you don't know."

Cathy frowned slightly, not out of anger but out of suspicion.

"Can I take a message regarding that file, sir?"

She grabbed a pen, squeezing it firmly between her thumb and her forefinger.

"No."

She let go of the pen.

"No?"

"No."

"You won't leave a message for Mr. Clawson?"

"No."

"Then what in the heavens do you want?" The words just flew out of her mouth before she even had the time to think of them.

There was no answer. Silence dawned on that moment as though she had reached the eye of a storm.

"Hello? Sir, are you still there?" she regained politeness, already regretting her flare-up.

"Yes."

"How can I help you, sir?" she sighed deeply so as to conceal her quavering tone of voice.

"You can't."

"Then what's the purpose of your call?"

"It is not me that needs help."

"What?"

"It is not me."

"Then who is it?"

"It is you."

"You're calling to help me?"

"Certainly."

"Excuse me, do I even know you?"

"I do."

"You know me?"

"Yes."

"How do you know me?"

"*How* doesn't change the facts."

"What are you saying?"

"What I said."

"Sir, I don't know who you are and what you want so I'm just going to hang up now and if you're looking for Mr. Clawson, please call back in a week and I'm sure he'll be glad to help you with whatever legal advice you're in need of. Anyhow, I'll tell him that you've…" she paused. "…that someone's called and asked for him."

"Nobody is asking for him."

All at once, she hung up with a thumping heart. Her eyes wandered back to her computer screen and her hands brushed over the keyboard in a graceful wave, ironically without the slightest idea about what to type next. Even so, she wrote the name of her grandmother, then that of her mother followed by her own and, and nothing. She stopped there, unable to figure out what would come next.

The phone rang anew.

She watched it ring.

The cursor on her computer screen kept blinking and as she pondered upon the name of her future children, oblivion roamed as a ghost in her hand, for she couldn't come up with even the slightest of a name.

Meanwhile, the phone just wouldn't stop.

Overwhelmed by a mounting sentiment of frustration, she lifted it off the hook so as to put an end to its deafening tone.

"Hello!" she yelled as though to scare off a gathering of birds.

"Hello...? I'm sorry. I might have dialled the wrong number. Did I call Clawson's?" the voice at the other end of the line questioned shyly.

"Uh... yes, yes this is Clawson Inc, how can I help you sir?"

"My name is Robert Jefferson. I'm calling from a company called Leasepark. May I speak to Mr. Clawson please?"

"Oh dear," she said out loud although she had only meant to think the words.

"I beg you pardon?"

"Mr. Clawson is on a business trip you see and can't take your call right now. Can I take a mess–"

"This is the strangest thing! Have I really dialled the right number?" the man asked infuriated.

"Well of course. What makes you think you haven't?"

"What makes me think–? First you answer the phone as if this was some kind of a cheap burger diner and then you tell me the man is on a business trip?

"He is in Miami and is planning on staying the whole week."

"This is ridiculous! Put him on the phone right now or I shall make a report! You don't send demand letters to people and then deny their calls!"

"Sir, I ensure you he is not at the office–"

"Enough! What's your name?"

"Cathy Peterson, sir."

"Peterson, put me through right now!"

"Sir, I can't, I told you he's–"

"Listen here young lady! Mr. Clawson called me personally about five minutes ago from his mobile, telling me he'd like to discuss the file with me. He told me he was en route to the office and that we could perhaps reach an agreement were I to call him back at the office shortly."

"What? That couldn't be–" she paused.

"Are you calling me a liar Peterson?"

"No of course not, sir, it's just that–"

"That what?"

"It's just that Mr. Clawson told me he had to catch a flight to Miami today."

"Well he didn't. He should be back in by now. He told me he was just about to park the car."

"Well sir, don't you think that Mr. Clawson would have called you directly from the office when he'd arrived instead of from his mobile while parking the car?"

"I don't know how the man thinks. He has got a strange jargon too."

"How so, sir?"

"First the man calls without introducing himself, asking me whether I am willing to help myself and when I answer that I don't know what he's talking about he tells me that that doesn't change the facts."

At the sound of his words, Cathy let go of the phone in a moment of confusion, it tumbled down onto the desk with a thump.

"Hello? Hello?"

With stapled breath, she picked up the phone, bringing it back to her left ear.

"Sir," she said nearly short of breath.

"Yes, what's the matter?"

"The man you talked to is not Mr. Clawson."

"But he told me his name was–"

"It is not. This man called me a few minutes ago too you see."

"Is this some kind of a joke or something? Because I don't feel inclined toward humour at this very time."

"No sir, it is not."

"Then who is the man who called me, and how could he possibly know about the Leasepark file, and most of all, how the hell did he get my number?"

"I don't know that yet, sir, but I'll call Mr. Clawson right away to inform him of the facts."

"You'd better do that, Peterson, and call me back today or I'll–"

"Of course! Bye-bye Mr. Robert, uh Jefferson…"

No sooner had she hung up to dial than the phone rang anew.

For a moment, she watched it ring in apprehension, but the idea that this could in fact be Mr. Clawson himself, wondering what the hell was going on, came on too strong, and at last she gave in to it.

"Cathy Peterson, welcome to Claws–"

"Have you thought it over?"

"..son Inc."

There was a brief silence, only betrayed by her panting breath.

"Mr. Jefferson?"

"Have you thought it over?"

"Who is this please?"

"I told you. That doesn't change the facts."

"Oh God! Stop harassing me will you, or else I'll call the police right now!"

"There is nothing the police can do for you."

"I can see where you're dialling from. I can see your number on the display."

"No you cannot."

"Yes I do." Her voice was trembling.

"Very well. Then what is the number you see on the display?"

"I…"

"Yes?"

"I don't have to tell you that!"

"You see. You cannot see any number on any display simply because I am not dialling from any place you'd be aware of."

"What do you mean?"

"I am not speaking through a phone."

"Then where on earth are you calling from?"

"Nor from any place on earth for that matter."

"You must be out of yourself or your mind."

"In a way I am. You could say that."

"I'm calling the police this very moment."

"Don't, Cathy. It wouldn't do you any good."

"How do you know my name?"

"I know many names."

"At that very moment Cathy's gaze wandered across the keyboard to the computer screen, the cursor still blinking, as if dying to know the next name to be typed.

"Oh you do?" Her voice suffered a sudden change of tone, embracing sarcasm.

"Yes."

"What's the name of my mother?" she questioned with mounting self-assurance in her timber.

There was a brief silence. A wry, almost wicked smile slowly formed at the corner of her mouth as if she finally had proven her interlocutor wrong.

"Gertrude," the voice spat out, stinging her ears as though it had been a shot of venom.

The smile withered as fast as a flower on the verge of autumn. Her eyebrows frowned, twisting the tiny wrinkles round her eyes.

"How do you know that?" she bellowed. Had there been fear or apprehension in her voice a little earlier, it had now been substituted for a mere feeling of anger.

"I told you. I know many names. I know, for instance, the next name to be typed on your computer screen."

Her heart pounded at an anxious pace, hammering in her chest so hard that it almost made its way out.

"Who the hell are you?" she moaned, tears in her eyes.

"Don't be afraid," the voice replied, wholly unaffected by her little outburst.

"How do you know these things?"

She was rocking on her chair, to and fro.

"I know the future, Cathy. I know the future, the present and the past."

"That's ridiculous!"

"I don't belong to the ridiculous."

"What do you want from me?"

"I want you to listen, Cathy, very thoroughly."

"I'm listening." Her voice quavered. She wiped her lips.

"I know how much you're longing for a child, and a husband for that matter. I also know you can have these things and you will soon write a new name on the screen, for you will soon meet someone. Someone to share your life with and procreate."

"Are you promising me all those things?"

"Yes."

"Is this some kind of a silly joke?"

"No."

"What's the catch then?"

"There is a catch indeed, yet a very small one."

"Don't linger! Speak!"

"You can have all these things, yet you will not have them, unless–"

"Unless what?"

"Unless you do exactly as I say."

"And what do you say?"

"Tonight, when you're about to head home. I want you to take the bus."

"I have a car. Why should I take the bus."

"I want you to take the bus straight home with no unnecessary stops."

"I can't. I have to head downtown and buy my mother a present. It's her birthd–"

"I already know that mind you. There will be no presents tonight for your mother. You need to do exactly as I say and take the bus home. That's the catch! It's as simple as that."

"What? Are you mocking me?"

"You shouldn't think I am."

"Why would I do as you tell me? For what reason?"

"I'm afraid I can't tell you the reason. Actually, that is about all I can tell you."

"Why?"

"Were I to tell you more, I wouldn't be able to promise you anything."

"Don't you think your little fairy-tale sounds a bit farfetched?"

"Nothing that I know of is farfetched or has ever been."

"That's enough, sir! You talk as if you're drunk!"

"Drunkenness is a virtue for humans, Cathy."

"And you're not?" She smiled wryly, but the timber in her voice betrayed her incertitude.

There was no answer. Silence bowed to her question as though it had been a villainous one. At the other end of the line, there wasn't so much as the sound of his breath, and the soaring quietness suddenly aroused her curiosity.

"Are you still there, sir?" she uttered discretely but the question was asked to no avail for silence persisted inexorably.

She hung up, turned on her chair and began slithering on a train of thoughts. Who was that man? What did he possibly want from her? Everything appeared so ludicrous, yet not. He knew so much, didn't he? Perhaps too much for it to be a joke, and the more she thought of it, the more uneasiness gradually took hold of her mind. Somewhere deep inside, anchored in the abyss of her subconscious, a voice echoed with glowing timber. It was calling out her name, yet she didn't hear it, for she didn't care to listen either.

***

Time didn't linger. It passed unnoticed like a ghost soaring by. Seconds turned to minutes, minutes to hours and before she knew it, day had bowed to a cold December night, the winds of which squalled on her windowpane like a frozen beast desperate to get inside.

"The weather is worsening. Only twenty minutes to go," she whispered almost inaudibly as she glanced at her watch, screaming at her from behind a shelter of sapphire, embraced by a cluster of diamonds and gold.

Outside, the snowstorm thrived. Beautiful yet deceptive, for behind the beauty lay a beast untamed. She left her chair, stumbling toward the coffee machine as she laid eyes on the perturbed firmament.

"A last one before I leave," she thought as the machine filled her cup with ardency.

She slurped, turned back toward her office and let out a sigh. Somehow, the storm weighed on her, and although she took pleasure in the cosy, wintry ambience offered by a month like December, she felt somewhat saddened by the rapidly darkening hours.

For they were darkening as the future to come, and she took a sip as though she didn't know, as though the man's murky words hadn't reached her mind the way they should have. Hence, she stood shy of the machine, empty gaze, reflecting her absentminded expression as she lacked awareness, an awareness all the more devoid of prospect.

Then, it struck her, rising out of the blue as though to catch her unawares.

What had that man meant to tell her?

"Where did he call from?" she mumbled between sips.

And most importantly, who *was* he?

In her mind, questions soared without answers and the more she pondered the less she understood, and the less she understood the more her future seemed to blur in a damp cluster of colours, as if immersed in tears.

All at once, her thoughts led her to her past, or was it the future? One anchored in her heart in indistinct snapshots. She frowned to recall, her gaze darkening at the pace of her thinking. She began to discern, if very faint a light, one shimmering at the end of a distant tunnel.

"What is that?" she questioned aloud in the remoteness of her office.

Unconsciously, her eyes began to peer through the window of her mind. A window seemingly divulging a future ahead. One not so much made of snow as of powdery whiteness. A white virgin of the night, yet too virgin to be good, too virgin to fit in the world.

For a moment, she thought she had seen some kind of a crossroad, and wouldn't that be quite a cliché? A crossroad as a symbol of her future? A subliminal imprint in her subconscious of what was about to happen were she not to open her mind. Were she not to listen to the conceit of that man's eerie voice.

"What am I thinking of?"

Laughter overpowered her as though it had been an antidote, freeing her from superstition. A superstition now all the more imminent in her daydream.

"This is pretty hilarious, isn't it?" she spoke aloud as she took another sip.

Only this time, that sip didn't taste so much of coffee as it did of bitterness.

She laid the cup on her desk and grabbed her seat. First, a former laughter turned into a sarcastic smirk, then into an innocent grin.

"I mean, it must be mustn't it?" she shoved, in an attempt to convince herself.

All at once, her seat felt less comfortable as if that grin of hers had suddenly succumbed to superstition.

The warmth of her office seemed far from reach, and the more her thoughts drifted loose, the more her seat seemed to embrace the cold winds gusting outside.

"Can there be some sort of truth to be deterred in that phone call?

Her eyebrows frowned again and the window in her mind opened anew.

She peered. Now she could see clearer. The crossroads wasn't really a crossroad. It was a roundabout, one surrounded by a gloomy, wintry night. A night that had given in to misty gusts of ever-whitening snow.

Beyond that point, everything seemed to blur, yet there was something in the way. Something glimmering faintly as snowflakes slowly feathered to the ground.

"What can it be?" her lips moved but there was no sound.

She smirked.

"How odd. It feels like a dream. Kinda like before falling asleep when you start seeing images, pictures, visions in your mind."

Her smirk vanished.

"But this isn't a dream, now is it?"

Her lids closed out the faint lights of the office. She concentrated, frowning even more.

"What is that thing glimmering in the middle of the roundabout?"

She sighed. Inhaled. Sighed again.

"If it glimmers it must be metallic, right?" she questioned silently.

"Right?" she pleonasmed aloud but silence was her only witness.

Her lids opened and her gaze was drawn to the window which was spoiled with ever-whitening flakes.

Then the words rang in her head as a thousand bells from afar.

"Drunkenness is a virtue for humans, Cathy."

A virtue for humans. It kept ringing until the words began to loose their meaning.

"...a virtue for humans..."

"And you're not?" she had smiled.

But it had been a wry smile. One filled with incertitude and apprehension.

"What if?" a voice spoke in her head.

"What?" she answered as if the voice had come from something alive. Something living inside her.

"What if the thing whom you spoke to wasn't human?"

"The thing?"

"Yes the thing. It knew too much to be human, don't you think?"

"I don't know what I think!" she rejoined.

"You know what?"

"No! What?"

"I don't think it was."

Silence dawned back on the office. It screamed to be heard, screamed to be noticed.

"I don't think it was," the voice renewed, as if to fight back that betraying hush laying its nest like a layer of dust.

"You're pathetic," Cathy sighed and took another sip.

"How does it taste?"

"What?"

"How does it taste?"

"I dunno, like coffee?" she shrugged.

She rolled her eyes.

"I'm not talking about the coffee."

"No?"

"No."

She frowned.

"I'm talking about your life."

"What about it?"

"Well. How does it taste? Hoe does your life taste?"

"It doesn't taste. It's just a life."

"Just a life?"

"Yes… I guess."

"And the cup is just coffee?"

"Right, I s'pose so."

"I think you've been seriously misled."

"How so?"

"Well, to compare a lame cup of coffee with your life."

"But I didn't! You did!"

"I asked you how it tasted."

"Yes."

"And you told me it had no taste."

"I guess it tastes like coffee."

"And your coffee has no taste."

"Not anymore."

"Aha!"

"What?"

"Aha!"

"How do you mean?"

"There you go!"

"Explain yourself, dear."

"Dear? Don't call me dear, I'm your subconscious."

"Oh yes I forgot."

"So I noticed."

"So what are you telling me?"

"What I meant to tell you is that ever since you spoke to that man, or to that thing as I'd like to refer to it, the coffee has lost its taste."

"How come?"

"Pretty bad sign if you ask me."

She nodded in agreement, grudgingly.

"It has lost its taste because you have chosen in your mind not to listen to what he had to tell you."

"So?"

"So perhaps, what he told you is about to have an effect on your life and thus on the coffee that you drink as of the moment you choose not to listen to him. It is bound to affect all that you taste for that matter."

Cathy sighed.

"Now you're being silly."

"Perhaps. I'm just telling you what I think."

"So what should I do?"

"Well if I were you, I'd certainly listen to the substance of his words. Read between the lines."

"But they had no substance, mind you."

"Mind you. Interesting choice of words. I'm your mind, mind you."

"Sorry again."

"No worries."

"Should I really listen?"

"He knew too much, Cathy, way too much didn't he?"

"Yes he did."

Her lips trembled slightly as she sighed before taking another sip.

"It's never a good sign when people know too much. Is it?"

"I s'pose it isn't."

"In my eyes, he is not human. He is something else and what he told you might be a well founded warning."

"Not human? Not human? Where do you think you are? In a science-fiction story?"

"Well I'm talking to you ain't I?

"I suppose."

"I'm your subconscious and I'm talking to you, little Cathy."

"Yes," she sighed.

"So don't mention science-fiction!."

"I won't."

"Good."

"He might not be human."

"No he might not be."

"What is he then? A Mothman professing?"

"Could be."

"Oh that's ridiculous," she said out loud.

"Is it?"

"I'm a grownup."

"Why take any chances?"

She sighed.

"You saw the glimmering metallic thing from afar on the roundabout, didn't you?"

"Yes I saw it."

"You saw it the way I did little, Cathy."

"Yes."

"And yet you're a grownup."

"Go away!"

"What?"

"Go away! I don't want you around in my head like this! I'm starting to think I'm loosing it."

"As you wish, Cathy."

All at once, the voice retreated back where it belonged, giving way to silence, the presence of which weighed on Cathy's shoulders as a heavy subliminal load.

"I must have had too much coffee," she smirked as she stopped the cup shy of her lips, trembling slightly as she strove to resist the tempting beverage.

"I'm starting to hear voices now," she uttered in sarcasm as she rose from her chair in a determined move.

"It's time to put an end to this. It was just a silly phone call. A nut! Somebody kidding around!

"Neither more, nor less." a voice rang at the rear of her head.

"Go away I said!"

"Go aw–"

The phone rang anew. It rang like a thousand bells from a distant church afar. One ominous and sinister by its presence, its presence in Cathy's mind.

At first she let it ring, gazing in apprehension.

The ringing ceased, instilling a brief moment of peacefulness before it began to ring anew.

Cathy lifted the earphone off the hook and threw it on the desk in a wooden thud.

She watched it in horror, raised eyebrows, the skin wrinkling around her eyes in the faint yellow shafts of the damp office.

Silence overwhelmed the room almost instantly. It exhaled against the air like a ghost panting for cold mist.

Cathy pondered, looked away, then pondered again.

"What do I do?" she thought.

"Bring it to your ears," the voice ran across her head.

"Go away!"

"Bring it to your deaf ears, Cathy! Before it's too late. Perhaps it already is."

She seized the phone, gave it a slight shove then threw it back on the hook.

Her heart thudded like a hammer, her breath cold as the whitening ice outside.

"Goddam it!" she swore. "I must be loosing it. I gotta stay focused or I'm'na loose it!"

She fell back into the warmth of her chair. A brief sensation of shelter climbed up her spine before the words came back to her as the doomsday bells that they were.

"That's the catch! It's as simple as that."

The catch. The catch! What's the catch?

Thoughts began to collide. Words confined.

"...take the bus home. That's the catch! It's as simple as that, as simple as that, as simple as that, as simple as that..."

The voice vanished in a fading echo bouncing in her mind. It bounced and bounced until it rang anew. The phone, that ever-ringing phone, and with insatiable vigour.

She seized it again, her hand quavering a bit as she did, her lips abiding to her fear, black and white. Black as the night. White as the ice.

"Who is this?" she yelled firmly as if it had been the fourth of fifth call placed by a never-learning, obstinate salesman much too eager to introduce his latest brand.

At the other end of the line, silence roared. Silence, yet not quite. For if one listened attentively, one would discern a faint moan. One so faint that even a trained ear would have to muse and frown.

As she stood pondering, mouth agape, Cathy didn't understand it. It was the moan of the storm. Faint gusts of winds brushing across the earphone at the other end of the line. Faint gusts and the panting of the flakes breathing against her ear.

"Who is this?" she repeated, her heart thumping at a faster pace now. At a much faster pace.

But the moans persisted. The moans and the silence behind them. That ever-betraying silence.

Cathy lent her ears to it. She listened with thoroughness and all at once she knew. It dawned on her out of the blue, just like that.

She knew damn well what she was paying heed to. Those sounds at the other end of the line. They were the sounds of the future, that ominous future which the man had spoken of. She was hearing the storm of a close upcoming, one to come soon, one to strike when least expected were she not to abide to the man's ludicrous words.

Yet in her mind she knew better. At least something told her she did. Something called common sense and reason. Something rational and logic.

She closed her eyes, instantly letting go of the phone, letting it crash down onto the floor in a loud thud.

She opened her eyes, only to discover pieces of plastic scattered across the floor.

That was it! Gone once and for all! No more moans, no more voices confined in her head. The whole thing was a scam. A pretty disturbing scam, she had just decided.

And all at once, as she leaned forward to gather the pieces, her eyes opened again, only before her desk in the same room with the same phone safe and sound before her.

"Oh my God," she uttered wearily. "It was all a dream. Nothing else but a silly dream."

She sighed in relief, got up from her chair and bolted past her desk toward the window, where, the storm howled like a creature of the night. Hungry, filled with greed, it unleashed its fury against the pane, Cathy's sheltering windowpane.

"Soon the storm will dampen down," she thought as she brought the cup to her trembling lips so as to take a deep sip. "Soon it will dampen down and I'll be on my way to the store."

She sank back into her chair. It felt warm and safe, and the coffee. The coffee tasted good again. Nothing wrong with it. Nothing wrong at all!

She mused aloud, laughed and pondered. Her gaze fell on the computer, as impervious as the night itself. There, blinking on the screen; the words, the names she had written whilst that man had called. They were all there, virgin, untouched. Yet she was convinced that they no longer had any meaning. For they were the fruit of superstition, of an imagination flowing all too much in abundance, and that dream, that silly scattered dream was the price she had to pay for being blessed with that gift.

She smirked, pulled a wry smile and exhaled. The sky seemed to look down at her with a nod of assent. She had defeated her foe. She had won the little duel involving herself and her alleged subconscious mind. There were no more voices ringing in her head like a set of sinister Doom's Day bells echoing from afar.

The ice was broken. Literally. Between her and her mind and she had no more fears, no more apprehensions as to the future to come. That icy future and the glimmering metallic thing on the roundabout at the end of the road. And those moans, those ever-gusting moans.

"What a bunch of crap!" she exclaimed as she slammed the cup on her desk. Slammed as if to emphasize her certitude with regard to the matter.

"There's no way in hell that I'm settling for the bus! Not in that storm anyway!"

By now it had begun to soften a bit. Gusts of wind gradually turned into a frozen breeze hovering across the misty road in a white silken-like sheen. Before Cathy's eyes the snowflakes danced with grace below a rising moon and the yellowish whiteness of the firmament cast a shallow shaft on her fulsome visage.

"Once a tempest, then a zephyr," she uttered poetically as her attention was drawn back to the coffee machine at the other end of the office.

She turned around and began heading for it at a shambling trot.

"The coffee doesn't taste anymore uh?" she jested in sarcasm as the black liquid abundantly flowed into the cup, spreading out a sheltering odour of well crafted grains across the air that she breathed.

"A little cinnamon wouldn't have hurt," she thought as she plunged her lips into the soft, black surface of the brew.

She grunted, all too aware that she had been abusing the little black drug slightly too much today.

"At least, you can't get drunk on coffee!" she giggled.

"Drunkenness is a virtue for humans, Cathy," a voice whispered in the dampened hush of the lingering air but she didn't hear, for her thoughts were elsewhere now.

She bolted back to her desk and paused shy of the glass, the luster of which seemed to glimmer fiercely in her eager gaze.

Now the storm had practically ceased and the hectic dance of the storm had become less than a faint memory in her mind, her alleged subconscious mind.

She drank her coffee by the window, contemplating the snowflakes as they fell, and the wind as it lifted them back up again. Ten minutes had passed. By now her thoughts couldn't be further from the man on the phone, and all she was focusing on was the present she had to get Gertrude.

She laid eyes on her watch again, and even as she did so, impatience started to grow inescapably. It felt as though it had begun devouring her, inch by inch, second by second.

Not feeling able to hang about any longer, she slammed the cup on her desk next to her keyboard and seized her fur coat. "What difference would it make?" she thought. "Ten minutes here or there?"

Mr. Clawson would never find out anyway. Besides, were she to stay the required ten remaining minutes, there would be no further calls anyway. She knew that by experience. Nobody calls after quarter to five.

Without lingering, she turned the computer off, activated the alarm system and began bolting toward the door. She knew she would make it to Seer's if she hurried, granted of course that the storm wasn't too much to cope with.

Hastily, she dashed down the stairs to the garage, so eager that she couldn't wait for the elevator after she'd pressed the button. No thoughts were wasted on the strange man on the phone, nor to what he had told her. Instead she threw the car door open, and before she had the time to sit down properly, she turned on the ignition.

The motor hummed and roared with the same eagerness as its master. It delivered a trivial, abridged thump only to bellow as the car accelerated out of the garage. There it met with the winds and the snow, outwardly painting a scenery of whiteness and freedom. In her eyes at least.

She turned the wipers on, keeping a hand on the steering wheel.

The radio voiced as a companion of joy. Up ahead, delight awaited with roaming keenness, and luckily enough, the traffic didn't present itself too dense. If truth be told, there were barely any cars on the road at all.

"How could that be?" she reflected aloud as she turned the knob so as to change to a better station.

Before her eyes, and in her rear-view mirror, the streets were nearly deserted.

"Deserted during rush hour..." she uttered with aloofness. "How odd."

It couldn't be for the storm.

"Well, why bother? The more the streets are empty the better the chances are that I get there before closing time."

She smiled, but the smile wasn't reflected in the gleaming shafts delivered through the windshield by the passing streetlights.

She sped up. The lights were green. There were no pedestrians to pay attention to. Not in that weather. Besides, the traffic lights invited her with a greenness hard to resist. She hit the gas a little harder. The car responded instantly by one more infamous hum.

"This is my lucky day," she said, pulling a smile as the car headed blindly for the roundabout a few yards ahead. "No traffic jam, no pedestrians, and probably no need to stop at the roundabout either. I'll be at the store in no time."

All of a sudden, an awkward sentiment had climbed her spine. The former feeling of fear that she'd not make it in time had now been substituted for mere enjoyment. She had found pleasure in racing against the clock. Especially now that she seemed to be in the lead, and the pleasure was such that she clearly had no intention of counteracting it.

The wheels glided on the packed snow underneath, seemingly spinning faster and faster under the blind advance of her vehicle.

On her right; a streetlight.

The car roared by. Ten yards left before the roundabout. She threw a glance to her left. No cars in view. Her foot is on the pedal, her hands on the steering wheel, grabbing it firmly. She could feel enjoyment mounting, the accelerator underneath her foot. And suddenly a thought hit her.

"That is why the man on the phone wanted me to take the bus. He wanted me to miss the enjoyment, the bliss," she jested with herself."

A smile embraced her lips. Her eyes glimmered, reflecting the yellowish shaft cast by the streetlights up ahead.

Then on her left something caught her eye. Her gaze ventured toward the object, only to realize a pickup truck had just emerged out of nowhere.

She hit the brakes.

The wheels spun and whirled.

The tyres hit patches of bare road and screeched.

Before she knew it, her car was already crossing the stop sign up-front, crashing voluptuously into the pickup's front bumper and anchoring itself into its metal shell. The impact was hard, throwing her forward as her car's advance was brought to a halt.

Despite the seat-belts being on, her forehead hit the steering wheel with what was felt as a deaf thump, for no noise reached her ears. She shut her eyes only to reopen them with stapled breath. The pain hadn't been too hard, at least. She swore, cursing at the snow as it kept falling impassively, unaware of what had just occurred, there in the middle of the deceptive roundabout, encompassed by the white sheen of an impervious white gold.

Through the fissures in her cracked windshield, she could see the driver jumping out of its pickup truck, arms waving in the air and shouts stinging her ears.

For fear he might show himself hostile, she took a step out of her vehicle, apologizing all she could and thinking of a valid excuse to come up with. Yet, overwhelmed by anger, the other driver didn't seem to listen. Instead, he kept growling as his eyes uncovered the damages.

"Look at my car!" he bellowed. "Look at what you've done you stupid idiot!"

She stood in front of him, silent as a goat before a wolf. She gazed about her. Of the two vehicles, hers was the one which had absorbed most of the impact, the motor having literally been slashed apart. His truck on the other hand, aside from severe scratches in the finish and a demolished front bumper, had succeeded in maintaining its shape, more or less.

Once again she presented her apologies but the driver didn't seem the least bit interested. Instead, cursing litanies and filthy words slipped out of his mouth as though he had gotten into a trance.

Cathy walked back and forth in the snow. She glanced at her watch. In all the confusion, she was still thinking of her mother. Somehow, making it on time had grown into a very important task for her, and suddenly the thought of pleasing her mother with a present that she had not yet bought weighed on her like a plague.

The store would close in fifteen minutes and she knew she'd still stand a chance if she were to catch a bus. The bruise on her forehead didn't ache, after all.

Turning around, she threw a sideways glance at her demolished car and tried to address the driver again.

"Look, in the collision my car was shoved to the ditch at the side of the road. So apparently, it doesn't obstruct the traffic by any means."

The driver had stopped cursing, yet from all to judge he was more preoccupied by the scratches in the lacquer than by her little speech.

"Here's what we'll do!" Cathy began as she felt time closing in on her. "I really need to catch the bus so I'm not going to be able to wait for the police or the tow truck. I really hope you understand."

Nervousness was climbing up her spine.

"How could I be so stupid," she murmured as she felt the snowflakes wetting her lips.

"This is my card. I work for Clawson Inc. just a few blocks away from here. Please give me a call and I'll pay for all the damages okay? But I really cannot stay and like I said my car doesn't obstruct the road."

She held out the card but the driver didn't care much for it.

"Would you please take it," she said, feeling her voice shudder as she spoke.

The driver unreceptive, she bolted toward his truck and laid the card beneath the wiper on the windshield.

"Like I said, give me a call by tomorrow and I'll pay for all the damages that I've caused you."

Before she had the time to hear an answer, she was already en route to the bus-stop a hundred yards ahead, staggering forward in the snow and praying that she would make it before the police came.

***

She had stood there for five minutes now. Every now and then she'd cast a glance at the roundabout to check on the driver, his silhouette nearly melting with the scenery from the distance.

To all appearances he was still standing next to his car, seemingly walking around in circles and holding something to his ear as though he were speaking through a cell phone.

That calmed her down a bit. After all, it was not like she had sneaked from the accident scene or anything. She had left him her card. At least he hadn't come after her to refrain her from taking the bus.

Speaking of which.

It nearly emerged out of the blue, braking in as the doors opened on the stop where she was standing.

She took a step aside, waited for the other passengers to walk off, then stepped on board, nodded at the bus driver, but he didn't return her salute.

She grabbed a seat at the rear, casting a backward glance at the roundabout before the bus roared forward and her eyes wandered down to her watch. She had eleven minutes before closing. She should be there in five, leaving her six minutes to do her majestic shopping. That should be enough.

The bus dashed through Landcaster Tunnel before emerging on the other side on 46th Street where, to Cathy's immense chagrin, a compact traffic jam awaited her disappointment. The bus slowed down and adjusted to a pace that would have had a snail lose composure.

She plunged her face into her hands so as to repress or conceal her tears and then bit her upper lip.

"Perhaps the subway," she thought.

She stared out the window, traffic building upon traffic, horns blowing at the corners of adjacent streets.

The nearest subway station would be on 45th Street. She knew that, but provided she would get there on time, she'd have to walk subsequently, for the store lay about a three or four minute-walk from the end-station. That'd leave her exactly two minutes to get herself to the underground.

To do that the bus had to stop about now. She'd have to take a shortcut and run through Colonel Avenue to access 45th Street faster.

The traffic jam before them thickened, obliging the bus driver to come to a standstill.

Cathy scrutinized the surroundings, her eyes longing to meet with a station where the bus would release its passengers. At first she saw none, but as her gaze bordered the 46th and Colonel junction, she found it, a few yards ahead, awaiting the bus' arrival with eagerness, yet not as much as she was.

Her watch gave her less than a minute now, provided again that the bus would stop promptly, but the stop lay ahead and the jam made it look so far away.

She rose from her seat, her forehead ghastly with sweat and now throbbing from the bump on the steering wheel.

"Sir!" she called from the rear, addressing the chauffeur at the front.

"Sir! Can you please open the doors right here and let me off? I'm sort of in a hurry, you understand."

At her words, the bus driver didn't so much as turn around, much less blink. Instead, he remained focused on the road before his eyes, either deaf or pretending.

"Sir!" she bellowed, now aware that time had finally caught up with her and that it was probably too late anyway.

"Would you please open the doors!"

Again, no reaction.

She gazed about her, seeking eye contact with the other passengers but they were all too busy sighing, looking at their watches or swearing silently.

Giving in to the circumstances, she sat down, her eyes filling with tears, which somehow, she managed to repress. There would be no present for Gertrude tomorrow, nor the day after.

***

That night, Cathy went to bed with a burdened heart. She slumbered yet didn't sleep well, tossing and turning in a mixed state of consciousness and sleep.

Outside, darkness roamed like a whore. It taunted her with despicable visions of landscapes and smiling teeth. And just when she was about to give in to a deeper sleep, the phone rang with insatiable vigour, waking her up in the twinkle of an eye.

She rose to her feet, embraced by white satin sneakers as she lifted it from the hook.

"Hello?"

At first silence soared, but as she slowly but surely slipped from her weariness, she thought she'd heard a moan, as if someone at the other end of the line was lamenting or worse yet, weeping.

"Hello?" she repeated, but the moan remained a moan.

Feeling tiredness catching up to her, she hung up, glanced at her watch and returned at a shambling trot to her bed.

The time was three o'clock, sharp.

"Who'd be unaware enough to call this late at night?" she mumbled as she laid her weary head on her pillow.

As she turned off the lights, darkness dawned on the room once more. A roaming silence laid nest. Minutes passed, gloom dwelled.

Then without warning, the phone rang again, this time it seemed louder.

She hurried toward the stand, answered with a sigh, then listened as she lent her ears to an answer.

Again, the same moan as she'd heard previously.

"Who's this?" she uttered in annoyance.

The moans were now substituted for a series of short-lived sobs, and for a moment she'd swear she'd recognized the voice.

"Mother is that you?"

The moans turned into grunts then eventually disclosing words and muttered sentences.

"Mother?"

"Serge?" the voice sobbed, letting through a burdened sigh.

"Mother?"

"Serge, is that you?" the voice wept.

"No it's Cathy, mom. This is my number. Dad is not here."

"Serge, it's Gertrude, Serge, it's Gertrude!"

"What's the matter mom? You seem all shook up! Has anything bad happened?"

The voice at the other end of the line exhaled noisily, as though to release an immense amount of pain.

"It's our daughter, Serge… It's our daughter…"

"What?"

"Something terrible's happened! There was a car accident, Serge, a car accident!"

"Mom, what are you talking about?"

"It's Cathy, Serge! It's Cathy! She crashed her car tonight…"

"Mom…?" Her voice shuddered like a leaf.

In an instant, her thoughts brought her back to the man in the pickup truck, the bus driver and the impassive passengers of his, the crowd's impassive faces in the subway train on her way back home. None of them had addressed her, let alone met her gaze. None of them had acted as if she'd even been there. Not since the accident. Not since.

"Oh my God…"

She felt her voice quaver. What are you saying? What are you saying?"

At the other side of the line, Gertrude uttered a deep sigh, and as she plunged her tear-wrecked face into the palm of her left hand, she sobbed against the speaker, shaking her head, shaking her head...

FEAR OF THE DARK   *Erik Jayce Landberg*

HELL IS THEM

FEAR OF THE DARK   *Erik Jayce Landberg*

HELL IS THEM

"All rise!"

The voice ran across the room half-unnoticed, at least to the defendant's ears, who was shrouded by an eerie, white silken mask, didn't so much as move an inch from his cold, moist chair.

"May the defendant rise!" the voice rejoined all too loud to be jesting. It was that of the judge.

Yet, to the jury's surprise, the defendant seemed to linger on like a lifeless corpse who had suddenly been struck by death. His eyes were shrouded. He couldn't see.

A mild tumult arose in the room which was damp and misty, surrounded by grey stony walls reminiscent of a cellar, or perhaps even a cell. They were dreary, confining, and behind them the ominous presence of Doom's Day bells ringing from afar. Ringing with unquenchable greed, one aiming at the defendant, the ever-condemned defendant.

It was a courtroom, at least as said by those who sat there, those of the clan whose visages were obscured by dark masks, the texture of which seemed far too rough to be silk.

All at once, a utensil hammering on a moist desk urged the multitude to quickly regain their composure.

"Quiet! Everybody quiet! I demand silence or this court will be adjourned!"

"Leave him be!" a voice spoke from behind a black shroud. Black as the night.

"Who said that?" the judge bellowed in rising antagonism.

"It came from the jury, Your Honour," a voice echoed in the multitude.

"From the jury? Who would be so foolish as to–"

"I did, Your Honour!" a man rose to his feet, high and tall so as to be seen.

"Be seated! Who gave you permission to speak!?"

Behind the tiny eye-holes in the judge's mask, something shimmered. Something angry and heated.

"Your Honour–"

"Take your seat back in the jury!"

"I only meant to say that it makes no difference whether the defendant is to remain seated or–"

"Quiet!"

"…at least when it comes to the outcome of the case."

"Quiet you fool!"

A tumult arose anew, embracing the courtroom with a sudden feeling of impending doom. One not so much aimed at the defendant as it was now at *him*, *he*, that fool who had dared open his mouth unsolicited. Groans and moans filled the room in a mounting macabre melody. It rang in one's ears, as if a dark chastisement was to be pronounced, and for all to know, perhaps it was.

"How dare he?" dark voices mumbled from within the multitude.

"How dare you speak your mind?"

"Your Honour, I only meant–"

"Sink right back into your seat or I unveil you on the spot and declare you a threat to the purity of our race!"

Silence dawned on the cellar not quite promptly, summoning one and all to hold their breath, for as from that moment panting for air no longer seemed righteous.

"Is that what your are member of the jury? An imminent threat to our race?"

"Of course not, Your Honour!" he stammered before sinking back into his seat in a deaf thud, not unlike that of a stone hitting sandy ground, one as dry as his lips were now.

"Don't mock us! Don't mock our superiority!"

Silence screamed. Blood rushed through temples.

"I am deeply sorry, Your Honour. I assure the multitude it will not happen ag–"

"Blasphemy!" the judge bellowed as his hammer hit the dusty moisture of his soggy wooden desk. "Blasphemy!"

Shadows roamed by from the mild oil-lamps casting a dampened yellowish shaft on the multitude's shrouds. Hearts thumped, teeth gnashed, and as silence feathered down on the room like a puff of dust, the defendant uttered a slight moan, one inadvertently gurgling out of his dusty throat behind that white mask, that eerily virgin-white mask.

"Defendant!" the judge bellowed. "Speak your name!"

Another moan came out, but that one by inadvertence too.

"I urge the defendant to stand up and speak aloud!" the judge's voice roared.

He frowned behind the mask, his eyes alight as though bound by a devilish spell. They shimmered again. They shimmered before the multitude.

"May I?" a silhouette rose up out of the shadowy spot next to the yellow shaft flickering on the defendant like a ghost.

"May I what?" the judge retorted.

"May I ask for permission to speak, Your Honour?"

"Permission granted. But speak your mind fast!"

"So I will, Your Honour. So I will."

Moans and whispers were heard in the dampened silence soaring within the walls.

The judge gave a nod in assessment so as to summon him to his words.

"As the defendant's advocate, Your Honour, I must inform you, the jury and the audience that it has come to my knowledge that the defendant is not the master of his domain."

"How so?" the judge grunted.

"The defendant cannot speak our language, Your Honour."

Once again, moans overpowered quietness, as if blasphemy had been spoken out of vanity.

"Cannot speak our language?" the judge rolled his eyes behind the dusk of his mask.

The advocate shook his head almost ashamed.

"Illiterate?"

He nodded.

"I'm afraid so, Your Honour."

"Then I presume he must be one of those *illiterate frogs* as they refer to them up there," the judge put on a disgusted look.

"He's no *frog*, no."

The multitude sighed out, in relief.

"Not only is he accused of being impure but he is also illiterate. Does he have a language of his own, that… that illiterate being?"

"Yes, Your Honour. A foreign language."

"What kind of inferior race doesn't know how to speak our language?"

Laughter filled the courtroom.

"From what I understand, he doesn't consider himself as impure or inferior."

Laughter was emphasized by giggling noises.

"Hush!" the judge spat.

"How do you know that for a fact if you can't communicate with him?"

"Well…"

There was a brief moment of silence.

"Well what? Speak!"

"Well, I happen to be a little conversant with his language, Your Honour."

All at once, whatever laughter was left lingering vanished in the wink of an eye.

"You do?"

The advocate nodded.

"Are you impure as well?" the judge questioned in an attempt to jest.

Laughter filled the room.

His heart beginning to thud a bit, the advocate shook his head with a smirk, only that smirk was veiled by his mask.

"No, Your Honour," he replied, panting slightly for air. "I used to be an interpreter."

"Very well. So I suppose you can act as one during this very session?"

"I'd be glad to, Your Honour!"

"But before you do. There is just one little thing."

"Anything you ask, Your Honour."

"I'd like you to withdraw your mask!"

"I beg your pardon–"

"Do NOT question my authority!"

"Your Honour–"

"Unveil yourself! I want to see to it that you're not impure too," the judge smiled but it was a smile of disdain.

"I assure you I am not foreign, nor impure for that matter."

"Very well. Do it then!"

Faced with no other choice but to comply, the advocate pulled on the piece of tissue shrouding his grudging visage.

First appeared his mouth, revealing a pair of pouting lips the colour of which seemed to fade at the contact with the moist air. Then, compelled to abide, the rest of his face was unveiled like a virgin on a honeymoon bed.

Sheltered beyond his mask, the judge frowned, cast a suspicious glance at the advocate's confounded visage and began to muse silently.

"I don't know," he started. "You seem a little bleak to me."

The multitude's eyes set on him like a thousand knives as his hands began to tremble. Silence laid its nest as an invasive bird.

"Don't look so distressed!" the judge spat pulling a wry smile. "Pay some respect and shroud your face!"

"Yes, Your Honour," the advocate sighed as he promptly obeyed.

"Now, I'd like to see the defendant step up to the stand."

The advocate leaned forward and whispered something foreign in the defendant's right ear.

At first he didn't so much as grunt, but when he was summoned anew, he mumbled something incomprehensible in his mask, only to stand up and yell at the top of his lungs seconds later.

"Dear one," the judge rejoined sarcastically. "The defendant is clearly not the master of his domain. What did he say? Translate!"

"He said, I quote; *'Don't you know who I am?'*" the advocate hurried to reply.

"As a matter of fact we don't! Therefore I order you to speak your name loud and clear!"

The advocate reached for his ear once again so as to translate.

No sooner said than done, the defendant began shouting again in his foreign language, saliva almost penetrating his virgin-white shroud.

Moans ran across the courtroom.

"Order! Order!" the judge bellowed as he hammered on his desk. "What did he say?"

"I… I don't know, Your Honour. He spoke so loud and fast. I didn't quite get all the words."

"You're a foreigner, defendant! A foreigner. Thus, you have no rights. You have only obligations. Do you understand?"

Panting for air and still quavering slightly, the defendant sank back into his chair without uttering a single word. All at once, he seemed to return to his former condition of impervious, corpselike state.

"You are being held here on charges of impurity. You're a disarray to the superiority of our race! Now before we pronounce a sentence, how do you plead?"

Without lingering, the advocate replied swiftly,

"The defendant pleads not guilty, Your Honour."

"Not guilty? It's a disgrace!"

Silence soared briefly until it was disturbed yet another time.

"I ask you again. How do you plead?"

"Not guilty," the advocate replied after having conferred with his client.

"Are you aware of the fact that pleading not guilty will cause you to serve a sentence much more atrocious than if you were to confess and admit?"

The advocate leaned forward and whispered in his language; "Get a hold of yourself! You need to plead guilty, otherwise I cannot account for the consequences!"

"Is this your last word?" the judge gazed inquisitively at the defence.

"I don't care!" a reply came in foreign words. *"You're all condemned! You're all corrupted and influenced by the communists! The communists and the j–"*

"Quiet you mortal fool!"

"You're all going to Hell! I'll see to it that you do!"

"The defence had better tell the defendant to compose himself!" the judge bawled. "What exactly did he say?"

The advocate remained silent, then shook his head as though pretending he did not understand.

"What language is that anyway?"

"Your Honour, it is–"

Gusting like a blast of air, a voice rose out of the blue.

"I'd like to call my first witness to the stand, Your Honour!"

The voice belonged to the prosecutor. Tall and haughty, he was standing firmly in the shades of the faint yellowish sheen shed by the moistened candles in the ceiling.

"Very well, you may proceed," the judge waved dryly.

"I call my first witness to the stand!"

"This is ludicrous! I urge you to cease this masquerade once and for all. I have wasted enough time here!"

The defendant was out of himself.

"Again, quench him!"

Two guards dressed in black gowns from head to toe stepped out of the shade bordering the left wall. One of them reached out a hand and grabbed the defendant by the arm.

"Let go of me you traitor! Don't you know who I am?" he yelled as best he could. Yet no one in the jury, nor in the multitude, understood. No one save for the advocate, of course, who failed to translate.

"I believe handcuffs wouldn't be out of place," the judge ordered in sarcasm as the silhouette walked down the aisle past the benches, toward the stand.

Another guard, also shrouded from head to toe, stepped forward and held out a book with a very peculiar symbol depicted on the cover. One not as ominous as mesmerizing.

"Do you swear to tell the truth and nothing but the truth so help you–?"

"I do," the silhouette interrupted as she momentarily stepped out of the murky area behind the stand to take a seat in the dusk of a chair next to the judge's elevated desk. Unlike the rest of them, her face wasn't veiled.

The prosecutor bolted forward, as self-assured as ever, his eyes flickering through the holes in his mask.

"The day it all happened," he began only to pause a few seconds later as if to ponder. "The day it all happened, the day the defendant was caught and brought here by our men."

The silhouette nodded.

"That very day were you with him?"

Another nod was uttered in assessment.

"Were you aware?"

"Aware of what?" she asked dryly.

"Aware of his impurity."

She hesitated, then spoke.

"Well no, I haven't considered–"

"Objection!" the advocate spat like a squirt of poison. The prosecutor is trying to mislead the witness, Your Honour!"

"Overruled!" the judge spat as loud as the walls were damp.

"May I...?"

The prosecutor rolled his eyes in sarcasm.

The judge nodded in assessment. "Come to the point fast! I have a sentence to pronounce!"

"Very well, Your Honour!"

Frowning slightly, he turned again toward the witness and pursued his deeds.

"Where were you when we caught the defendant?" the prosecutor pursued, eager to escape the judge's mounting impatience.

"I was next to him," she answered in her severe foreign accent.

"Next to him, where?"

He emphasized *where* as though to assert that the judge's impatience was now invading him.

"In the room."

Her voice was feminine yet assertive, as though she didn't quite understand what *he* or *they* were accused of and what consequences they were facing.

"In the room, huh?"

"Yes."

"And why were you in that room?" he grinned in wryness.

"We had no choice."

"You had no choice? There is ALWAYS a choice."

"Your Honour!" the advocate objected.

"Overruled!"

"At first we attempted to flee but we soon realized there was no use. So–"

She was rolling her *R*s in a firm yet appealing way.

"So?" the prosecutor thrust.

"So he wanted us to flee by way of a different–"

"The defendant?"

"Yes."

"Continue."

"At first I didn't want to but he said it would be for the best because…"

She hesitated.

"Because what?"

"Because they were after us."

"Who were after you?"

She raised her eyes and her gaze met with his not quite in arrogance.

Then came the words, emphasizing the latter even more.

"Don't you know?"

She spoke in such a flat absentminded tone that it almost scared the hell out of the prosecutor, who answered with nothing more than a grunt.

"Everybody knows!" she raised her voice.

A faint commotion burst out at the rear of the courtroom.

"Quiet! Quiet!" the judge spat as he hammered the moist wooden desk of his.

"I won't tolerate any arrogance from an inferior race! Do I make myself understood? Now speak, what happened next?"

"Inferior?" she questioned not quite with pride and conceit, her gaze wandering toward that of the judge, fire in her eyes.

The tumult grew all the more loud.

"Quiet! Or I will adjourn the case!"

"Who are you to speak in that tone of voice?" the prosecutor retorted.

"Don't you know who I am? Don't you know who *he* is?" she snarled.

She pointed in the defendant's direction. He was snarling too as he mumbled something imperceptible yet audible enough for all of them to inhale his lack of eloquence.

"How would we? You were just brought here as a witness."

"Quiet!"

The hammer fell anew.

"By what means did you two attempt to flee?"

She rose from her chair. The prosecutor puckered his brow.

"May I?" she asked as she tucked both her hands into the left pocket of her gown.

The judge threw the prosecutor a sideways glance so as to ascertain that she didn't carry anything sharp, or worse, a weapon.

The prosecutor answered with a faint nod, as though to approve of her deeds. The judge copied.

"By means of this," she said out loud as she trembled, yet firmly held a little round, white object squeezed between her forefinger and her thumb.

"What is this?" several of them grimaced.

"It looks like a pill!" others pursued.

"It *is* a pill," she uttered flatly, before sinking back into her chair with a deaf thud.

"You were going to escape by way of a pill?" the judge enquired as a grin slowly formed upon his blood-thirsty lips.

She lowered her eyes and shut her lids.

"It didn't work," she uttered with a sigh, as though in regret.

"What is it? A magic pill that opens doors in the wall?" the prosecutor roared with laughter and so did the rest of the jury.

"Objection, Your Honour!"

The defence advocate rose from his chair, peering at the prosecutor in a reproachful air.

"I demand that the session be adjourned! He is trying to mislead the witness."

The judge didn't seem so much affected as he was impervious.

Meanwhile, the defendant barked in an – to all of them – unknown language, the nature of which painted their wraithlike faces and visages with revulsion. Only no one could witness it there behind their shrouds.

"Have him stop!" the judge hammered.

Yet by now, the defendant was out of control, mainly at the view of the pill Eva had held in her hand less than a minute ago, or was it two?

"Make him stop!" the eerie judge rejoined in a despiteful pleonasm.

Two tall silhouettes hastened forward, one of them holding what looked like a fork, only a giant one, out of proportion, three pointy daggers shining skyward. Unlike everybody else in the courtroom, the two silhouettes melted in as shadows, their gowns black as a widow, their faces masked like coward thieves. They paused short of the accused and seized him in a tight grip by both his arms.

"Objection!" the advocate bellowed.

"What are the despiteful words the defendant is yelling?" the judge asked, as yet unaffected by the advocate's opposition.

"Speak!" the prosecutor ordered the witness.

"May I, Your Honour?" the advocate attempted but was almost at once required to hold his tongue.

"We want to hear it from the witness herself."

Eva gazed back at him in sheer wander.

"He is saying he doesn't understand why you brought him here and what this masquerade is all about," she began.

"Yes?" the judge approved.

"He says you all ought to be aware of who he is and that there will be consequences once he gets out of here."

"Consequences?" the judge grinned.

"Get out of here?" the rest of them burst in laughter, casting wicked sideways glances at one another as only demons could.

Eva's voice began to quiver at their words. She began to understand this was no ordinary trial and that she might not only be sitting in the witness chair. She began to wish the pill had worked. She shut her eyes as though to close their shrouded faces and their burdensome voices out of sight.

Once the laughter had settled, the prosecutor asked.

"What exactly were you running from?"

"Them," she answered, her eyes still closed. "Them," she repeated.

"And the pill was supposed to save you two from them?"

The defendant was still shouting foreign words of wisdom but no one understood. No one but the prosecutor and Eva, whose mind was now elsewhere. Miles away from there. Miles away from the room where they had been trapped and found, and, eventually brought here before a faceless jury. A court as heartless as they once had been. The two of them, living in dirty deeds, delusion and utopia.

"What is he saying now?" the judge's voice pierced her daydreaming mind.

"He demands that the shroud be taken off his face. He demands to be heard. He says he is ready to take consequences for his acts. He says that, would he have the chance to go back in time, he would do *it* again and not change a single thing."

By now she whispered rather than talked, for deep in her mind she knew more than *he* did, it seemed.

"What else?"

"He demands he be released so that he can face the consequences with pride."

"Pride? Released?" they roared with laughter.

"What else?" the judge waved at the jury so as to let her speak.

"I wished the pill had worked…" she whispered but they all heard.

Laughter turned into a grin. A wicked one for which there were no words.

The judge leaned forward.

"The suicide pill?" he grinned all the more and although she could not see it, she could feel it.

Her eyes still closed, she answered with a faint nod.

"What if I tell you," the judge began. "What if I tell you it did?"

All at once, her eyes opened before a smiley judge whose shroud sheltered his deeds.

Her mouth was agape now, her pores sweating as never before. She tried to speak but no noise came out.

"I'm not sure *Mademoiselle* has understood the true implication of this trial," the prosecutor added.

"Are you aware of where you are Miss…, miss…," the judge thumbed through some musty sheets of paper, as though to uncover her full name. He brought his hands to the mask concealing his visage and withdrew it just as quickly. It revealed a long, edgy nose and a skin darker than hers. "Someone get me my spectacles," he asked as he thumbed further through his scriptures.

Meanwhile the two silhouettes at the sides of the defendant laid hands upon the mask of the accused, preparing to unfold his face to a jury now more eager than ever.

"Don't you know where you are?" the advocate whispered gently in her ear as she strove to catch her breath.

"No, where am I? Where are we? Wherever we are, I plead not guilty!" she bellowed.

"Plead?" the advocate exclaimed. "It's not a question of whether you plead or not. You're already found guilty. My task is nothing more than to try to lower your sentence."

"Guilty of what? I only married him! He gave me no choice! Everything he did against them is his own decision!" she yelled in a final attempt to avoid whatever could be avoided.

They all stared back at her.

"Gentlemen, you can all withdraw your masks. She just admitted to his dirty deeds. Our witness has witnessed against him. It is time for the sentence."

One by one, they began unveiling their sombre faces and the – in her eyes – unbearable star revealing on their foreheads. It was a star she was all too conversant with, and only at that point did she realize that the pill had indeed worked. That neither one of them had actually survived. That this was in fact nothing else than Judg–

"All rise! At my signal, withdraw the shroud from his eyes so he can see!" he ordered, pointing at the defendant.

The two dark silhouettes were ready to abide. The judge threw one last glance at the manuscript and lowered hands.

All at once, light pierced his pupils as he set eyes on the moist cellar for the very first time, and when his gaze met with the eerie Star of David engraved on their forehead he shrieked at the top of his lungs in that bloody foreign language none of them could grasp.

"Hölle sind Sie!" Hölle sind Sie!"

"Are found guilty of race impurity before the jury, to the first degree, Miss Braun and the defendant are hereby sentenced to–"

And as the judge uttered a sentence of an entire afterlife in *their* company – *them* in the jury with that eerie Star upon their heads – for all time and eternity, he shrieked like a girl at the sight of a spider.

He shrieked and shrieked, as though the chastisement could not have been chosen better, for in his mind, and in

his mind only, *Hell was them, Hell was them!*

FINAL CURTAIN

Erik Jayce Landberg

FINAL CURTAIN

A shadow in the doorway.

"Halt! Who goes there?" the old man in the leather chair asked.

A voice as dark as its shape.

"Lucifer my dear."

"Lucifer?"

The shadow nodded, encompassed by a burdening gloom, betrayed only by a faint shaft of light.

"You mean, the Devil?"

"Indeed," he grinned, his hand brushing against his silken tie in a gracious gesture as though to approve of his name.

The old man's gaze wandered down to the fireplace, the flames of which danced with fury as their master approached at a daunting pace. He pulled a wry smile, uttering a sarcastic little laughter that almost made him cough, one not so much filled with dread as with conceit.

"What can you possibly want from me? I'm as religious as ever. Been all my life!"

"Oh, is that a fact?" the King of Darkness rejoined, all but astounded.

"Ask the angels! I suggest you leave by where you came from. I'm afraid you're wasting your time in my presence."

"See that's exactly what I came here for."

"How so?"

"Time. That's what I came here for. It's time to take you home, to summon you back to your own breed."

"Home?" the old man attempted to say but his lips didn't abide, nearly too dry to obey.

"Yes, home to hell," the devil sighed, as impervious as death itself, his eyes glimmering as he spoke the latter word, his breath ever-smelling of death.

"That is ludicrous!"

"I believe it is in the eye of the beholder, now isn't it?"

The old man licked his dry lips, staring eerily at the creature's glaring pupils, obscured behind black shades of dusk.

"I urge you to take your business elsewhere."

"You are my business."

"I don't believe you. It's not likely to happen." His voice quavered slightly, and so did his wrinkled hands.

"How so?"

"I've been faithful to my religion. I've read the scriptures as often as I could!"

"So?"

"I attended the services each and every Sunday. And most of all, I've followed every rule there is. I've even refrained from marrying the one that I loved, owing to the fact that she was not a member of the church and thus could not be saved. Only God knows how much I loved her. I've done exactly what was expected of me. I even broke contact with my father who wasn't religious enough to serve God and… I've dedicated my life to my religion, gave all my savings to it, all I own. Look at me I'm a poor man, poor to serve God. So many sacrifices," he sighed as his gaze fell down onto the wooden floor, "so many sacrifices."

The beast laid a speckled, clawed hand on his shoulder as though to give him comfort.

"I know. I am very proud of you. You did my deeds well," the creature spat out as a squirt of poison.

"What?"

"And you've raised a judging hand at your fellow beings, I like that," it smirked.

"I… I don't understand," the old man stammered, "I've been praying every day, I've done everything that was expected of me. Why doesn't God take me to heaven?"

"Heaven? God?" the being burst out in laughter, "If you're intention was to go to heaven, why did you follow me instead of God?"

"But I didn't follow you! I followed my religion!"

"Religion? Religion is my invention, not that of God. My product, the cause and solution to man's every problem throughout all ages since the beginning of dawn. The appetite for greed, hatred, wars, vengeance and vanity. I am indeed very proud of my trademark."

"Do you mean that all these years, I've been devoting my life to… to nothing else but–"

"Fire and brimstone awaits dear. It is time to go," the devil nodded, revealing a gaze so horrendous that the old man's heart ceased beating almost at once.

"I don't want to go with you!" he yelled, his throat feeling as dusty as ever.

"Think about it. Better reign in hell than serve in heaven, isn't' it?"

"No!"

"No? I see you humans are a very naïve and stubborn race, very naïve and… evil."

"You can't be serious! How can this be? I've prayed to God, I've dedicated my life to–"

"Not to the God that you think."

"Are you telling me that all these years have been wasted, cast away worshipping you?" he gasped for air, his heart thumping like a hammer dying to break through the wall of his chest.

"Indeed my dear, indeed."

Painfully, the old man rose from his chair to his feet, facing the creature's evil visage, so as to prepare himself for the worst, as though he had finally given in to the idea of demise. Doom's Day bells rang from afar, but loud enough to sting his ears, confine his head. Loud enough to deafen his fraught cries.

"Indeed," the devil neoplasmed as he penetrated his face by means of ever-sharpening claws, tearing it open, blood-red. Blood-red as the gates of hell."

ABOUT THE AUTHOR

*Erik Jayce Landberg is a Swedish author, short story
writer, artist and renowned musician.
He resides in the city often referred to as The Venice Of
Northern Europe, namely Stockholm.*

Erik Jayce Landberg

FEAR OF THE DARK   *Erik Jayce Landberg*

Also available on Paperback:

IMMORTAL

Victoria Publishing Ltd.

ISBN 978-1-105-64425-2

IMMORTAL
A Novella

Erik J. Landberg

Fear Of The Dark **is also available on Hard Cover:**

Victoria Publishing Ltd.

ISBN 978-1-105-64928-8